Several Glorious Months

A Diary of Murders

Short Story Collection

by Sarah Cook

For more information, email: sarah@sarahcookwriter.co.uk

First paperback edition May 2024

Edited by Steven Cook, Elena Barnard, and Louise Havard
Cover design by Beth Morris

ISBN - 9781739347048 *(paperback)*

www.sarahcookwriter.co.uk

For all my dark goddesses
and those who worship them

TRIGGER WARNING:

Several Glorious Months is set in the world of Diary of Murders and deals with equally graphic content.

The positives: consensual sex, BDSM, femme-domme, male sub, ropes, ties, whips, references to orgies, and public sex.

The negatives: domestic violence, PTSD, alcoholism, baby loss and miscarriage, and references to sexual assault and violence.

Very much like Diary of Murders, Several Glorious Months explores in greater detail the marriage of Miriam & John, and their dark and devastating love, this is not a romance. There is no HEA for these two.

If you ever need to talk about any of the issues raised, I am always here!

All my love,
Sarah

Short Stories:

The Engagement Dinner

17th September 1895

John Bennett and Miriam Clayton had met and fallen in love with one another in a matter of days. Unbecoming to how societal creatures lived, the pair had even consummated their relationship, over and over again without much thought to how scandalous it would be if anyone were to ever find out. Within their short time together, a month, more or less, they had found an eternity with one another. Neither of them cared about what other people might think or say – their love was deeper and richer than time itself.

For an ordinary couple, two days without your lover was normal. Adequate, even.

For Miriam and John, it was torture.

On Tuesday 17th September 1895, Miriam had to draw a very small line in their courtship, though she was wildly against doing so. She strolled into his office as soon as he arrived. Slamming the door, and locking it tight, Miriam had a look on her face that was both sad and sultry. John chuckled softly. He was not at all surprised about her entrance, it had almost become a daily occurrence. In fact, within seconds of her appearing, he was growing stiff with delight.

The power this woman had over him was electrifying.

"My aunt is in town," she said cautiously, "I am afraid she'll wish to be my escort. I cannot sneak off to see you."

"Oh, quite right." John nodded though he did not agree. He wanted to worship her body and soul every night until the end of time.

Occasionally he forgot that Miriam's family was filled with lords and ladies that adhered to convention rigidly. Miriam came from wealth but did not flaunt it. Like her father, she poured it into charities and the hospital, for the betterment of their patients.

Her ferocious spirit, and perpetually frazzled manner, also made it hard to picture her as some sort of debutante that he had to court traditionally. It was easy to forget that she technically was part of that world, especially as Sir Fredric didn't seem too fussed with customs either, often forgetting or simply not caring that Miriam and John spent time together alone.

The disappointment must have been clear on his face because Miriam sauntered over to him, sat down on his lap, and kissed him deeply. He wrapped his hands around her back and groaned against her lips, hoping to stop time to keep her there forever. When they broke free, he clung onto her fiercely, leaning his head upon her bosom. There was a fear that if he were to let go, she would tumble away from him, and he had spent so long trying to find her. He wished to take her there and then.

"A parting gift, perhaps?" Miriam read his mind. Slipping off his lap, she bent down before him. She unfastened his buttons and prised his member free from his trousers. He was practically throbbing for her already so when she touched him, he gasped. Gently, Miriam started to stroke him, keeping her gaze on his eyes. John let out a ragged breath as her hands moved deftly upon him. Then she took him into her mouth. He sighed loudly, hesitant of being so loud that other staff members could hear him. Yet the way she moved her tongue and hand upon him was brilliant. Guttural moans caught in his throat as he bucked into her mouth. Miriam made small whimpering and gagging sounds as she pleasured him, making the experience even more exciting.

"Are you close?" she said breathlessly, stroking him fast and ferociously. As she placed him back into her mouth, John wondered if she asked because she was fearful that she'd get another shot of semen in her face. He groaned at the memory.

"Yes," he seethed, gripping onto her hair unexpectedly.

Then suddenly she stopped. She looked up at him as she stopped moving her hand and let his cock fall from her mouth. His eyes widened from the shock, and he gritted his teeth. *What was she doing?*

"All in good time John," she said with a wink. Lifting herself off the ground, she wiped saliva off her lips and brushed her dress down. John blinked at her like a depraved man would having been denied his next meal. "My instructions are simple. You are not allowed to touch me, or touch yourself, until I say so. Do you understand?" John stared, half-incredulous and half-impressed at the notion. Miriam folded her arm sternly. "I asked if you understood?"

"Yes," he replied in barely a whisper. The idea of being in her control even without her being around was too tantalising to resist. He wondered if he had the mettle to obey.

"Do not believe for one second that you can fool me. I will know." She nodded at him then made her way to the door. He didn't even dare fix himself up in front of her, letting his frustrated feelings hang there. Before she opened the door and disappeared into the busy hospital, Miriam turned. Their eyes caught across the office as the atmosphere was thick with wanting. She broke out into a huge smile. "Oh Dr Bennett, try not to look too agonised."

And she left him… uncompleted.

John spent the rest of Tuesday trying to place Miriam at the back of his mind so that her absence did not trouble him greatly. In his endeavour to distract himself, he worked in surgery for most of the day and tended to patients long into the evening. At first, he thought he was successful. He walked exhausted into his Camden boarding house room with nothing on his mind but the busyness and calamity of hospital work. There was still a red stain upon his skin from his bloody operations, and his mind only echoed the agony of sick people.

Yet as he collapsed on his bed, too weighted from the day to even remove his suit, John found the memory of Miriam sliding through his senses. Almost as if she had been waiting for a quiet moment to come and cause chaos within him. He didn't realise how very used to her being he had become; he was still expecting her to waltz into his room as she had done so many times before. When Miriam didn't appear, John sighed and drifted off to sleep with the thought of her lips and the frustration they had left him in earlier that day.

He awoke Wednesday and cursed his own weakness. As he entered the hospital, knowing that this would be the first day since they united without her, John tried to be strong – holding on to the man he was long before Miriam Clayton had entered his life. But his office was filled with the scent of her. He stood aimlessly, like a lost child, wondering whether his mind had gone completely. But, sure enough, the room was engulfed with her perfume. It was so much more than just the puff of lemon and bergamot; he was certain that he could smell her sex and flesh. It was as though moments before his arrival she had sat in one of his chairs and pleasured herself until completion. It was an idea so devious that Miriam had to have done it.

When he found a pair of her drawers in his desk, still damp from excitement, John concluded that his theory was correct. Pawing at the fabric, he could not help himself and he brought it up to his nose to breathe in that familiar and fantastic aroma. The anticipation was too much. His heart agonised as much as his prick, painfully stiff in his trousers. He was so achingly close to breaking the rules... *How could she ever know?*

Sternly, he placed the drawers back and sighed loudly to no one at all. He busied himself with work but the scent of her haunted him for the rest of the day.

Now it was Thursday, the day of their engagement dinner, and John tried to quell the rising hunger he had for her, but it was becoming impossible to ignore. Miriam's morning gift to him was a photograph. It sat on his desk quite nicely, in an ornate silver frame. It was a simple picture of her: She was dressed smartly in a fashionable, frilled dress. She had a face of concentration but with a sly smile. Though the picture was grey, her dark blue eyes stared straight into his soul. The present was too nice and ordinary for his fiancé, and he tried desperately to deduce her plans.

That puzzle hung over his head as he went to the day's board meeting. But a wonderful memory also gripped his mind. Last time he was in this room, merely a week ago, Miriam had bent him over the table and beat his buttocks until he relented. He couldn't possibly think about procedures and policies at this meeting when he could still see his heated palmprints on the brown wooden table.

Plus, he was bound to see her today, and John was eagerly awaiting her arrival once more at the morning's meeting. Instead of Miriam, however, he was dismayed to see Matron Lockett walk through the door.

"I have a note from Dr Clayton. She says, 'Gentlemen, you'll be delighted to learn that I am detained on a serious patient matter. Matron Lockett will serve as my replacement for today's meeting as she will adequately take you to task if she sees fit.'"

There was a grumble from the room that was silenced by an immediate glare from Matron Lockett.

She turned back to the note but faltered. Surprisingly, her stern features fell. She hesitated over the words with a slight grin on her face. Looking upwards at John, she coughed politely. "Try not to look too disappointed, Dr Bennett."

John flushed red whilst the men around him started to chuckle gently. It was a strange sensation. John had been known as a man of quiet privacy. Yet his courtship with Miriam was already gossiped about within the hospital halls. It seemed he simply couldn't hide how besotted he was with her, even now. So, he hung his head down low, trying to ignore the under-the-breath remarks and faces that leered at him. As Sir Fredric began the meeting, John took a pen and opened his notebook, hoping that others would follow suit.

However, his eyes immediately landed on a shocking sight.

In the pages of his notebook lay another photograph.

Only this time, Miriam did not look like a sensible genteel would-be-wife as she did before. It was a racy boudoir photo. Miriam was standing in her undergarments, corset, and boots. She was tightly cinched, and her breasts were plumped. She stood in a commanding position, with one foot on a chair next to her. In her hand was a small, wooden cane. She held it with a fierce expression on her face.

John gulped loudly and immediately slammed the notebook shut, fearful that one of the men surrounding him, or Matron Lockett for that matter, would see the risqué photograph of Miriam. The sound ricocheted loudly around the room, causing everyone to immediately silence and turn to look at him. His face turned a deeper shade of red.

Sir Fredric smiled politely though he was slightly annoyed at the interruption. "What is it, Bennett?"

"Oh, my apologies Sir Fredric," John said quietly and waved his hand in the air, trying to dismiss the event, as though there wasn't a salacious photo of the Chairman's daughter writhing within the pages of John's notebook. "There was a fly. Luckily, I caught the pest."

No one said anything further. The picture burned in John's mind alongside both the scent and the feel of her that Miriam had teased him with. His entire faculties were flooded. He was completely ravenous for anything – a taste, a touch, a tryst. He'd take as little or as much as he could get.

Tonight, John thought hopefully, *tonight*.

The door had become beastly. Caught in the creature's sights, Miriam hovered in the hallway of her aunt's lavish Chelsea home, completely unsure what to do with herself. She looked at the door then to the clock and then back at the door again. Though it was an hour until the dinner, and thus his arrival, Miriam Clayton would've given anything to see John walk in that very second. Or the next one. Or the next one.

She'd only move when a plate of food would pass her by. Whether it was meats, cheeses, or sweets, Miriam pinched whatever she could from the waiters' plates and stuffed them into her face. Eating bits here and there was the only thing to keep her from dissolving into pathetic longing.

The game was intended to rouse John. She had made sure that every sense of her stalked him. A perfume spritz. A pair of drawers. A photograph or two. It was all in order to tease and tantalise her would-be husband in her absence. However, as fun as her games were, they similarly made her tense. Because, ultimately, the ruling came from another's request. Though Miriam had used it to her advantage, hoping that John was salivating for her this very second, it had not been her will. Frustration had mounted within her since she left him on Tuesday morning.

At least I can touch myself, Miriam thought to herself with a cheeky smile. She reached for a plump, red strawberry that walked by in a gold-rimmed glass bowl.

A small, slender hand batted the fruit from Miriam's fingers. She looked up and found her Aunt Isobel holding onto the bowl. Miriam's face went red – half-indignant and half-apologetic for having been caught.

Isobel sighed. "Miriam, I wish you wouldn't dither around, you are rather getting in the way."

"Forgive me," Miriam said sharply, "perhaps it would be better if I locked myself away for the evening entirely. After all, it is only *my* engagement dinner."

The forceful, sarcastic nature of those words did not faze Aunt Isobel who merely rolled her eyes dismissively. "Very droll Miriam. May I say that are no longer a child? I am merely suggesting that you help, rather than stare at the door as though it were about to gobble you whole."

"I am sorry," Miriam said, hanging her head down low. To show she was truly repentant, she grabbed the next plate that walked by – which happened to be a bowl of grapes - and insisted on carrying it. Aunt Isobel nodded and made her way to the dining room. Miriam dutifully followed but kept moaning. "I am rather apprehensive about the whole evening. Why must we go through this social rigmarole? I'd marry John..."

"'... tomorrow if I had my way.' Yes, you have made your whole stance on the affair perfectly clear," Isobel replied. They entered the dining room together and Isobel instantly tutted. Despite carrying the strawberries, Isobel began to straighten the silver cutlery and plates. She would move the place names next, muttering on who hated who and couldn't possibly sit with one another. In between her grumblings, she turned to Miriam and said, "Forgive me Miriam, if I simply wish to add some decorum to this *very* short engagement."

"Damn decorum!" Miriam said, throwing her arms up wildly into the air, despite the fact that she was still clinging onto the plate. A few loose grapes sprang loose and made their escape. They rolled away. Isobel tutted. Whilst still clutching onto the strawberries, having failed to find a home for them, Miriam's aunt bent beneath the very long table.

There were many guests coming tonight. Most of whom didn't know Miriam or John that well at all. Miriam had seen the list of people coming and immediately made a fuss. Apart from her friends and close family, she couldn't stomach the rest of them. They were mostly men and women from Isobel's societal coterie who'd much rather gossip than use their wealth and privilege for the greater good. When she had seen the invites, Miriam had made a studious effort to remember not to invite them to the actual wedding, knowing the exclusion would send them into a frenzy.

When Isobel returned from retrieving the roving fruit, she said in a strained breath, "It is expected of young ladies such as yourself when one wishes to court a gentleman."

"But Aunt Izzy, it just seems very superfluous seeing as John and I have already..." Miriam stopped herself. Flashes of John's naked body flushed through her, causing her cheeks to burn further. She was so hot that she was afraid of setting the tablecloth on fire as she put the grapes on the table. She searched for an appropriate word. "… courted."

"For my benefit, Miriam, please." Aunt Isobel muttered with a grin, finally placing the strawberry bowl down in the centre. "When you are married you can do whatever you so wish."

"Hmmm I believe I shall," Miriam said, swiping another strawberry and devouring it quickly before Isobel could slap it out of her hand again. She stuck her tongue out at her aunt like a disobedient child. The pair then burst into polite chuckles.

Miriam had lost her mother when she was baby. She was too young to have any memories and was not impacted by the loss in any great way. Any thoughts of her were constructed from stories and photographs. Though, at times, she wondered what her life would have been like if her mother had lived. Miriam had a devoted father and a loving aunt. Isobel was one of her closest motherly figures, alongside her housekeeper Hettie. Isobel might have been stern in her approach to social standing, but she was also kind and considerate. She had carried that spirit long through the years of hell she had been unjustly put through because of her violent husband Charles. Miriam often pondered on the unassuming strength Isobel had.

The pair were close enough to jibe at one another without much harm. They had similar polite chuckles and wild cackles. In the quiet that followed their laughter, Isobel took a few moments to inspect her niece. Whenever her aunt or father went quiet like this, their eyes glassy as they gazed over her, Miriam wondered if they were thinking about her mother Anna. Isobel reached over and kindly stroked Miriam's cheek, before saying. "You look beautiful, Miriam. The dress is exquisite."

Miriam could not help but let out a little squeal of delight, immediately grabbing the dress and swinging it from side to side. It was a baby pink garment with a scoop neckline. Climbing up the skirt and upon the puffy but short sleeves were vivid red roses. In fact, the entire evening had centred around the flower – there were many varieties that filled the rooms and adorned the tabletops. She'd even placed a few in her plaited hair. Each and every one served a purpose – to completely devastate John when he walked through the door.

It had its desired effect. The minute he saw her, John was frozen in the mouth of the door. He wavered on the step, fully aware that Sir Fredric was beadily watching his reaction. Miriam looked radiant – as pretty as a princess – yet her eyes glowed with dark desire. He swallowed air quickly, trying to catch the breath that she had taken. The flowers on her dress and in her hair danced within his mind. The roses entangled with her very being, he thought of that wild mesh of vibrancy and violence that had awoken in them both. John's mind raced in two directions. There were the usual notions of her writhing naked below him as he had his wicked way with her. But also, he wanted to take her far from this place and hold her tightly, protecting her from the rest of the world and all its thorns.

It wasn't just John who was caught in the moment. Miriam too was stunned into silence. John was the handsomest and gentlest man she had ever known, and still he burned with a bright passion that matched her own. Standing in the doorway, he was dressed in a simple tuxedo – black tails and trousers with a white waistcoat and bowtie. Yet he looked heavenly and devilish all at once, his wanton needs blazing in his bright blue eyes. As John walked slowly over to Miriam, her heart raced so madly that it panged and pained in her chest. The power this man had over her could move the earth. All at once she wished to take him in front of everyone and take him far away from this place. What adventures they would have if they just ran away from society.

Suddenly John was stood inches away from Miriam and the extraordinary scent of him wrapped around her causing her to instantly gasp.

"May I?" John said in a quiet whisper as he softly bowed to her and tentatively reached out his hand.

Miriam shook her head, denying him permission. A slick smile spread across her face. "No. Not here. I am afraid of what we may do."

"Indeed," John grumbled, knowing he was moments away from exploding. He brought his hand down and wiggled his fingers. She was right, of course. He too was certain he'd do unbecoming things to her if she gave him one iota of skin.

Miriam realised that she was flushing and instantly regretted wearing pink. She had suddenly become a beacon of the colour. They stood awkwardly opposite one another, not sure what to do with themselves and utterly frightful that their carnal urges would take over. They smiled timidly at one another.

As Sir Fredric approached them, he chuckled loudly at the pair's hesitation. Luckily, he misconstrued their yearning as shyness. Laughing, he slapped John hard on the back. "Come man, there is no need to be so nervous."

"I too would be nervous if I were marrying Miriam Clayton," whispered Michael Jenkins to John as he came into the conversation. He tried to keep it low, for only John's benefit. However, it was not low enough. Both Miriam and Michael's wife

Adelaide, who was clutching onto his arm, had heard, and scowled together.

Miriam pursed her lips and turned her sights to Michael. The look was enough to make Sir Fredric grimace and grab a drink before rushing away to find his beloved sister-in-law. The minute Miriam's eyes caught Michael's, his face immediately grew red. He hoped that he hadn't upset her enough to receive yet another tongue lashing in front of his peers.

However, she kept it short and curt. "Michael, you are a Doctor, are you not?" Michael's eyes widened. There were a few beats where he wondered on whether or not he should answer. When Miriam gestured for him to do so, he nodded slightly. "So, I assume you are fully aware of anatomy." She pointed to the side of her head. "These are ears, they help you hear. I use them quite regularly. Do you?"

Michael bowed his head somewhat, but John smiled wildly. As did Adelaide. She let go of her husband and reached out her hand to Miriam. "Well, hello there." There was a delightful American twang to her voice to her calm, collected voice. Her hazel eyes sparkled delightfully as she continued, "I am Adelaide Jenkins. I do not believe we have had the pleasure of meeting."

Miriam took her hand and shook it vigorously, blushing somewhat at the beautiful blonde lady. "I have seen you at functions before but no, we've never been formally introduced." She cocked her head to Michael. "I wonder why that is?"

"Oh well, Michael is deathly afraid that we'll become the best of friends," Adelaide replied, and a flash of trouble streaked through her eyes as Michael said her name sternly to stop her. She dismissed this then scooped her arm into Miriam's and brought her close. "My dear husband was right in that estimation. I like you already. Come, you must tell me *everything.*"

Both John and Michael looked bemused. They stood dumbfounded as Adelaide whisked Miriam off into the party. Michael swallowed nervously and muttered, "Oh, I do not like this."

John, however, was worried for a different reason. He did not want Miriam to disappear again, having hungered for her since Tuesday. Now he was finally by her side, he wanted to drip his yearnings into her ear. He wanted to tease her in all the ways that she had been teasing him. Most of all, he wanted her to release him from his torment so he could touch her.

There was a slight fear that Adelaide would steal all of his fiancé's attention for the entire evening. But as Miriam was walked away, she turned her head to John and kept her eyes solely on him. He grinned goofily, tipping his glass of champagne to her, and watched until she was out of view.

By the time dinner was called, the betrothed pair had unfortunately found themselves parted for the first hour of the evening. Though, unbeknownst to the crowd they both were wracked with the same thoughts – of which room was best to fuck one another in. They smiled and nodded at the polite conversations of their acquaintances but were clouded as memories of their trysts played like reels behind their glazed eyes.

At least, at dinner, they could sit and talk to each other.

They followed their friends into the dining room. As people fawned over the place settings, Miriam and John sighed contentedly at seeing one another again. At the top of the long dining room table was a smaller table with two chairs next to one another. Both Miriam and John silently loathed the idea of being propped up at the head of the table so that everyone could stare at them. Yet as they took their places, they realised it was bliss; a small wooden cloth-covered island for the two of them. They could whisper their dirty thoughts, and no one would be any the wiser. As the wine was poured, both gripped onto their separate glasses, trying to stop their hands from wandering. Yet there was an undeniable charge that passed through them. Their hearts raced in time.

After a few beats and a few sips of liquid encouragement, John placed a little red velvet box on the table. He muttered quietly, "As we are making this official."

He nudged it closer to her. There was a hesitant moment between the pair as they gazed around the room, hoping that no one would see and encourage John to propose on bended knee and slip it on her finger. That would be breaking Miriam's strict instructions. Luckily, people were already in high spirits and too busy enjoying the starter course to notice John's action.

Miriam gingerly reached over and opened the box. "Oh John," Her pulse caught in her throat. "Oh, it is beautiful."

"It was my mother's," he said nervously, trying to swallow memories that pooled in his thoughts. Miriam gasped at the admission. She slipped the silver ring on and then stretched her fingers out to admire it. It wasn't the perfect fit; it was a little tight on Miriam's fingers as she slid it down. It wasn't very expensive either, a hand-me down through generations. It was scuffed and there were scratches on the deep purple gem that he hadn't had time to smooth away. Yet it was rich in sentiment.

There wasn't very much left by his parents after they died. When John moved down to Kent, everything was packed into a suitcase. Anything of any value, he sold to pay for an education in order to escape the clutches of his abusive aunt. Throughout it all, he kept this wedding ring. It was a token of his mother – the only reminder of his humble roots. Even his accent was beaten out of him. Giving it away to someone else meant a great deal more to him than if he were to buy the most expensive diamond in London.

He hesitated, fearing that when she inspected it closer, she would see it was a tatty pauper's ring. Yet the way Miriam gazed upon the jewellery – with her mouth agape and her eyes wide and pensive – it was as though it were Queen Victoria's own band. It made John love her more. Without speaking of the ring's meaning, she had understood it completely. Miriam smiled earnestly. "Tell me about her."

"Oh, she was very resourceful, but she was kind..." John offered a slight smile. "She worked hard - long after father died. Though, she still made time to read us a story at night. I cannot quite recall what she looked like. I just remember dark-brown hair and green eyes. And her laugh."

In a reverent way, Miriam inquired. "Do you miss her terribly?"

"In a manner, yes," John replied quickly, trying to cover the shakiness in his voice, "but I was young and that was so many years ago. One learns to live with the loss."

Miriam nodded then reached out a hand. It hovered over his for a moment. She was clearly wondering whether she should break her own rules to give him a comforting touch. Catching her eye, John shook his head, fearful that if she did, he'd dissolve into all the tears he'd been holding back for decades. Instead, she placed her now ringed hand on the table – millimetres from where his lay so that at least some heat and electricity could still pass through them.

John's heart raced not just from the way her hand was dangerously close to his but from Miriam's uncanny ability to uncover all his secrets. The pair shared a commonality in having mothers who had long since parted this world. Neither of them knew how to really speak about their respective losses. Miriam spoke about her mother in a matter-of-fact way, having never known her long enough to build that bond. John, being a man of little words anyway, had never truly spoken about it at all.

Despite this, every time Miriam looked at him, or asked him questions, John could not help but give a little piece of himself to her. They said nothing more on the matter, but they stared at one another intently. It did not matter that the food had arrived and was taken away from them before they had a single bite. It did not matter that their friends and family could see them, gazing longingly at one another. It did not matter at all. They had this sweet space reserved only for them.

Suddenly there was a tap on a glass that broke the haze. They jumped, snapping their hands back into their laps as though they had been caught in a scandalous position. The crowd grew immediately silent as Sir Fredric stood up. His booming voice echoed across the heads. "Ladies and gentlemen, I wish to thank you all for joining us on this happy occasion. We are here to celebrate the impending nuptials of my wonderful and darling daughter Miriam. Some may be shocked at such a quick turn of events, though not entirely surprised. One only has to be around the pair to recognise that they are well suited. Even now, they cannot keep their eyes off one another." There was a small chuckle and the betrothed pair blushed. "So please, raise a glass and join me in welcoming the exceptional Doctor John Bennett as my new son." With all eyes on him, John's cheeks burned further. He raised his own glass to the toast in hopes to hide behind it. Sir

Fredric bowed his head and tipped his glass politely to John. "I believe you will make a fine addition to this family. Now it is time for my daughter to announce the wedding date."

Miriam smiled as she joined her father in standing. John caught a flash of mischief in her eyes. He breathed in somewhat excitedly, expecting Miriam to deliver a thousand insults to the people around them. However, she kept it brief. "The third of October."

There was an alarmed and animated murmur from the diners. Miriam might've, from time to time, adhered to societal conventions but she had a particular talent for stirring up trouble when she saw it necessary. She stayed standing for a little while, relishing in the wide-eyed faces of the crowd around them.

"Two weeks?" John was excited and nervous all at once as Miriam sat back down. To everyone within the room, the quick and short engagement was a shock. To the couple themselves, it was a long, long time to finally be united as one in every sense of the word.

"Yes, that was the earliest I could book." Miriam scowled. "Father and Aunt Izzy were quite insistent on using the village church. It is where they both got married." She then whispered, "Between you and me, I believe it is cursed. Look at the evidence!"

John began to laugh heartily though he unconvincingly said, "I am certain time will fly by."

Miriam glowered at him. He could practically see the carnal images dancing through her mind. "Hmmm, are you certain you can last that long?"

"Without you as my wife?" As he cut into the cold steak in front of him, he looked around to make sure no one was watching him, lowering his voice so it sat quietly beneath the chatter. "Or without touching you in all the ways I wish to?" Leaning as close as he could to Miriam, John whispered, "Either way, it is torture."

Miriam did not have the answer for him. For a short while she said nothing at all and continued eating her food. As she picked up her glass of red wine, she turned to him and whilst sipping slowly said, "Have you followed all of my instructions?" There was a flash of torment in his eyes as she questioned him. He nodded gently and a rush of seething hot air left his mouth. Glee filtered through her at that very moment, even though she was similarly tense from lacking his body. What she said next, then, was also an instruction to herself. "Try not to look too pained, Dr Bennett."

Under the table, Miriam leaned down to her skirt. She pulled it up and removed something from a garter on her leg. John tried not to look, biting into the meat to stop himself from biting into her flesh. Suddenly, she slipped something into his trouser pocket. The sensation of her hands near his crotch caused him to twitch somewhat as he nearly lost all control of himself. Using all his strength, he tried to keep deathly still. When she pulled her hand back, she gave him a quick squeeze on his thigh. The very action nearly caused him to spill over. He let out a small gasp.

John had never been more thankful that Sir Fredric had walked around and interrupted their conversation.

After that, the rest of the evening went by in such a blur. There was dining, drinks, and dancing – all of which proved difficult without touching his betrothed. But, without warning, it was time to say goodbye. Sir Fredric, Aunt Isobel, and Miriam were lined up against the door as people filtered out into the evening. John was last in line, clenching his hands into fists and letting them go out of anxiousness. Were they really going to be parted for two weeks? He wasn't entirely sure what he was going to do.

Yet when he was face-to-face with Miriam, her blue eyes sparkling gleefully at him, all that urgency and need pulsated through him. John knew he had to act. A small violation. To see her come undone momentarily. He leaned forward and kissed her on the cheek softly before whispering darkly into her ear, "Forgive me, I could not resist."

The way she exhaled told him everything. He winked at her before stepping out into the evening, charged with enough electricity to illuminate the entire world.

In the carriage home, John watched London stroll by. He was as bright and beaming as the incandescence of the city. There was a chatter in the air as people filtered in and out of theatres, pubs, and more. Smiling to no one in particular, John was as alive as the place he called home. The city was striking in all its vivaciousness and matched the rhythmic pulsing heart within him. He was thankful to be by himself, musing on the evening and the soft skin he had finally skimmed from his love.

With a gentle chuckle, and finally, with no one around, John slipped his hand into his trouser pockets to pull out Miriam's final gift. It was a small envelope. He brought it up to his nose and smelled her perfume upon it. After a few beats, he slid his finger into the paper's crevices and tore the envelope open. Falling into his lap was one final photograph.

Immediately, John let out a small, suffering, sigh. The photo was indeed another of Miriam. But there was no dress. No corset. No cane. Nothing. It was Miriam completely nude. She sat on a simple wooden chair, with her legs crossed so as to not show her privates completely. Her breasts were free, however, and her nipples erect. She leaned her head in her hand. Her expression was the same as it had been in the previous photos. Her eyes bore into his spirits so much that it was as though she were real. John could practically smell her sex and hear her voice as she called out to him.

In a moment, John wondered how she had produced such a photograph: Who else had coveted the naked body of his fiancé? He groaned at the very thought of it.

There and then, John realised he may not have the constitution to wait two weeks without Miriam. He could barely survive the evening without pleasing himself to this picture of her. He sighed and knew if he were to go home right this minute, he'd forsake her ruling altogether.

Signalling to the driver to stop, John got out of the cab and walked the rest of the way home, Strolling slowly by the river and slipping through the shadows of the night, John mused on the devilish nature of his fiancé. How blissfully devious Miriam was. He laughed to himself as he paced through the city, winding down its curved paths and cobbled streets until his feet grew sore. Though they were not as agonised as his spirit was – caught wonderfully in the web of Miriam Clayton.

John's entire body was shattered when he reached his boarding home in Camden. He climbed the stairs with no other thought than collapsing onto his bed and drifting to sleep. However, as he unlocked his room door, John was greeted by a figure on his bed. Dressed entirely in pink, with roses crawling up her dress, Miriam looked like an angel. Orange hues from the fireplace fell upon her milky white skin and chubby frame. Miriam turned slowly to him. As heavenly as she looked, flames danced riotously in her blue eyes. In a calm manner, she beckoned, "Hello John."

"Miriam!" John replied quietly, closing the door behind him, and locking it tight. For a while, he was dumbstruck. He blinked, believing that she was simply a mirage from an exhausted doctor's frustrated mind. So, when her figure did not disappear, he suddenly said, "You are here!"

"A fine observation, John." Miriam broke out into a sly smile. She inhaled, her breath jagged with pleasure and need. Her glorious breasts heaved in her corset as she did. She continued in a matter-of-fact manner: "Yes, I could not help thinking on how futile photographs are. I slipped away as soon as I could."

"Oh, thank goodness!" John took off his cape and hat quickly. It had not escaped him that his kiss had had its desired effect on Miriam, unravelling her entirely. He made a small note that no matter how in control Miriam was in their relationship or sexual exploits, John could always make her falter for a short while. He relished that somewhat.

Yet when John loosened his necktie, Miriam raised her hand. He halted immediately. "Do not think I have forgotten your infraction tonight. You broke the rules."

John nodded. "Quite right."

"Kneel before me John," Miriam said, patting the space and air before her. "You deserve to be punished."

He nodded again. Slowly he walked the short distance from the door to the bed and fell to his knees before her. Looking down upon him, Miriam was filled with so many urges that she practically burst through her corset. The way his blue eyes darted all over her made her unearthly. How foolish she was to deny herself this man, not when he devastated her so. She wanted to shower him with pleasure always. As well as pain, of course.

Even though he was ready for her new ruling, Miriam had paused for a long time – unexpectedly holding her breath. Miriam reached down and from her stocking, she produced a small, wooden cane and exhaled with an unbridled elation. The cane was the exact one that she had been holding in the photograph. John's eyes widened at its appearance. His eyes grew even bigger when she slapped it in her palms sharply. "Roses to stop?"

"Yes," John seethed, shuffling eagerly on his knees.

"Oh Doctor Bennett," she muttered, leaning down so her tight plump breasts were practically in his face. John could not stop staring at them, holding himself against the urge to ravage them entirely. She took her finger and ran it down his jawline softly. Then she lifted his chin, so that his mouth was dangerously close to hers. As their eyes met. Miriam laughed, "Try not to look too excited."

The Invitation

Thursday 19th September 1895

The hospital ward was quiet.

On her own, and somewhat afraid, Marie looked around at the empty beds. She had only visited this place twice before, but there were always one or two people here. Always women, with injuries just like hers. A broken nose, bruised eye, a swollen jaw. There was always someone waiting alongside her, a mournful echo of one another's crimes. It was a horrible reminder that there was more than one terror on the streets of London. Yet, as odd as it may have seemed, Marie sometimes was comforted by the fact that she wasn't the only one tarnished by brutish men wielding their brutish fists. She had seen women of all classes here, sharing a familiar curse. With a hefty sigh, Marie resigned herself to the fact that it was a good thing that the Lady Gray Ward was empty.

That fact did nothing to lessen how alone she felt.

A singular beam of light scraped through the thin basement windows at the top of the ward. It shone on Marie. Sitting on the edge of the bed, she cradled her left hand in her lap. Marie was no doctor, but she knew it was definitely broken. The base of her thumb was protruding at an unusual angle, and over the course of the morning, the skin around it had become the oddest blend of purple and red. Marie would try to move it ever so slightly and pain would reverberate throughout her, making her feel sick. As she inspected the injury herself, Marie could see flecks of dirt and mud that she had yet to wipe off. At the sound of footsteps, she immediately licked her good thumb and gingerly tried to clean the boot print from her hand. A shadow blocked the light, and Marie froze, hoping that if she did not move, the figure would not have seen her actions.

"You cannot hide this from me," said the voice above her. In that moment, Maire looked up and saw Doctor Clayton. She was silhouetted by the sunbeam behind her, but her features were no less distinguishable. Despite being younger than Marie, the buxom doctor looked down like a school headteacher would having caught a naughty student. Doctor Clayton even folded her arms.

Behind the doctor stood the equally scary Matron Lockett, whose weathered face looked as though it hadn't smiled in decades. The image of Doctor Clayton and Matron Lockett together was enough to bring a mountain down to its knees.

Marie was suddenly very frightened that she'd get rapped knuckles if she dared fly into excuses. Instead, she merely looked down on the floor. "I am sorry, Doctor Clayton."

"Why do *you* apologise?" Doctor Clayton said in a tone both kind and stern. She then tutted gently before taking a seat beside Marie, causing the bed springs to wheeze as if they had been holding their breath. The doctor then nudged Marie playfully. "I think we can dispel with the formalities now, can we not, Marie? Call me Miriam."

"Oh!" Marie gasped. The name illuminated in her mind, bright and burning. It was a kindness she thought she didn't deserve. Not only had Doctor Clayton – Miriam - remembered her name, but she had extended a friendly courtesy. It caused tears to well up in Marie's emerald-green eyes. She tried to hide them by jovially saying, "Miriam. Oh, I like that. Very pretty name. Miriam Clayton."

Miriam smiled gently as a way of thanks. She then reached into her skirt pocket, producing a small silver watch. Looking up at Matron Lockett, she said with an air of disappointment, "Matron, I am afraid I must absent myself from today's board meeting." Miriam reached into her pockets again and removed a small piece of paper and pencil. She quickly scribbled a note, folded it, and handed it to Matron with a sly grin on her face.

"Please attend in my place. I've a note for the gentlemen for you to read aloud."

"Oh Doctor Clayton, I do not want to be a burden…" Marie began.

"Nonsense," Matron replied in a curt yet courteous manner, "I am more than honoured to. I bet my presence will pale them." Matron quickly nodded with an air of finality on the topic before leaving the ward, leaving Marie and Miriam alone on the bed together.

Marie's face burned, half-indignant and half-embarrassed from Matron's response, though she meant well. The sharp footsteps of the older nurse petered away into the atmosphere and as soon as they disappeared, an uneasy quiet filled the ward. The young doctor sat patiently beside the weary patient.

Marie held her breath so as to not disturb the silence. In the seconds that followed, a little bird dancing in the courtyard chirped around the sole window of the ward. Marie sighed at its song. Miriam had said nothing, as though she too were content to listen to the birds for a while. An unexpected calm before the certain storm that was sure to follow.

Marie could sense it all around Miriam. The angered words she was about to say. The pitying glances that she was about to throw. The urgent pleas she was about to deliver. In this moment, Marie regretted ever coming to the hospital. Doctor Clayton and Matron Lockett were being kind, but their kindness and generosity hit the pit of Marie's stomach like droplets of poison, coursing through her insides with fire. Marie did not want people to waste their time on her, fussing over injuries that she had acquired through her own folly.

The bird finally flew away. A teardrop rolled down Marie's cheek. Miriam brushed it deftly away before saying in a slight whisper, "Do not blame yourself, Marie."

Marie spun her head quickly to meet Miriam's eyes, slightly aghast that the doctor had read her mind so clearly. She went to respond fast, but Miriam had already reached over and began to tuck loose strands of Marie's red hair behind her ear. The motion cooed her more so than words ever could. In the gentlest of tones, Marie said, "I was drunk."

"That is hardly cause for such violence."

"I laughed at him."

"I am sure he is risible enough to warrant such an insult." Miriam chuckled but stopped when she saw how silently distraught Marie had become. She gave another sigh before she repeated, "Do not blame yourself Marie."

"Doctor Clayton…" Marie replied desperately before stealing a breath from the atmosphere. The sharp intake caused more tears to roll down her face. She dared not cast them aside, she let the stream of them tumble from her with the aching sadness.

"Miriam, please." Then the doctor took Marie's good hand and gave it a kindly squeeze. Marie echoed the gesture.

There were only two times before where Marie had been in this ward and encountered Doctor Clayton. The first time was for a black eye and the second time was for a broken nose where Marie had bled all over the doctor's blue and white striped blouse. Each time, Doctor Clayton had grasped Marie's hand so fiercely and waited for a response. When Marie squeezed back, it meant Miriam had permission to fix whatever injury Marie had.

Doctor Clayton tended to Marie's wounds warily as though Marie was a fragile and broken glass ornament. She lightly took the broken hand and slid her delicate fingers across the bruising. Carefully she examined the wound, apologising every time Marie winced or grimaced. "I'm afraid I need to reset the bone. Forgive me, this is going to hurt."

Marie took a deep inhalation, before nodding to Miriam, who very quickly pushed the protruding bone back into place with a short snap. Marie did not cry out but squeaked with the agony, causing Miriam to mumble another sorry. The doctor then grabbed some gauze and began to wrap up the wounded hand before reaching into her pockets. As Marie watched Miriam remove a small bottle of laudanum and a spoon, she marvelled at the many compartments hidden within the skirt. Happily, Marie took the spoonful of tincture, as a warming feeling spread throughout her gut.

"Thank you, Doctor Clayton." Marie smiled weakly after she was fixed. Then suddenly gasped and corrected herself. "Oh, I mean Miriam!"

Miriam did not chastise Marie this time. Instead, a small grin appeared on her face as she patted Marie's knee gently, and breathed out, "Speaking candidly, you will not be able to call me Doctor Clayton for very much longer anyway."

"Wh…" Then Marie burst into the biggest of smiles. "… Are you getting married?"

Indeed, I am."

Marie squealed with joy and went to clap her hands. Remembering her wounds, she settled on gently placing them together, putting them up to her mouth as though she were trying to hide the bright beaming smile on her face. Miriam bristled from the joy emanating from Marie before the younger of the two looked off into the distance.

In this quiet moment, this almost frozen beat, Marie watched as sparks of lightning flashed through Miriam's eyes, and a gleeful grin crooked on her face. On the young woman's cheeks grew pink roses, slyly blooming alongside her thoughts. Beautiful petals unfolded upon Miriam. As Marie watched, a longing pang hit her stomach: She recognised that look. She had worn it well once.

That youthful charge of hopeful love - both exciting and frightening all at the same time. Seeing it echo on Miriam's face caused a different type of blushing to grow on Marie's cheeks: One with thorns of envy.

To dispel the wicked jealousy and tirade of memories that threatened to overcome her senses, Marie reached over and grabbed Miriam's hand. "Th-that is wonderful news!" A beat. "You seem really happy, Miriam."

"I am!" Miriam smiled gratefully, placing her own hand on Marie's. Then she let out a gasp of joy and said, "You should come to the wedding!"

Marie blinked out of shock before she threw her head back and laughed loudly. Wild uncontrollable cackles that ricocheted off the walls of the ward. Still gripping Miriam's hand, Marie giggled and chortled. However, when she caught Miriam's eyes and realised that the doctor was not laughing along, she abruptly stopped. "You don't want the likes of me at your wedding!"

"I would rather you than any of my aunt's tedious social parasites," Miriam scoffed. She then went back to pushing Marie's hair behind her ears. "But I insist that you come. You'll be my guest of honour."

"That is very generous Miriam, but I can't. You know I can't."

Miriam continued the calming motion of playing with strands of Marie's hair before she said somewhat absentmindedly, "At the very least, think on it."

Marie responded with a resigned, polite nod.

Thursday 26th September 1895

The room was not quiet.

The sound of strident snoring stirred Marie. Truthfully, it had kept interrupting her throughout the night, making Marie restless. She laid awake, her head throbbing and her mouth dry from last night's liquor. It was a cold autumn morning, yet it was stark with sunlight.

She stared at the ceiling, counting the wooden panels, though by now she had the number memorised. Anything to distract her from the noise that reverberated through her sore head. The source of such a sound was Detective Blythe who slept beside her, unaware that the morning had come to beckon him to a more respectable life. His slumber rolled over her terribly, shaking reminiscences from her foundations.

Whenever a trick stayed later than he should, invading her sleep in such a cruel manner, Marie always thought back to the first time she had had sex in this bed. It had been thoughtful. The man had touched her in bright and brilliant ways, making her feel warm and wanted. The first time since her husband had passed away. It had reminded her of a fairy-tale if such stories could happen on the steps of public houses in Soho.

Marie had sat half-cut in a small corner of The Furnace. She had slid the last remaining pennies across the wood of a small table in the corner, wondering whether another gin or a room would keep her warmest at night. A man dressed in a velvet burgundy suit had approached her quite kindly and offered to pay for a drink. The first of many for the evening. Sparks glowed through his brown eyes, enough to heat her so brightly that she feared setting the entire place on fire. They swapped stories, they sang songs, and as the night petered out, he had taken her hand and guided her upstairs. They had made love throughout the night.

This is how Harry Wright gets his workers. It had happened to Marie so many years ago, and it had happened to many girls since. He seduces them so softly that they don't realise they are being swindled. He plies them with drinks and promises of shelter. He showers them with affection so beyond anything that they had ever known. Only in the morning, as stark and cold as this one, does he demand repayment.

Marie had heard from other girls on how their pimps would leave marks – tattoos or burns as though they were branded cattle. Harry's mark was much more insidious, it lingered deep beneath the skin. An unwanted and unmoveable desire that curled within her soul. The more that he degraded her, the more that he beat her, the more that she yearned for his approval. She'd give anything to go back to that sweet first night where Harry took her in his arms and made love to her so considerately.

Occasionally, when he was drunk, Harry would wander into Marie's bed, and she'd forget every cruel thing he ever did to her. Because all she longed for, more than anything, were those first tender touches. Marie thought about them every morning. Every morning for the past five years. Every damn cold stark morning.

"Psst."

The short sharp sound sliced through Marie's head. She winced immediately, scrunching up her face to dispel the ache within her temple.

"Psst. Marie!"

She groaned, sitting up in bed slowly, though her body was crying out not too. As Marie looked around her room, she haphazardly smacked her dry lips together, the remnants of last night's gin repeating on her tongue. It wasn't long until she found the source. Her door was slightly ajar, and in the gap Marie caught a blurry glimpse of blonde scraggly hair and grey sunken eyes. A hand-waved frantically at her, the movement added to the whirlwind within Marie's mind. She squinted at the figure to get a better look. "Oh Alice," she said with a groan, "what is it?"

"Come here…" Alice then looked behind her as she said hurriedly, "… Quickly. I've got something for you."

Marie huffed and pouted. It was far too early to leave the confines of her bed. The sun had barely risen though the light of it was kept trapped behind the dull, off-white clouds. Marie herself was only awake from the ripples of snores and calamitous thoughts. Even sitting up was a struggle, she wished, instead, that she had closed her eyes and pretended to still be in a deep sleep. Alice continued to frantically wave at Marie, causing the latter to lift herself from her sunken mattress. The act caused Detective Blythe to groan and roll over, the springs squeaky under his weight. The sound of it caused Marie to freeze, as though she were deathly afraid of him waking up. She waited a few beats until she heard the honks of his snore again.

Padding over to the blond-haired woman in her doorway, she sighed and repeated herself, "What is it Alice?"

"Oomf, what's got you all out of sorts?" Alice replied, a smirk appearing on her face, "I'm in two minds now whether to give you this or not."

"Give me what?"

"This!" Alice then reached into her cleavage and produced a small, perfectly white envelope that was now somewhat creased from being nestled in her bosom. She waved it around in front of Marie with a playful glint in her eyes. As she laughed, Marie could smell fresh gin on Alice's breath. The scent of it caused Marie's headache to worsen and her stomach to flip. She had no time for games. Frustrated, she tried to get the envelope and soon snapped it viciously from Alice's hands. The sharp action caused Alice to silence and frown. "Well, that wasn't nice."

Marie didn't listen. Instead, her hands pawed over the envelope. On the front was her name, written in beautiful, golden handwriting. As she ran her fingers over the letter, she could smell the faintest, familiar puff of lemon and bergamot. It shifted in Marie gently. "Where did you get this Alice?" she said faintly.

"Well, I was just minding my business in the bar and there was a knock on the door. Gave me quite the fright it did. Nearly dropped my gin. Ha! I was all spooked-like as this person tried to open the door. Then this slid under it! Thought it best to get it to you quick. You know, before Harry woke."

"Where is he?!"

"Oh, who knows where he hides!" Alice said with a scoff. She had lived at The Furnace longer than Marie did, and yet neither of the pair knew the place very well. Just the bar and their rooms upstairs. There were secrets in the woodwork here. Harry's other great trick was disappearing for long stretches of the day, appearing at the most inopportune moments to collect money, deliver beatings, or sleep with them. The two women had the same chilling thought and looked carefully around the hallway in case he was there. Alice lowered her voice, "Well, in any case, best hide it in case he is about. Could be money!"

The generosity of Alice's actions finally hit Marie. Though there were only a few of them taking lodgings in the brothel upstairs, they weren't all so kind to one another. Each woman had their own experiences which weighed on their soul and found it easier to scurry themselves away in their rooms with their clientele. Alice, however, was the opposite, especially when she wasn't drunk. Giddy most of the time, she was eager to make friends with all the women in The Furnace, as though it would soften the blows. Before the night rolled in, Alice and Marie would often natter over drinks like societal women in teashops. It was the part of the day Marie would look forward to the most. Any other person would, understandably, be curious and clever enough to ransack the envelope for money. Alice, however, had brought it straight to Marie. A kind gesture. Marie exclaimed gently and reached over, grabbing Alice's forearm, and giving it a squeeze. "Thank you."

"You're most welcome," Alice chuckled, and then lowered her voice, "mind you, if there is money in there I expect to be rewarded for such a generosity." She laughed loudly before she bounced down the hallway to her room.

Now sitting timidly on the chair by her dresser, Marie held the envelope preciously. With the shimmering writing catching the morning sun, there was such promise in the idents of the words. Flipping the envelope over, she exhaled and finally prised it open.

There was a small singular pink card. She tentatively pulled it out, her eyes widening as they gazed over the lush details. There was more gold lettering, flowing ornately over the card, within a blooming frame of colourful painted flowers. Holding the precious thing, she read:

Dearest Marie,
You are cordially invited to the wedding of
Doctor John Bennett and Doctor Miriam Clayton
at
The Clayton Manor
Clayton Village, Northamptonshire

Thursday-

A loud groan interrupted the air, causing Marie to panic, shoving the invitation down onto her lap like a naughty schoolchild. Immediately she looked up at the man on the bed. His eyes were opening and closing slowly. Cautiously, she looked back into the envelope again. There was money in there. Several pound notes wrapped up within a small piece of paper which had written upon it:

For the train ticket.

The loud exclaim of bedsprings shrieked in the air. Marie immediately shoved the money and the invitation in her drawer, slamming it shut. She looked up and smiled politely at Detective Thomas Blythe who similarly nursed a hungover head as he sat in his drawers on the edge of her bed. As always, he did not look at her immediately. Instead, his face grew redder as he reached down for his trousers, causing his suspenders to jangle from the movement.

Marie's face equally flushed – partly because she was now sitting on a secret, and partly because of this rotten routine the pair had entered. She grew indignant, and instead began cradling her broken hand in the other, gently poking and prodding to procure the pain.

"Marie?"

The sound of her name caused her to look up. As he was buttoning his shirt, Detective Blythe had for once during their mornings caught her eyes. He said nothing about the new connection. She smiled nonchalantly, "Yes Detective Blythe?"

He grimaced. "You can call me Tom now, Marie." He slipped on his grey tartan waistcoat before he found his matching jacket. He sighed and said, "You would be candid with me, wouldn't you Marie?"

"Tell you what?"

"If Harry… were… you know… causing you harm." He hesitated as he wrapped his necktie around him. "I could…"

Marie cut him off with the loudest of laughs. "Oh, Tom." She stood up and walked over to him, still chuckling underneath her breath. She reached up and began to help him with his tie. "What could you do to help me? We're both under his thumb."

"I do care about you Marie," Blythe said in response.

There was much that Marie wanted to say in return; the imposition of this conversation had made her both sad and angry. The way he had said this, with a seething hot breath, told her he was being truthful. Yet they both knew that he had a wife waiting for him to get home and as an upstanding man of the law, if anyone knew Blythe was soliciting, he would be ruined. Besides, if Blythe wanted to do anything to help her, he would've done so by now, instead of paying Harry to fuck her over and over again. She wanted to scream all this at him. However, she smiled weakly and said, "I know."

Blythe removed the wallet from his jacket and pulled out the usual amount of notes, walking over to her dresser to put it down in the same place as he had always done. Then he removed a smaller bundle and turned back to her. Kissing Marie gently on the cheek, he carefully put the remaining notes into her hand, before leaving her behind in The Furnace.

A small tear rolled down Marie's face. She let it slide, not daring to brush it away in case the action caused more tears to come. She paced back to the invitation in her drawers. Removing the money from the envelope, she added it to the bundle before she walked back to her bed. Hunching down, she carefully and quietly wriggled out a floorboard. A faint pop sent shivers down her spine. She stayed still for a moment and listened for a beat. Within the hole in the floor was a book of nursery rhymes. A book she had bought when she was eighteen. She had carried it with her for over twenty years. However, in the pages, she had hidden an envelope full of cash that she had collected over the years. Quickly, Marie placed in the new notes, and put everything back carefully.

As though nothing had transpired, Marie sat back at the dresser and read the invitation again, more carefully this time. Her heart fluttered excitedly in her chest. As she studied every detail, she thought about the thrill of weddings and marriage. How desperately in love people can be that the world melts away beneath them. That special charge of hope as the future becomes that much clearer and the world becomes a little bit brighter. She remembered how those feelings possessed her once. Before she knew it, Marie was crying softly. She longed so intensely to be in love like that again. Her life now felt like one big lie.

Memories pounded in her heart and her head until her eyes caught sight of the date. A simple thing that turned a chill through her. An icy grip froze all thoughts and emotions. The tears immediately stopped. There was no sound as the air was ripped from her.

The invitation had read:
Thursday 3rd October 1895.

Thursday 3rd October 1895

The pub was quiet.

This wasn't entirely unusual, after all it had just barely opened. The barkeep was still arranging the stools and removing barrels as the woman walked in. Truthfully, she was somewhat surprised that the pub was opened so late into autumn, but knowing the owner, she knew the shrewd business mind that hoped to catch any straggler walking up and down the seafront on a cold, blustering afternoon.

During the summer, Margate was the hub of tourism. The seaside town bustled with visitors from all over the country, hoping to enjoy the sun and a moment's peace from whatever life they led. The sandy shores were flooded with people of all kinds, their shrill squeaks perforating the air with joy. The piers were alive with entertainment – rides, arcades, and pubs like this one offering theatrical shows.

But as the sun began to wane, so did the tourists. Margate grew into its usual state of hibernation as the new season came. Only locals and the occasional visitor would walk the wooden boards of the piers and the stone pavements of the town.

As the woman sat on the stool, looking around the vicinity and leaning back against the bar, she knew better than anyone that pubs never really go out of season. Even ones that stood close to Margate Jetty, overlooking the turbulent sea as it crashed on the shore with a whoosh. You could even hear the creaking sound of the pier wood as the tide slammed against it. Some poor wretched soul was always in need of warmth – from the drink or the establishment itself. For now, it only sheltered her, and the poor bartender who was forced to work.

The name of this pub had caused the woman to hover outside for a few moments. It always did whenever she was in town. The Little Nan, after all, was named after her – Nancy Castor. It hadn't always been named that way, mind. It had changed within the past decade or so. When Nancy was a child, when her last name was MacDonald, and her parents owned the bar, it was called The Blackbeard, and had as much pirate paraphernalia as you could think of.

Now it had become a shrine. All across the walls were framed newspaper clippings and photographs of two little children.

Musical prodigies who wowed with their humorous dances and comedy routines. Little Nan, and her older sister, Jolly Jane. The MacDonald Sisters. There were even costumes from thirty years ago, hanging on the walls. Their tiny little sailor outfits as they tap-danced and sang ditties about sailing the sea that loomed all around them. Their near-daily routines proved popular with both the locals and the tourists that came to visit. The two girls didn't mind too much about working tirelessly on the stage. They enjoyed the limelight and the fact that they danced together.

The very thought of it caused Nancy's cheeks to burn. She turned away from the décor, the homages to her, and instead focused on the swill of gin at the bottom of the glass. She wasted little time in finishing the drink and ordering herself another. The bartender was a young man in his twenties, with short, dirty-blonde hair, and a round face. As he poured her another, she tried to look for someone familiar in those features, whilst hoping that he wouldn't do the same. As he refilled her beverage, he must've noticed her staring because his cheeks flushed and he said, "Local?"

"London," Nancy gruffly mumbled. It wasn't entirely a lie. She did live in the city, as she had done for nearly twenty years. But Margate was where she was born, and it was where she was raised. Though the smog of London overwhelmed her, Nancy could still taste the salty air of her old home. She breathed out. "Paying relatives a visit."

"Ah, young'uns?" The young man gestured to the book of nursery rhymes on the bar next to her.

The shock of him noticing caused her to instinctively grab the book. Flustered, she slid it into the small bag hanging around her shoulder and hung her head lower. "In some manner yes," she said quickly, gripping the glass tightly with her right hand. Then with her bandaged left hand, she pointed to the photograph of herself and her sister above the bottles of spirits behind the bar. "Did you ever see them perform?"

The bartender looked behind him and then chuckled. He turned back with a glint in his eyes. "Oh, no, before my time. Though mother says I'd seen their last performance when I was a babe." The admission curdled in Nancy somewhat and she downed her drink again before signalling for another, rummaging in her pockets for the loose coins. As the bartender poured more gin for her, he said, "Admirer?"

Nancy was somewhat thankful that the young lad hadn't recognised her. Had she really changed that much? She guessed two decades was a long time and he had never met her before. She didn't look much like those pictures and the grey images couldn't capture her bright red hair. Though that itself was greying at the roots. Her face was ragged now – dishevelled and aged from the world and her fondness for liquor. As she looked at the photograph – two blurry children in the middle of a performance – Nancy realised that the spark had gone. The jovial glint that was clear in the beaming smiles of the young girls in front of her. An unparalleled joy. Had that really gone from her? So much so that no one looked at her and saw that happy, bright, young thing from so many moons ago. Tears filled her eyes as she said lowly, "Oh well, I'm an old school acquaintance, you could say, and there were a few times I happened to see them perform." A beat. "What happened to them?"

"Oh well, Jolly Jane runs this here establishment. And Little Nan…" There was a dreadful pained pause before he continued softly. "Alas, the pair became estranged when Nancy eloped with some fella in London. Word is that she died ten years ago. Tragic, really."

Nancy did not bristle at this revelation, dismayed at her sudden early demise. If anything, she tried to stop a smile creeping on her face. The act had prevailed, and no one knew otherwise. She could flit through her hometown unnoticed. How strange it was to be one's own ghost. She breathed out in this afterlife and muttered, "Now that is a shame. Always fond of that one. Does Jane still reside in the Shallows?"

The bartender paused and eyed her quizzically. "Yes."

"Figured I'd give due diligence and pay my respects whilst I'm here."

The bartender nodded. Nancy finished her remaining drink, feeling the gin hit her for the first time as she stood up from the stool. She stretched her back from the pain of being hunched over. Reaching into her bag, and flicking through the pages of the book, Nancy removed some notes and hesitated before she slid over a generous amount. The young man thanked her as she walked out into the streets she once called home.

The walk from the pub to the Shallows Road was a familiar one. A path that she had taken countless times since she was a child. There was no great thought needed for her legs to make the journey. She moved slowly, however, keeping herself close to the buildings, submerged in whatever shadows they could offer her. She was fearful that someone might recognise her. Even if she knew that the spark that once possessed her was now dead.

As the walking brought Nancy closer and closer to her sister Jane, the last words that were screeched at her came blazing through her mind. Every footstep made the memory cling fiercely to her mind. The wretched tears stuck to her face as Jane screamed about the legacy she and their now deceased parents had built within the pub; the painful screams that burned Nancy's throat as she roared about the life she was owed since being trotted out as a performer since she was kid; and the slamming of fists upon tabletops as they viciously argued over her unexpected, out-of-wedlock pregnancy, just months after meeting a young bank clerk named Joe Castor. The last words Jane ever said to Nancy, screeching as the eighteen-year-old stormed out of the cottage for the final time, was that Joe Castor would be the ruin of her.

Walking up this beaten path, as the rows of houses appeared, those words smarted in Nancy's brain. She hated how true the statement was. The relationship didn't start that way. In fact, the pair moved to London and for the first five years, everything was fine. They were determined to prove their families wrong – those who had scorned their very fast engagement and marriage. They had a small flat in Bermondsey, Nancy worked in a clothes shop in Mayfair, creating clothes for high-end clients, and whilst they lost the first baby, and the second, and the third, they were more than content. They worked hard for one another, they loved one another, and even had friends who helped them thrive. They fell into a routine and had roughly five years of almost boring bliss.

And then...

Then it all went wrong. See what Nancy didn't know was that Joe had ambitions far beyond his station. Or, at least, she had dismissed the very notion of it, whenever he excitedly brought up his ideas on how they could make money through investments. Nearly every time she smiled, and nodded, but put the idea into the back of her mind, knowing that whatever bright spark Joe had would fizzle before it blazed brightly. She would've been more than happy living in the comfortable humdrum.

What Nancy couldn't see was that it was breaking Joe, bit by bit. His ambition ate at him until one day he was sacked for losing a lot of money. The company that he had served for so long had slammed the door without another single penny. It had disgraced him so badly that he found it impossible to find work again in financing. Instead, he picked up odd jobs and a nasty habit of using alcohol to numb the flame of wanting that still nestled in his chest like a disease.

A year later they downsized to a single room in Whitechapel. Despite being forced into closer confinements; the pair were growing distant from one another. See, what Joe couldn't see, was that the loss of their children was doing a similar thing to Nancy. She had several miscarriages until she was 23. Just before Joe crashed out of the stock markets, at their brightest moments, Nancy gave birth to a seemingly healthy young girl. The pair were so excited that they immediately called her Marie – a name that Nancy had loved since she was eighteen. Unfortunately, rubella would take the child before she was six months. Nancy stopped naming her children from then on. Over the years, she birthed two more children, both of whom died before they reached one. Disease and then malnourishment. With her husband spending more time in the bar than at home, Nancy was a shell of who she was, broken into a million pieces. Shattered in so many different ways, her final pregnancy came when she was 27, just as Joe died and just as she was made redundant.

The Shallows Cottage was finally in view, bringing Nancy out of her terrible memories. The light was low, the last of the sunlight hidden behind the clouds turned the sky into a horrible dark blue as though the depths of the ocean had dripped into the sky. Though the home was nearly shrouded in darkness, she traced the familiar patterns of stone with her eyes. Behind the walls, lay unknown emotions. There were orange lights in a few windows. She focused on the images that flitted through them, as though she were watching a film. Her sister Jane tended to a handful of children, all of different ages. The scene panged in Nancy, and she was overcome with the urge to rush through the door.

Twenty-two years is a long time to spend apart from one another. The rift that started as a crack grew and grew until it was a cavern, too impossible to cross, and too hard to shout over. Both women were stubborn at first, choosing to hold steady to their anger rather than forgive. One too proud to admit fault, the other too ashamed about the life she now lived. The very humiliation of it kept her frozen to the top of the path instead.

Nancy reached into her small bag and produced the book of nursery rhymes. Nestled between the tall tales and the colourful characters was the wad of cash that she had been saving for the whole year. She took a deep breath, and quietly opened the wooden gate, trying carefully not to let it wheeze out, and she tentatively walked down the pathway of her childhood home. Usually, Nancy would push the envelope of money through the letterbox and run away fast and far before anyone had a chance to catch her.

This time, however, Nancy placed the tatty, old book that held the notes on the doorstep and knocked quickly. She ran but not far. Instead, she found solace in the same bushes she had crouched in ten years ago. Tonight, however, in the freezing dusk, she watched as the door opened, producing a small streak of amber hues – the small streak of home. Nancy was hoping to see her sister Jane but tonight, fate had a different gift for her.

Instead, from the warmth, a teenage boy emerged. The sight of him caused Nancy to gasp quietly. *Nathan.* He was lanky but with a round face like hers, and a big nose like his father's. Even though the light was low, she could see the sprig of ginger hair protruding from his head. The boy curiously bent down to pick up the book. He turned it over and looked out into the distance for a short while. When Nathan could see no figure, he sighed heavily and took the book, stuffed full of money, into his home. The door closed, and Nancy pushed her hand against her mouth to stifle loud sobs.

The bartender wasn't exactly wrong. Nancy Castor was dead. She died when the shop she loved to work at went bankrupt and she was left unemployed. She died when her husband drank himself into a stupor before drinking himself into an early grave. She died with every miscarriage she had. Then when each child died. A little death each time.

Her final child was born three months after Joe died and survived for three years. She didn't name him Nathan until he was one. At three, he was suddenly gripped with scarlet fever that brought him desperately close to death himself. Now Nancy had so few means to save him. So, she bundled her son Nathan in the last good rags she had, grabbed his papers, and used the last of her money to travel back to this seaside town. Her hometown. There she found her old childhood home where her estranged sister lived. The place was warm and inviting. She held her sickly son in the dark one last time before she placed him on the doorstep with a note saying that Nancy Castor and her husband were dead. It was a formal note, but it was charged with great importance. Could Nancy's sister Jane please look after the child as if the boy was her own? After all, it was Nancy's last dying wish. If that would not sway Jane, then there would be a yearly allowance for the pair, to be given every year, on Nathan's birthday. The third of October. This very night.

On that fateful evening, Nancy knocked desperately on the door as she did just now and ran into the shadows to watch. Back then, it was Jane who answered, and found the child. If Nancy was unsure whether her older, stubborn sister would do what was asked of her, then the look of abject horror on Jane's face as she read the note solidified it. Jane crumpled into tears, as though the words she wished she had said to Nancy tumbled out of her. It took all of Nancy's strength not to rush forward and embrace Jane. Instead, she stayed cold and steadfast in the shadows, watching as Jane picked up Nathan, and took him carefully inside, into the home where he had been for ten years now.

So, Nancy Castor walked away from her son, each step killing the remains of her as she made her way back to London to earn the promised allowance. When she returned to the city, Nancy started a new life. She changed her first name to Marie, a name that she had loved since she was eighteen and kept her maiden name MacDonald as a hopeful reminder of her life by the sea. For a while, she sewed dresses in a factory during the day and worked as a barmaid in the evening. Every penny she saved, she put it in an envelope for Nathan. Over the years, it became easier to drink gin to keep warm and soon, she was fired from her factory job.

From then on, Marie worked daily in a pub, serving, cleaning, and entertaining, performing as she did when she was a child. She'd stay in one place until she was caught sneakily drinking gin on the job and was promptly ousted. This became a yearly routine as Marie flitted from place to place, from pub to pub, from person to person. Yet throughout it all, and despite her dependency on alcohol, she always saved money for the allowance.

Five years ago, Marie found herself a permanent job – one that did not mind if she drank and could keep her in comfortable enough lodgings. From that point on, she was a fixture, and a favourite, at The Furnace, especially in the brothel upstairs. The last bit of Nancy died the minute she met Harry Wright.

That's not to say her ghost did not always return. It did so annually, without fail, on the third of October, her son's birthday, and the last day she ever saw him. Nancy would wake in place of Marie, and she'd be overcome with the urge to visit the sea. At the earliest hours of the morning, she would sneak out of The Furnace as if it did not matter at all, and she would catch a train to Margate. She would walk the pavements and wooden piers that she had when she was a child. She would traipse up to the Shallows. She would deliver the money that she had been secretly saving.

Mile by mile, track by track, and step by step back to London, Nancy Castor would die all over again.

Today, on his thirteenth birthday, Nancy stood longer in the bushes than she expected, trying to capture a glimpse of the life she longed for. It wasn't until the children began to head off to bed that Nancy realised the time. Suddenly the world of Marie MacDonald beckoned her violently.

As Nancy ran to the train station, she wondered why she was returning to the cruel and unkind city, with all its monsters. Surely Nancy could stay here, bridge the divide, make amends, and stay in the kindness of her old home.

As Nancy boarded the last train home, she knew why.

Nancy Castor was dead.

Marie MacDonald's life was in London.

There were even, at times, soft tender, hopeful touches.

Harry Wright slammed Marie's head against the wall of her room. He pressed his hands into her cheeks, squeezing them tightly as she wriggled against him. The bang reverberated through her head that was already aching with the day. She clasped on his wrist, desperately trying to pull him from her. With his free hand, he brought up the invitation and shoved the card close to her face.

Who's this Doctor John Bennett then? Payin' customer? You been 'oldin' out on me, Marie?" Harry slammed her head back against the wall again. "Or is 'e your lover?"

In the haze of the morning, Marie had forgotten about the wedding entirely. When she had not returned to the pub for the evening, to earn her keep, Harry had ransacked her room and found it – bright pink with gold lettering like a glaring admission. As she walked through the door, he gave her little time to explain.

Desperately, she wiggled in his grip again. For the struggle, Harry threw her head back again, and squeezed her cheeks tighter. Marie pooled enough strength to stammer out, "I... I... I... I never met him, I swear Harry."

Harry Wright leaned his rotten teeth closer to hers, the stench of ale already on his breath. He pushed the card against her and watched as her eyes terrifyingly gazed over it. "Do you fink me a fool Marie?" A small smirk of realisation crept onto his face. "Oh... is it 'er? She the one you run to when you need fixin'?" Marie said nothing but unwillingly answered when she stopped wriggling in his arms. "I see. Fink you're friends, do ya Marie?" Spittle from his nasty mouth landed upon her cheek. Marie tried desperately not to cry but tears filled up her eyes. "You're just a charity case to 'er. Somefin' to make 'er feel good about 'erself."

The words struck Marie so hard that Harry let go of her instantly, knowing that she would not escape him now. Instead, Harry chose to fondly stroke her cheek with almost loving touches. Marie tried desperately to stem the tears from her face. She brought her own hand up to her nose to brush away the snot. "Right you are, Harry. Right you are."

"She don't care about you like I do Marie," Harry said, kissing her gently on the cheek. So tenderly that it caused ripples of remembrance to shiver down her. She gasped inadvertently at the touch, trying her best not to entirely melt into them.

Suddenly, Harry swung his cane up high and brought it down – fast and hard. Marie tried to squirm out of his grasp, but it was too late. Soon the silver cane down crashed down on her cheek bone, landing on the same spot he had just kissed her on. The agony rippled through her, waves of hurt and caused her to cry out. She collapsed to the floor, cradling her face with her broken hand as she felt the heated blood pour from the wound. Harry crouched down beside Marie as she tried to compose herself. "Why don't you go see this Miriam Clayton and get yourself sorted out again? Then you can come back here and work twice as hard to make it up to me, darlin'."

The Lady Gray ward was quiet.

There was no one else there, which, as Marie had come to learn, was a good thing. She sat, and with her bandaged hand, held rags up against the wound on her cheek. Instead of the pain, she turned to distractions. The shadows of the night mixed with the oranges of the gas lamps like lighthouses upon the horizon. Though there were no birds chirping in the courtyard, Marie listened to the dull roar of the gas lamps, picturing large waves that swept up against the ocean. The footsteps that echoed from far away wards made her think of ships mooring up against the dock. If she closed her eyes, she could still taste the sweet, salt air upon her tongue.

When the door of the ward swung open, an amber hue of warmth stretched across the floor. In the doorway stood a figure, and for the briefest moment, hoped it was many different people. Joe, Nathan, Jane, and even Harry on the night they had first met. She knew that Miriam could not be there. After all, today was her wedding day in the country. How Marie longed to have gone there instead and started somewhere anew with a possible friend by her side. Yet she had wasted the invitation on a ghost story.

The figure moved forward. The stern yet substantial Matron Lockett had walked in, Marie tried desperately not to weep as she rotted away, a sunken ship submerged in the shame. Abandoned in the fray. Alone in the abyss.

Alone. Alone. Alone. Alone.

How long had she been alone?

Halloween

Thursday 31st October 1895

There had never been a silence as grave as this one.

It permeated the Bennett household like a thick fog. As soon as Miriam stepped into her home, she was suffocated by it. The mournful mist darkened her mind with absolute dread instantly. After the door clicked shut, she was greeted with the quiet of the home. There was seemingly no roaring fire nor clock chimes, though they were both moving. There was no rustling movement or a cheery greeting. Just the stillness. When it hit her, Miriam's cheeks flushed with the wrong kind of anticipation – one that was expecting conflict. Breathing in deeply, she turned to face the source of this calamitous cloud.

Stewing in his emotions, John was standing in the living room, leaning against the mantle. In one hand, he clutched onto a glass of brandy. In the other, he held his golden ornate pocket watch, which was attached to his black waistcoat, adorned with a white, shiny web detail. He was staring at the little face of time that had ticked all evening. Each time that little black hand moved, his tempers flared. Watching the seconds go around and around, over and over again, without Miriam's arrival had only stoked a rage in his gullet.

He didn't need to tell her that he was mad. It was rare that John spoke in anger, but Miriam knew when he was upset. She always knew. His annoyance lay in the way he gripped his glass to ground himself, it resided in the furious way he furrowed his brow, and it twisted in the taciturn way he tightened his lips.

Instead of shouting at her, which he had every right to do, he brooded on the evening and her actions. The silence was much worse than any raised voice. Unable to breathe under the quiet judgement, Miriam tried to fly into excuses. "John I—"

"An hour, Miriam," John said calmly, though there was a quiver to his tone that alluded to his emotional state. He slammed the watch shut with a loud click. The action made her jump somewhat. Slipping the watch into his pocket, he continued, "I have been home for an hour."

"I am—"

"And before that, I scoured the streets of London looking for you." He did not look her in the eyes, fearful that he'd either soften the minute he looked at her or start screaming his emotions loudly. He swallowed to steady himself. "For how long, I do not know, but it mattered not. You had vanished."

There was another long pause that pulled the air from her lungs. In an attempt to alleviate the heated haze that had descended in her home, Miriam half-joked, "I see we've forgone my ruling." When John's nostrils flared as he closed his eyes briefly, releasing some of the hot air that had pent up over the day, Miriam bent her head down. "I am sorry."

John took another sip of his drink and another sharp intake of breath. "Where were you?"

"The hospital."

"The hospital?" John replied with an indignant scoff. "Can I enquire as to why, on our one day off together, after what you had promised, you headed there?"

Wavering still on the outskirts of the room, Miriam hesitated. The shaky nature in which he delivered his questions showed that he was not only angry, but he was also hurt. Though ashamed that she had caused such upset, Miriam knew she needed the space. "It is the one place I can think." There was a beat. "I was offended."

"Well, that was apparent," John said with no discernible tone. "What with the way you stormed out of the theatre, I believe the entirety of London could tell you were insulted tonight."

"I do not believe you are being very fair, John."

John rolled his tongue across the inside of his mouth as he chuckled resentfully. He finally turned to meet her eyes. The apologetic look on her face nearly melted him from his chilly mood. Instead, he pursed his lips and seethed out of his nose again, wishing to linger in the anger a little longer. After all, as sweet and as beautiful as his wife was, he still did not understand why she had fled into the night. "How do you wish me to be, Miriam?"

She didn't know how to answer. The events of the day and the evening were still pounding extremely in her heart and mind…

A terrible storm raged on Halloween, hours before it brewed in both Miriam and John.

A clap of thunder on a midweek morning caused John to startle awake. His heart thudded deeply in his chest as he laid there nude in bed. Wrapped up in the silk of his sheets, he uncurled himself and turned over to lay on his back, as he waited for the rumbles of his heart to ease. Whilst his eyes softly opened and closed, he reached across to his gold ornate pocket watch on his bedside cabinet. Through different squints, he deduced that it was after 11am.

Groaning, John placed the watch back on the cabinet. It sounded out with a metallic clank. He took a deep breath and exhaled with a smile, running a hand across the bed in search of his darling wife.

The bed was empty.

The silence that had now settled within their bedroom, the highest room in their quaint town house, was a curious one. Since they had married and had moved into their home mere weeks ago, they had always risen together. One would assume it was a necessity. They did, after all, both work at the hospital. But that wasn't quite it. No, the pair woke together for selfish reasons. It was impossible to enjoy a singular minute awake without the other. Not when there was a world to face as one. It was almost as though they were making up for lost time - as though, from the beginning of creation, their spirits had been aching to collide so beautifully together. So, it was strange to John that Miriam was not there.

John let out a deep sigh.

Flinging the cream silk blankets from his body, John wasted no time in pulling a shirt and some trousers on. He had wished to enjoy the morning a bit longer. Between his busy work and his whirlwind marriage with Miriam, he had found moments of stillness to be few and far between. Not that the consummations and carnality weren't enjoyable. However, he'd be remiss to deny how annoyed he was that his day-off was interrupted by the disappearance of his young wife. He grumbled to no one at all when he left the bedroom. Despite his dishevelled appearance, having had little time to refine himself, he clambered down the staircase, huffing with each creak of the woodwork.

He had quickly reached the hallway and was about to reach for his dark grey raincoat when he heard a soft chuckle from the living room. "Well, good morning John."

"Ah." John took a couple of beats before he turned to the open doorway. There leaning over from her armchair sat Miriam. The fireplace crackled, casting hues of amber into her brown hair, and the grey morning. The flames altered those deep blue eyes of hers and made them look almost black as she smiled. He took a step towards her, sheepishly, like a scolded child would having been caught in a sweet jar. "You are still here."

"Forgive me, you were sleeping so deeply dear, I wished not to wake you from your well-earned rest." A beat. "Did you think I had vanished?"

He shuffled somewhat awkwardly before replying, "Yes."

"Where would I have gone?"

Another beat. "The hospital."

"Can I enquire as to why, on our one day off together, you thought I'd head there?"

John looked to the floor, his cheeks burning from the manner in which she was addressing him. He was being chastised for doing nothing wrong. The very idea of it hit his stomach and swiftly developed into excitement. "I… I…"

"You truly do know your wife," Miriam said with a smile. She did not move from her chair. Instead, she gestured for him to come closer to her with a singular finger. As he padded over, she watched him intently, savouring each move he made. "Truth be told, the thought had crossed my mind. But I promised both you and father that I'd try. And I am a woman of my word."

John chuckled at this somewhat. There had been only two instances where Miriam had taken time-off from her hospital duties. Their first weekend in the Manor and their wedding day. Their weekends since had been spent planning the refuge. Sir Fredric had told him once that even on Christmas Day, Miriam would visit the ailing in their wards. Most doctors took Sunday off for church, but Miriam was devoted to her patients and her causes and would inevitably find herself back at the hospital. Even if it were only for an hour or two. When John entered her life she did, indeed, make allowances for him – their evenings were spent entirely entwined and she'd take her breaks in his office. However, one of her father's wedding gifts had been an insistent day off and whilst he had planned it for the day after their wedding four weeks ago, it took much convincing from both men for Miriam to exact the present.

When John had reached the armchair, turning to face her, he could see that his tricky wife was making the most of her relaxing morning. She had curled her hair carefully in bits of fabric and was wearing a simple tea gown over her bodice. The layers of lightweight material blossomed across her body and puffed out at her arms, all in shades of ivory, mint, and pink. She was barefoot and propped her feet upon the footstool. Beside her armchair was a pot of tea, and in her lap was a book. *Hauntings* by Vernon Lee.

Yet despite the angelic way she looked; the way she smiled, the way she glowered, and the way she spoke to him made her desperately unholy. It sent a thousand shivers, each as delightful as the last, trundling through him. A slick smile spread on his face. He reached down and took her hand, kissing it gently. "Good morning, my dark goddess."

"Am I?"

"Hmm?"

"Am I your dark goddess, John?"

"Oh, most ardently yes."

"Then why aren't you kneeling?"

He wasted no time in dropping to the floor. The soft thud of his body upon their pink and blue rug made her smile. She kicked the footstool over to give him more room. He inched closer to her as she placed one foot on his shoulder. John was frightened of moving more, waiting for her to impart a ruling. Instead, he glanced upwards towards her as she stared down. In a venerable whisper, he said, "Forgive me, goddess."

"You are forgiven." There was a beat. "Now praise me, mortal."

Taking his cue, he began to kiss the milky skin of her ankle, as he did the first time they made love. Despite the command she had over him, she still laughed as his moustache tickled the pale flesh of her lower leg. Miriam didn't want to let go of her position too soon, and, to keep herself bridled for a little bit longer, she turned back to the book and began to read out loud. He caressed her foot with his hand as well, massaging it as his lips adorned and coveted the inches of her. As John found her calf, pushing her skirts up, he heard her loudly groan contentedly.

"John…" she said, unfurling his name within the aftermath of the murmur.

He paused and cast his eyes upwards to see her grin profusely. "Yes, goddess?"

"… I'm not wearing any drawers."

"Oh!" He dove back down to her leg.

Miriam giggled at his haste. She went to tell him to slow down, but the minute he placed his lips back upon her calf, he had understood her wordless command. Without uttering another ruling, John took a measured climb to her knee with his mouth, whilst his hand paved the way for him – coveting each freckle and each morsel as though he had never explored her body before. She continued reading, but as soon as Miriam's husband delved down her thigh - closer and closer to her warmth - the sentences became more scattered amongst her sighs. His mouth and tongue ran over her flesh studiously, savouring every scent and taste of her, as if he were uncovering cells he had yet to touch. And his hand…

Oh his hand, his hand, his hand.

And then, the doorbell rang.

The two women swirled their teacups.

As they did Miriam looked deep into dark brown liquid that swished with dark black leaves and herbs. They spiralled like a tornado, brewing from the top and spiralling across the bottom. Her thoughts delved into the fray as she gazed over each different fragment. Every tiny ingredient was crucial; the billowing bergamot, the turbulent tea, and the looping lavender all mixed to craft an exquisite taste. An instrument of relaxation and pleasure. She wondered if these notes knew they were to score a symphony one day.

What's more: Did they know they held the fate of the universe? Could they truly capture one's future? Were there secrets within the song that entwined in her little white teacup? She sighed as the elements settled. The soft rumbles outside of a passing storm added a backdrop to these brooding thoughts.

"Miriam?" Adelaide said. Her usual gentle tone had an undercurrent of concern. She reached over, tapping Miriam's wrist with her own laced-gloved hand. "Are you quite alright?"

Miriam took a deep breath, shaking her head softly to dispel whatever clouds had formed in her mind. She sighed and smiled, twisting her hand to take her friend's gently. She shook it lightly whilst saying, "Yes Adelaide, I am quite well." A pause. "Just discombobulated. I'm afraid days away from the hospital do not suit me."

"Even more reason to take them," Adelaide replied with a smirk, taking her hand back to pick up her tea and sip it gently. "Besides, quite selfishly, I enjoy having you all to myself without our husbands or the refuge getting in the way."

Miriam cheeks flushed. She didn't look directly at Adelaide, instead she gripped the white porcelain cup, dotted with floral swirls of pink and green. She took a sip of the tea. "Indeed. One should endeavour to do this more often."

She finally turned to meet the hazel eyes of her closest friend. They sparkled, as always, with kindness. Adelaide was carved for perfection. Even on a stormy Thursday morning, she had arrived on Miriam's doorstep impeccably crafted, as though the wind and rain were no match for the tenacity and steadfastness of her make-up and curls. If Miriam peered close enough, she was certain that she would not find a single freckle or hair out of place. A different type of red grew on Miriam's cheeks.

Adelaide paid no mind as she took small sips of her tea. "Where is John anyhow?"

"Oh." Miriam waved her hand dismissively. "He is at the market, getting supper for this evening."

"I am sure he was pleased to also have time away from the hospital."

"And I suspect Michael was happier this morning, safe in the knowledge that I was not at today's board meeting."

"Speaking candidly, Miriam, I think he is somewhat fond of you." Adelaide let out a singular honk of her laugh. "But yes, I must admit that there was a spring in my husband's step before he left for work." Another honk before she slammed her hand on the table. Unfortunately, she caught the end of her spoon and sent it clattering to the floor. It slid across the wooden boards underneath the dining room table.

"Fear not. I'll get it." Before Adelaide could react, Miriam had already dived underneath the cloth. There were a few seconds before she emerged, breathless and red faced. She was holding the small, ornate silver spoon. "Here we are!"

Adelaide peered quizzically at her friend, bemused at the rush. As she took the spoon back, wiping it with a napkin before placing it down on the saucer, she said, "I fear it is true what they say about couples after marriage. We all start turning out like the other."

"Good Lord, does that mean I am about to become quieter?"

"Or John more outspoken."

"God help us all!"

The pair burst into laughter before Miriam suddenly jumped slightly in her seat with a loud yelp. Adelaide frowned. "Whatever is the matter?"

Peering underneath the table, Miriam sighed. "Oh, silly me, I thought a mouse had run across my foot, but it appears it was just the tablecloth." She sat back straight on the chair, taking her cup which was now lukewarm. She took several hefty gulps and tried to compose herself. Her cheeks were still red, however. With a gasp for air, she peered at the content of the cups and gestured to Adelaide. "Shall I read yours and you read mine?"

"Why yes!" She passed over her own cup as she took Miriam's. "What a novel idea this is Miriam."

"Yes, I may be a woman of science, but I am electrified by the supernatural. Now…" She twisted the cup around in her hand. "Oh dear, I am afraid there is a dagger here."

"Oh my…" Adelaide gasped, snapping up from her own cup in her hand. "Whatever could it mean?"

"Well…" Miriam placed the cup down on the porcelain saucer with a slight clink. She picked up the book that had been sitting beside her. She flipped through the pages, running her fingers down the text until she found the desired word. "'A dagger at the bottom of the cup signifies that you need to be more approachable.'"

"Hmm."

"Or it could be a knife! Wait… yes… OH! 'A knife at the bottom of the cup means that you are having a good time!'"

"Oh yes, I like that one, let's go with that."

There was another round of giggles between the pair.

"Do not keep me waiting." Miriam passed the book over to Adelaide. "What does mine say?"

"Well, there is a ruddy big dog's head on the side of this cup which… let's see… Oh, well, well, well. It says, 'To have a successful year, you must learn to rely on others.'"

"A rather pointed cup, I must say."

The pair again giggled wildly before dismissing the tea leaf reading altogether. As their chortles and cackles subsided, they moved into a long chat, gossiping over socialites and hospital practices for a long time. What Miriam liked best about Adelaide was that she was a quiet, meditative person in polite society but in the right company, she spoke fast and at great length, as though she had been holding back words. What Miriam knew was that it was probably the effect of marrying her talkative husband. What Miriam wouldn't admit was that Michael, underneath his posturing, was somewhat of a good man. As she watched Adelaide speak, she thought about Michael's tongue and for a slight moment, wondered how it tasted.

Soon enough, the grandfather clock in The Bennetts' living room bounced out its chimes, causing Adelaide spring to her feet. "My goodness, is it three o'clock already?" She looked apologetically to Miriam. "I'd love to stay and chat longer, but I must pick up dinner. Do you have anything nice planned for this evening?" Adelaide picked up her belongings and placed them in her small handbag. On the table she had left out a compact mirror and lipstick.

"Yes, John and I are going to see a medium act. See if we can attune to the spiritual realm."

"Sounds ghastly." She leaned back to pull her boots on, tying them tightly around her calf. "I gather you have themed attire."

"Yes, cobwebs."

"Is that what is supposedly in your hair?"

"Oh!" Miriam gasped, bringing up her hands to her head, realising that she had left the bits of fabric in her hair. Embarrassed, she patted them gently. "I forgot."

Adelaide did not reply. Instead, she grinned slightly, half-amused and half-apologetic at her somewhat insult. She stood up and brushed herself down before she made her way over to Miriam. Before her brown-haired friend had time to stand up, Adelaide had reached the chair and begun to unravel the fabric. Tenderly. Taking her time, she untangled the web of curls that Miriam had created.

Miriam placed her hands flat upon the table. A silence had grown between the pair as Adelaide took a great deal of care with Miriam's head and the latter wished not to disturb the tranquillity. She also knew how dangerously close Adelaide was. A perfume of lilacs wrapped around Miriam's senses as Adelaide stood behind her. The warmth of her thin yet inviting body crept down Miriam's spine, causing her heartbeat to quicken. The fingertips that were unfolding within the hair were nearer her neck and the tension mounted second by second.

When that delicate touch happened, Miriam tried to hold in her gasp. The sensation of Adelaide's hands skimming the sensitive skin on her neck shivered down her spine. She thought about the pleasure those hands could do if they were lower on her body. Racing thoughts of Adelaide's nude and undone body soon followed the path down Miriam. A cavalcade of sudden excitement marched down her spine, through her privates, and down her leg, causing her toes to instantly curl.

John winced quietly as her feet accidentally scraped the skin of his chest and pulled at the hairs on his body. He seethed silently through his teeth and grabbed her ankle gently to release the sudden hold. When Miriam relaxed her foot, he smirked. He knew her body very well – enough to know that excitement coursed through her, causing her toes to react in such a manner. Turning his head, he could see Adelaide's boot-clad feet behind Miriam's chair. John stifled a chuckle.

He had been lying upon the floor for nearly three hours, with Miriam using him as a footstool. As instructed, he had to stay excruciatingly still and silent whilst his wife conversed with her best friend. Luckily, the table was long enough to hide him covertly, but he shuffled up against Miriam's chair just in case, careful not to slip out of the sanctuary of the baby blue tablecloth. At times, he almost held his breath, frightful that the American would be alerted to his presence. Plus, he was desperate not to break the rules.

The afternoon tea had gone on longer than both Miriam and John had anticipated when she shoved him under the table. They had both forgotten how much Miriam and Adelaide enjoyed each other's company. Their short friendship had blossomed into a fierce and loyal one. Once nestled in their home, Adelaide and Miriam would talk for hours. Lying on the cold, hard floorboards under their dining room table, John stayed steady. Even when his backside ached, and he grew somewhat weary.

It was not without its agonising teases and close encounters. Adelaide nearly kicked him in the face when she loosened her boots and a spoon clattered to the floor, sliding close to his face. He picked it up and handed it to Miriam quickly. Occasionally, when Adelaide would briefly leave the room to grab a drink from the kitchen or use the bathroom, Miriam would bunch up her skirts and open her legs to flash herself to her salivating husband. What glorious treasures she had in store for him. He'd give anything to taste her.

Knowing that Adelaide had teased some excitement from his wife proved impossible to ignore. John could only imagine the wetness that had spread between her legs when the toe curled upon his chest. An idea had already nestled in his brain the minute he laid down, and it had grown until he was consumed by the necessity. He had tried his luck before, pinching her smallest toe when the two women lightly joked about him. John's hands were still on her foot. After a singular second, he decided to take his climb again – moving faster than he did before, hiking his way to the peak quickly.

Miriam did not dare move underneath his caress, not when Adelaide was nearby. By the time he reached her knee, the lack of reaction caused John to hesitate. He paused, wondering if he was at the line he dare not cross.

"Yes…" Miriam sighed.

"What was that Miriam?" Adelaide replied.

"Yes!" Miriam said, slamming her hand on the table. "Thank you so much for doing that, Adelaide. I fear I might've left the house looking terrifying."

"Tis the season."

Then Adelaide's feet moved away from the chair.

Laughing quietly, John continued his climb down her inner thigh. She slightly opened her legs for him again and soon enough, he was making his way through her parting. When he found her entrance, he wasted no time in sliding a finger inside of her, placing a thumb on her sensitive spot. Miriam made no sounds but slouched the slightest bit down to make it easier for him. However, entering such a place had an exciting effect on him. He adored the way her warmth felt. Inexplicably, he moaned out of appreciation. Quite loudly.

Miriam aggressively shoved her foot on his mouth.

"What was that?"

"What was what?" Miriam said dismissively. "Oh, my stomach I'm afraid. I am utterly ravenous." Then she slid her chair back, causing John's fingers to fall out of her, and stood up. "Come, I'll see you to the door."

John placed his hand on his lips to restrain himself again, staying statuesque and still.

Savouring the scent of her on his fingertips.

The audience of the Gaiety were already in high spirits before the show had even started. John waited in the foyer, growing increasingly bothered by the noise of the chatter and the bodies that bounced and bounded around him. To centre himself whilst he waited for Miriam, he gazed at the giant posters on the yellow walls. They blazed with big purple letters:

Madame Mara
Medium and Psychic.

The live staged séance had been Miriam's idea – something spooky for this set of scientific sinners to indulge in. They had never had any great belief in the afterlife. They had seen too many good people suffer for them to be bound to religious rule or the idea of Heaven or Hell. However, with the many memories of men, women, and children dying at the hospital, they would readily admit that they held onto hope that there was something beyond this mortal realm. After all, they had vowed to one another to reunite there long after death.

John was overcome by an excruciating excitement that had nothing to do with the event itself. As he waited patiently for his wife to come back from the bathroom, he wriggled and gently bounced on his feet. He peered over heads, looking for Miriam. Anticipation bounded through him so joyfully that he felt like a puppy waiting by the door for its master to appear.

"I am sorry that took me so long darling, there was a frightful queue," came Miriam's voice from behind him.

John jumped and then accidentally bumped into a young blond-haired woman beside him. The collision caused her to spill her glass of white wine onto her hand. She huffed, shook her hand in disgust, and turned to him with a face full of anger. John's eyes widened at the humiliation, his face growing beetroot red. He opened his mouth but then closed it, saying nothing. The young woman looked pointedly at him, before calling him rude, and disappearing into the crowd.

Sighing, John placed a hand to his forehead and grimaced.

"Good boy," Miriam said softly, kissing him on the cheek. causing him to grin goofily. As low as she could, she then whispered, "Oh… and I am *still* not wearing any drawers."

John's eyes widened as he tried to halt a long-suffering moan in his mouth.

"Miriam?"

The Bennetts both spun around to see a small, old woman, dressed entirely in black and purple, behind them. She clutched onto a slender, black walking cane. Miriam exclaimed loudly, "Rissy!" In a quick moment, she wrapped her arms around the woman and brought her into an enveloping embrace. "Oh, it is so good to see you."

"The feeling is mutual," said the old woman in a thick French accent.

The pair broke the hug, but Miriam still clutched onto the older woman's free hand, both exchanging beaming smiles. John stood beside them. He would have felt awkward if it weren't for the glints and sparks that shone in Miriam's eyes. He adored watching them. This woman must be close for them to sparkle in such a manner.

"I did not expect to see you here tonight."

"I was visiting family in the city and was personally invited by Madame Mara herself. I found it intriguing. After all, one finds these days alone so very hard."

However, soon a sadness streaked across each of the women's faces. Miriam gave Rissy's hand a loving squeeze and said gently, "I was terribly sorry to hear about Claude. He was a good man."

"The best." The woman known only to John so far as Rissy smiled with a glaze of sorrow in her eyes. "Ah, but he lived a good life, and I had forty years of him." Rissy reached over and carefully stroked Miriam's cheek. "Forgive me for having to miss your wedding. We'd have both given anything to attend."

"Oh Rissy. There is no need to apologise."

"Is this him?" Rissy gestured to John. "Your new husband?"

"Yes!" Miriam squealed and excitedly pulled John forward, presenting him like a prize that she had won. "Doctor John Bennett, please meet Viscountess Clarisse Menochet."

John bowed gently as he took Viscountess Menochet's hand and kissed it. He then smiled as Miriam looped her arm into his. He said nothing. Viscountess Menochet looked quite quizzical at John before she chuckled, "Your aunt was right; he is a man of little words."

"Oh!" Miriam laughed rather loudly. "Forgive my husband, he woke up without a voice today."

"It matters not," Viscountess Menochet replied sincerely. "I should take my box. It was so lovely to see you, Miriam. We should have tea whilst I am back in London. Pleasure to meet you, John."

"Excellent work," Miriam breathed out after Viscountess Menochet had disappeared. John nodded, trying to stop a smile appearing on this face from the compliment. He did his job so very well. He obeyed superbly. He had not said a word since three o'clock that afternoon.

When the door closed on Adelaide, Miriam had finally released John from the confines of the dining room table. Standing up, John had chuckled, "Why do we need to visit a psychic, Miriam? When I now know what sits deepest within that magnificent mind of yours?"

Miriam had walked forward to him in the dining room and placed a singular finger upon his lips before she told him that, because of his infraction underneath the table, she was going to punish him. For the groan, John was not to say a singular word for the entire evening. They weren't to have sex either. Not until John could satisfy her rulings. Then she would have her wicked way with him.

Linking with one another, they walked into the theatre and down the aisle together. As the couple made their way to their seats in the middle of the fourth row, John had many questions on his tongue, and he was quite frightful they'd spill out. He was lucky, then, that Miriam had an uncanny ability to read his mind.

As she sat down, she said, "If you must know, I couldn't pronounce Clarisse when I was a child. The nickname just sort of stuck between us. They were close friends of Izzy and that bastard Charles. But I loved the Menochets quite dearly. They moved back to France when I was ten, but they always kept correspondence and visited whenever they could." She sighed gently as she tried to arrange her skirt comfortably, wistfully stroking the patterns when she had finished. "Forty years they had together. Queen Victoria herself had twenty-one. My... my... father had twenty." Miriam turned to look at John with light tears in her eyes. At the sight of them John reached over and took her hand tenderly, giving it the softest of squeezes. She gasped, "I've had you just two months and yet... the same pain."

The sentiment plummeted through John. He dared not dwell on the pain of losing Miriam nor on wondering how long he'd have with her. The thought was too impossible to bear. Instead, John leaned over and kissed her softly on the cheek, causing a small tear to slide down it. He knew it would be breaking the rules but in that moment, he wished to shower her with words of comfort. He went to speak but Miriam shook her head, frightful that anything he would say would cause her to dissolve into more tears.

Suddenly they were all plunged into darkness. The audience erupted into ripples of shrieks and giggles. Then the lights illuminated the stage as a creeping mist rolled over the floorboards. There was loud music and sound effects to mimic the very storm that was raging outside. Actors in masks danced throughout the aisles and on the stage rather dramatically. As they leered and jumped out at people, there were ripples of excitement. Everyone's mood was immediately heightened.

Gliding through the fog, the medium and her assistant took the stage. The evening took a drastic turn. A hush fell over the crowd. Forgetting her sadness, Miriam clapped her hands hurriedly, delighted, and eager to indulge in nonsense whilst John giggled at her new excitement. The middle-aged woman was called Madame Mara. She had long white hair that she covered in a purple, translucent shawl. She wore a tatty purple dress and boots. There was thick eyeliner on her face and blue eyeshadow. Her eyes were wide and unblinking as she shuffled across the stage.

In the centre of the stage was a table that had a crystal ball on the top of it, Madame Mara started to move her hands over the illuminated sphere. "Spirits of the otherworld. I am your conduit. Come to me now." She spoke in an exaggerated, but indiscernible, foreign accent. "Yes, spirits. I can hear you. I am your vessel."

Suddenly, the elderly woman began to violently twitch and writhe and moan. Miriam gasped loudly and gripped tightly onto John's hand. He turned to see her face, half-frightful and half-exhilarated.

Madame Mara suddenly collapsed on stage causing the audience to scream and chatter wildly. The pair of doctors both pondered whether they should rush the stage to check on her. As soon as they went to move, the medium sprang to her feet like a reanimated corpse. She stood stiffly in the silence before she burst into loud giggles that were unlike her accent from before. Madame Mara strutted across the stage with a youthful stride, almost as though she were drunk. She took the shawl from her head and wrapped it across her arms.

Her assistant was a young man in a suit, with dark hair and a thin moustache. He was there to ask Madame Mara questions about the supposed spirit which now resided in the old woman's body. "Are you Madame Mara?" he said in a bellowing voice.

"Wat?" Mara now spoke with a cockney accent. She shrugged and shook her head. "Nah, never 'eard of 'er."

"What is your name?"

"Polly!" She said gleefully. She then fiddled with an invisible hat. "See what a jolly bonnet I've got on!"

Small gasps burst from the crowd as recognition dawned upon them. The assistant continued his questioning, "Where are you from Polly?"

"Whitechapel, of course."

There was a short exhale of breath as Miriam stiffened beside John. She let go of his hand and balled her own into a fist. He steeled himself with caution. There was trouble brewing. It rolled over Miriam like the mist upon the stage.

"What was the last thing you remember, Polly?" said the assistant. There was a slick way he asked, knowing that the audience were in the palm of their hands, baiting them to reveal secrets of the horrific murders which stalked the city so many years ago.

"Whatcha talking about? Whatcha…" Then Madame Mara's expression changed. A sorrow-filled expression fell upon her face. "Oh God. I remember. A toff. A man. Oh, a gentleman. He's taking me out all fancy-like. He… He's grabbed me. A knife. There's a knife. Oh God, I am dead, ain't I?"

Then there was a loud blood curdling scream. Madam Mara collapsed again on the stage. There was a scattered applause and mystified murmurs before a curious quiet moved through the audience. Mara stayed still on the stage before it went to black.

"This is outrageous to profit from that woman's unjust death. Despicable." Miriam loudly sneered, garnering tuts and shushes from those around them. John said nothing, of course, caught tentatively between her ruling and the agonising wish to comfort her.

A singular spotlight shone on the stage. Madame Mara stepped into it. There was something so intriguing about how she stood. It was purposeful; holding herself as though she had a different gait and was weighted weirdly. She possessed something different – something unusual was caught within her. If John did not believe in ghosts before, he almost did in that moment. Madame Mara looked other-worldly.

The entrancing spell she cast would not last long. Because from out of her mouth, came a deep, rolling voice, not too dissimilar from an old man's. She mumbled out one name. Yet it was enough to bring the thunder of the storm to that very theatre.

The voice simply said, "Rissy?"

"Stop."

"Rissy?"

"Stop it now."

"Claude?"

"Is that you, my darling Marguerite?"

"STOP THIS! STOP THIS AT ONCE!" Miriam shouted from the audience, startling everyone around the pair. The act on stage stopped immediately. She had found herself on her feet. John gazed upwards. Her skin had paled to marble, John opened his mouth to say her name but snapped it shut, tightly fastening his lips. For the first time he was truly frightful of the punishment if he did. Instead, he timidly glided his fingertips over the back of her hand. She did not waver. She didn't even twitch. She simply glared in condemnation. Statue-like within her anger.

Madame Mara transformed back to herself immediately. In her usual croaky, unguessable voice, the old woman signalled for all the lights to be switched back on as she said loudly, "Who said that?"

"I did," Miriam said angrily, though she was acutely aware that all the eyes in the auditorium were suddenly upon her. Her cheeks flushed at the attention. Still, she was steadfast in her anger. "To use someone's grief in such an appalling manner. You ought to be ashamed of yourself."

There were murmurs of agreement. From the box to the left of them, Viscountess Menochet stared between Mara and Miriam, her expression indecipherable. This did not shake Madame Mara. Instead, her thin lips burst into a malicious grin. She moved forward on the stage with such confidence that she actually frightened Miriam. Getting closer, she lifted a creaky finger and thrust it in Miriam's direction. "You dare insult the spirits?"

"No," Miriam scoffed, "but I'll gladly insult you, you wretched old hag."

More gasps and laughter followed. Viscountess Menochet got up to leave. John wriggled in his seat, unsure what to do. His face burned with embarrassment, but he did not want to stop his wife, not when she was justified in her fury. Still, he slunk down in his chair as though he were hiding himself.

Madame Mara laughed. Then she turned the crooked finger that she was pointing upwards, worming it slowly to beckon Miriam to the stage. Miriam's mouth flopped open, shocked at the proposition. She clenched her hands and then extended them, hesitating on the spot. Yet the mockery that Mara displayed still incensed Miriam. She tightened her lips further and nodded softly. Without another moment's hesitation, Miriam made her way to the stage.

As Miriam climbed over her husband, John went to stop her but could only graze her arm so gently that he wasn't sure she could feel it in her fury. Her skin was hot to the touch. With all eyes still upon them both, John wished not to act further for fear of enraging not only Miriam but the entire theatre. He could hear them whispering and had never had a fondness for being the topic of such scorn. For a fleeting moment, he wondered if he should, as her husband, put a stop to this ordeal before it escalated further. Yet he knew the vicious whispers were nothing compared to the wrath he'd face betraying his wife's trust in that manner. Instead, he slid further down, wishing that the ground would swallow him whole.

Miriam glided across the stage, greeting Mara like duelling partners swimming in the mists of an early dewy morning. Their guns were poised to the sky, though no one knew what bullets the pair would be shooting. Standing before Mara, Miriam folded her arms, tapping her fingers across her skin as though she had been waiting there for hours. The older woman gazed over Miriam, though no one could discern her emotions. Uncomfortable under this scrutiny, Miriam played the only weapon in her arsenal – sarcasm. She waved her hand in a manner as to egg Mara on.

Mara grabbed Miriam's hand sharply, causing Miriam to gasp from the shock and the pain. It echoed across the breaths of the audience. John sat up immediately from the sound, curling his own hand into a fist. Flipping over Miriam's hand, Mara turned her penetrating eyes to the lines on Miriam's palm.

"I suppose you are going to tell me that I am to meet someone tall, dark, and handsome," Miriam sneered, causing the crowd to giggle with her. She winked at John. "Fortunately, that has already happened."

Aggressively Mara pawed at the lines. "No, but these hands have seen bloodshed. Lots of bloodshed." There was a curious mumble across the crowd as Miriam frowned. "You are a doctor, are you not?"

Miriam nearly snatched her hand back out of shock. She took a sharp intake of breath as there were excited noises from the audience. She flicked a worried look to John before turning back to Mara, placing the old woman under an equally scrutinising gaze. Miriam was wearing no outfit that would suggest that she worked in medicine. No wayward gauze slipped out of her pockets, and she was certain no stethoscope hung around her neck. There was no way from looks alone that Mara could place Miriam's profession. Besides, it was rare that anyone outside of the hospital would assume any woman was a doctor. Or inside the hospital, for that matter.

She had not spoken about her title either in the theatre. Not that she could recall anyway. In the seconds that were quickly evolving into minutes, Miriam tried to pinpoint Mara's face, flicking through recent patients. She hoped to remember someone that she had treated, attempting to unfold Mara's ruse. When no such memory appeared, Miriam's cheeks flushed. This woman was good.

Mara smiled, rolling her tongue inside of her cheek, knowing that she had procured the exact response she had wanted from Miriam. She gripped the hand tighter, and Miriam winced loudly.

Suddenly, John found himself standing.

"But there is more bloodshed here." Mara pulled Miriam closer, slithering her hand up the young doctor's forearm. She smelled of wine and tobacco. Mara said the next revelation in a loud, thundering snarl, "You think yourself so pious, my dear, but I see who you are. You have killed mercilessly also." Mara dropped Miriam's hand and pointed her bony finger again, so wildly that Miriam stepped back in fright. John made his way down the row. "You are a murderess! A monster! A fiend!"

As that crooked accusatory finger pointed viciously, the audience who had once agreed with her indignation was suddenly laughing at Miriam, clapping rhythmically, and chanting the very words that Madame Mara had thrown. "Murderess! Monster! Fiend!" How quickly the tides turn.

Miriam started to panic. She tried to look for John, but the crowd had blurred and melded into one. Her chest was instantly on fire as her skin began to itch. Adrenaline powered through her, and her stomach twisted in knots. She breathed jaggedly, trying to control her heartbeat that was thudding in her throat. She didn't want to be there anymore. She wanted Hell to swallow her into its infernal pit. There was already the heat of the flames.

Suddenly, Miriam was racing off the stage with tears in her eyes. Suddenly she was storming past her husband who had reached out for her. Suddenly, her heeled boot clacked furiously down the aisle. Suddenly, John was racing after her.

Suddenly, she was gone into the London night.

"Well, Miriam?" John repeated, breaking her out of her thoughts. "Do you wish to answer me or am I to stand here like the fool I have been all evening?"

"You are not the fool here, John."

"Then what is it?"

"What if Madame Mara was right?" Miriam said in such a hushed and revered way that John could barely hear her. She looked down to the floor as a prisoner would, preparing for the noose.

"*What?*" John muttered incredulously. Miriam didn't answer him. Instead, she turned to the drinks trolley by the living room door. The lack of response fuelled him once more. "Miriam, I do hope you are not taking those batty old woman's words as verbatim? She was saying such things to get a rise out of you. I might add that she was, indeed, successful."

"John…" Miriam muttered, interrupting his ranting as she poured herself a drink. Her hands were shaking as she brought it up to her lips and she spilled whisky down her shiny, grey dress, anointed with black velvet webs. "… Please."

The way her voice pleaded with him broke the raging resolve he once had. Though she had her back to him, John could tell that she was about to cry. He hated that he may have caused more upset and he hated how he could no longer hold any resentment to her, despite still being wronged somehow. "Miriam, what vexes you?"

She downed her drink and poured another. After Miriam shoved the whisky bottle down, causing a loud clang and a trembling of the glass bottles, she turned to face her husband with big, sad blue eyes. "May I ask you a question John?"

He sighed loudly as his shoulders dropped. The anger was quickly dissipating. In that moment, he wished to rush forward and envelope her in his arms. He said tenderly, "Yes, my dear Miriam, anything."

She walked towards him, hesitating on memories and musings that she had been going over and over in her mind since the séance. As she got closer, she could no longer meet his gaze and instead, turned her sights to the fire beside him. She stood opposite him by the mantle and drank hastily. People with sins to confess always interrupted their sentences with long pauses. His gaze grazed the side of her cheek. Miriam swallowed, "Have you ever killed a man?"

The question landed in the atmosphere like a lightning bolt. Miriam looked as though she was expecting to be struck on the spot. John had not expected Madam Mara's words to have shaken his wife like this – not when she usually found such acts so risible. So, he decided to answer truthfully. "I have had people die at my table."

"But that is not by your hand, John," she replied sternly, raising her hand wildly to drive her point home.

"No, I have not taken a life willingly, if that is what you are driving at." John said with almost a shrug. Then a realisation came over him in a cold, icy grip. "Miriam, do you mean to tell me that you have?"

After a sharp intake of breath, Miriam paused. Another grim silence started to fill the space between them. She tried to control her heavy breathing, but her heartbeat agonised in her chest. This was the final piece of her that she hadn't given him yet. That lifelong darkness that had brewed within her. That act that she had committed, so young and so furiously, had stalked her very being. That moment where she had transformed into something else.

The fireplace blazed wildly in John's eyes. He glanced over her as though she were unravelling before him. Miriam studied the colours of those flames that altered those usually bright blues into something she couldn't fathom. She wondered if that fire was a final judgement. That if she were to allow the confession to fall from her lips then he would cast her into the flames. But the drumming in her chest and every voice within her mind urged her to tell him. There was no going back from this precipice. Despite fearing that everything was about to change, Miriam nodded softly before bowing her head in resignation.

John mirrored her movement without a clear expression. It was just a nod to show he understood what she was wordlessly confessing. The evening was starting to make sense to John; why Madam Mara's words would cut so deep, why Miriam struggled to meet his eyes, and why she had found herself at the hospital. It was less to do with thinking, he surmised, and more to do with gazing upon all the good work that she had done since she had committed such a malicious act.

There was a nagging memory in the back of his mind – a conversation that had already turned his head a few months ago. John would be a fool to ignore the fact that he hadn't previously pondered on this very notion. There was something etched in Miriam's face that day. He took a sip of his drink and allowed it to burn down his gullet. He mused on the moment for the longest time. Then he replied, "Your uncle?"

The question caused Miriam to look up suddenly. Her eyes widened. "How did you..?"

Unexpectedly, John smiled slyly. "I have had my suspicions since you spoke of his death in the garden."

Miriam did not know what to say next. All the words she had been rehearsing in her mind were stalled. She had prepared herself for chastisement. She did not expect her husband to have guessed her sins so easily. He greeted them with nothing more than a mischievous grin. Was John aware of how she slipped into the Gray Mansion in the dead of night? Did he know how she climbed atop her drunken uncle? Could he see his wife as a young girl, pouring her father's stolen laudanum down Charles' throat, watching until he expired beneath her?

She hadn't detailed the murder yet somehow, Miriam sensed John knew it all. With that cacophony of thoughts, Miriam was suddenly aware that all her horrific ways had been uncovered. She turned away from him, so he did not see the tears that were still glistening in her eyes. Trying to smother the sobs, she downed the rest of her whisky. "So that blasted woman was right – I am a murderess! A monster! A fiend!"

Despite the warmth of the room, John saw Miriam begin to shake. He let out a kindly sigh before placing his glass on the mantel. He stepped forward and wrapped his warming arms around her body, pulling her close to him. He took her glass and put it down so that she was free to grab him back. "I see no monster nor murderess. I see someone who protected a person they loved. I see someone full of mettle that no man has." He kissed her gently on the cheek. "I see you, Miriam."

"But—"

"Sometimes one must do dark things for the betterment of this world. It takes great courage to do so," John whispered deftly, letting his words coo, and calm her. "Do you not recall what I said that day in the rose garden? Good riddance. He was the true fiend."

Those last words caused a wave of relief to flow over Miriam. She softened against him and soon melted into his embrace; blessed and forgiven. As he rocked her gently, Miriam leaned her head against John's. In a murmur as pensive and as captivated as when they first met, Miriam said, "Who are you?"

"I am but a humble mortal who adores you, my dark goddess." His words grew heated as one of his hands stroked her chest. He kissed her neck, tickling her gently with his moustache. It caused a ricochet of uncontrollable sensations down her spine. "I have worshipped you long before we met. Since the stars collided and scattered us across the universe, I was born to bask in your glory."

The silence which followed his words was one they both knew very well. It was charged with that unwavering yearning for one another. His mouth continued on her flesh, kissing parts of her neck and shoulder and back. He wished for nothing more than to tear her from her burdens as well as her clothes. Swaying softly from side to side, he anointed her bare skin with as many touches as possible. He even pawed at the spider necklace on her neck, following the intricate design delicately as though he were imitating what he'd do if his hands were lowered. Miriam reached around and stroked his crotch, his cock hardened behind his trousers as she did.

He broke the quiet with tender yet tantalising pleas. "I am at your behest." His hands slipped down her, slidingly into the back of her dress and grabbing the fabric. "I am at your command." His lips lavished her neck over and over again. "I am at your control," he growled.

"Praise me mortal," she uttered yearnfully, "worship me however you wish."

"Very well."

Using all his strength, he ripped the dress from her body. Miriam giggled at the ferocious way he tore and discarded her garments. They flew across the room. The insatiable pair wished to waste no time: Miriam wriggled quickly out of the crinoline whilst John hastily removed his jacket and loosened his necktie. The pair were both too hungry for one another to remove any more clothing.

In the whirlwind of animalistic need, John somewhat forcefully pushed her to the floor. She landed on her hands and knees, gasping gleefully out of the shock. As glorious as being in control was, from time-to-time Miriam enjoyed this rough play where John acted utterly ravenous for her. She heard him fumble at his trouser buttons before he knelt down behind her. Lifting the skirt of her chemise up over her body, they were both similarly thankful that Miriam had chosen to abandon her drawers today. John squeezed her plentiful buttocks as she pushed herself out for him. "Praise me John," she whispered voraciously.

It was not long till she felt his penis press between her legs. For a short while, he stroked the tip between her slit, up and down to enjoy the wetness as well as the glorious tease. She whimpered at the motions but bounced backwards brazenly.

John chuckled before he slowly eased himself into her, gruffly groaning as he did. She seethed between her teeth at the sensation of him filling her. Placing both hands on her hips to grip himself, John started thrusting into her with vigour.

The evening had elicited many emotions that he needed to release: the turbulent tension of all that teasing, the anger from their acute argument, and the damnation of her dark declaration raced in him alongside the lust of this loving reunion. With all the force of these tumultuous thoughts, he slammed himself into her over and over again with loud grunts.

Miriam encouraged his furious fucking, urging him to go faster by saying repeatedly under her breath, "praise me, praise me, praise me." Those words fuelled him further. He dug his fingers into her flesh and moved so hungrily that she whined loudly. Every now and then he'd slap her behind, causing her to shriek in delight.

This was certainly one of Miriam's favourite positions, when she would let him pound into her with his urgent and unrelenting desire. But she longed to kiss him and shower him with adoration. She pushed herself up on her knees and bounced herself upon him. John threw his arms instinctively around her, pulling her whole body against his. Leaning her head backwards, she found his mouth and kissed him greedily.

John slipped a hand under her top to massage one of her breasts. All the while the other hand slid down her body to find her aching spot. He lavished it with absolute attention. A symphony of squeaks and sighs fell from her lips. The sound of her song melted into him, and he couldn't contain himself any longer. He thrust upwards quickly before spilling his worship into her with a raucous moan.

Breathing heavily against one another, they stayed that way until his member fell out of her. Miriam relaxed in his arms, so he tightened his embrace around her chest and gripped gently onto her neck. She swallowed excitedly in the palm of his hand. His luscious soft voice said, "No no, my darling girl, it is not over yet."

His other fingers were still on her clitoris, and he began to quicken the motions as before. Leaning her head against him, she groaned. He knew her body very well. He hastened the perpendicular strokes as she became wetter for him. Writhing against him, pleasure radiated throughout her, and she wondered on his words from before. How sweet the universe was for allowing their souls and bodies to meet and entwine in such a perfect manner. As that wondering flowed over her, a familiar rise began.

With the movements and the moans she was making, John knew that she was close and was keen to see her come undone. In her ear, and with heated breaths, he dripped the precise words that'll tumble her into pleasure, "Praise *me*, Miriam."

As she climaxed, she cried his name loudly into the night.

They enjoyed each other once more in the fire's glow. The wanton
way in which Miriam called his name had caused John to harden
again and Miriam could never resist him when he was always so
eager for her. Truthfully, they wanted to just be naked and worship
one another without the barrier of clothes. They shed all their
remaining garments and made slow love, nude by the fireplace. It
was a tired tryst of two people who were already spent. When John
ejaculated, he shuddered deeply as he gave his last morsel over to
her.

Lying on the rug, their bodies were still entwined in every
sense of the word. Heated by their activities and the flames beside
them, they gazed into each other's eyes. Even though the pair were
exhausted, they were too alive inside one another's embrace to fall
asleep.

There they were again, caught in that sweet timeless place that
was reserved only for them, both wishing to stay there forever.
There was a soft sound of rain against the windows. The lamp
lights flickered as the wind wormed its way through the
woodwork. They did not care, nor did they feel a chill. They were
too enraptured by one another to be bothered by the bitter world
outside.

Miriam pondered on how they were forged by the same
exploding star that scattered their love across millennia. She
wondered who they were in past lives. Perhaps Persephone and
Hades, guarding the underworld forevermore with their dark and

devastating love. John was wrong, Miriam thought to herself in this moment, he was not a mere mortal. He was her saviour and salvation. And she'd never run from him again.

She didn't say all this, of course. Sometimes she was quite frightful of saying her feelings out loud as though the words would break the spell. Instead, she said it in the moans that left her lips, she told him in the way she allowed his hands to explore her body, and she loved him with the manner in which she accepted him inside of her. She promised wordlessly to bestow riches upon him over and over again until the ground dared to take their bodies. That no matter what, they will unite here in that special space reserved solely for them.

She didn't say all this, but John knew. He always knew. She needn't ever say the words to him. Especially not now.

After all, there had never been a silence as great as this one.

New Year's Eve

New Year's Eve 1890

Michael Jenkins was a man prone to accidents - in both action and speech. He had been that way since he was a child. He would often trip, slip, and bump into things as though he was born with an innate gravitational pull towards calamity. By the time he was thirty, Michael had already accumulated an assortment of scars that dotted his white, tanned skin.

His tongue would do the same for his reputation. He often spoke before thinking and collided with many people, causing many rows, heated confrontations, and scorned looks. Though Michael was a smart man – a Doctor of Chemistry, no less – he was, for lack of a better word, an idiot.

Still, if it weren't for his clumsy nature, he wouldn't have met her. Adelaide.

They first bumped into one another, quite literally, on New Year's Eve 1890. The Piccadilly Theatre hosted a lavish show and party every year, mostly for the pretty bright young things and socialites. This year was Michael's first attendance. Perhaps it was because he was slightly older than the crowd, or perhaps because he hated loud, garish parties, but Michael Jenkins found the entire evening ghastly.

The rowdy throng of people that were driven through the doors of the theatre were high-spirited and, of course, high in spirits. Both men and women guffawed and chortled so loudly that they were creating an unfathomable roar. The drinks were pouring plentifully and already the crowd was moving on a wave of intoxication. Michael had already caught a few scenes that caused his face to redden and his lips to tighten.

Everyone around him was moving with the more youthful times – that electric charge of the nineties that dared to innovate and inspire. Michael seemingly had stayed in one place, unable to move on from his upbringing. He looked out at the sea of his peers at odds with them all. His own generation was steadily abandoning the social conventions that Michael upheld dearly, especially the women. After all, his father had instilled in him the idea that a wife should be ornamental. Quiet things that took care of the household, their husband, and subsequent children.

Having mostly studied for the first three decades of his life, Michael had yet to find a woman who matched the ideals forced upon him at a young age. Looking out at the loudly laughing ladies, he miserably conceded that tonight, he wouldn't find that honourable housewife.

Sipping at a glass of red wine, he dutifully followed his colleagues like a reprimanded child, pouting over sore, beaten knuckles. The young doctors, roughly around the same age, worked together at the St Bartholomew's Hospital. They had all been eagerly planning the night with the promise of excitement and intrigue. They hadn't even ventured into the auditorium, but the foyer and stairs were alive with performers – circus acts and magicians. All of his friends would point at the pretty spectacle and prod one another in jovial jibes. As more people drove into the theatre, Michael sighed loudly, wishing that he'd spent the evening in his local. Or at his sister Catherine's as he usually did. Or anywhere really.

Anywhere but here.

"Come man," said Doctor Damon Hargreaves, St Bart's junior physician, who rolled his eyes at Michael's audible annoyance. He was a man of average height, round, and flirtatious. He had a different woman every week. He and Michael were friends of comfort – thrown together because of work, rather than a liking of one another. Damon slapped Michael on the back, causing the latter to spill his wine over his hand. "Try not to look so wretched.

There are festivities to be had." Damon then nudged his friend gently. "Not to mention women."

"Damon…" Michael said, shaking the remnants of red liquid from his hand, "… finding a woman at a place like this would be like courting the prettiest pig at the farm!"

Wildly, Michael lifted his hands in exclamation, causing the wine to escape his glass and hit the person directly behind him. There was a small yelp which caused Michael's face to flush further – mirroring the very drink he had unwittingly drenched someone in. Slowly he turned around to find a beautiful blonde woman in a blue bustle dress, dripping with his libation. He gasped at the sight, his eyes widening as quickly as the stain was. "Oh, my goodness," he stumbled immediately, trying to reach for his handkerchief to clean her up. "Please, please, forgive me."

There was a short huff of hot, heated air. The woman looked up from the stain and glared at him, a fire burning in her brown eyes. "Whatever for?" She had an American twang to her voice. "Ruining my favourite dress or insulting my entire gender?"

Michael said nothing. Instead, he lowered his head, unable to meet her gaze. Still, it burned him. After a few short, stilted beats, the woman huffed again then pushed past him, colliding aggressively with his shoulder as a final note to their predicament. The impact bruised him. Yet as it panged, he followed her, watching until she had disappeared into the crowd. For the rest of the evening, Michael looked out for that yellow ringleted hair and those heated hazel eyes.

Alas to no avail.

Adelaide Jenkins climbed into her carriage and immediately the tears filled her eyes. Though she was alone, she slammed the door of the cab in angry protest. She wished that the silly stupid man could sense her rage, all the way on the stairs. She hoped it reverberated throughout him. As the carriage started rolling, she huffed and folded her arms, ready to start crying – but found that she was too angry for that.

Partly because she blamed herself. She looked down at the fabric with a hefty sigh, unlocking her stance and pawing at the baby blue cotton and silk. What a waste, she thought to herself, holding the damp fabric between her fingers, hoping she could magically remove the wine. Since she had stepped foot in the British city, Adelaide had immediately brought colours back into her wardrobe, having worn black for almost two years. Now her favourite shade of blue was patched with horrid stains. In a fearful thought, Adelaide wondered if her husband was cursing her from beyond the grave.

It was not as though the pair had loved one another to warrant such a haunting. Yet even the coldest of men treat their wives like prized possessions. Perhaps the moment Adelaide had shed her grieving skin, Graham had risen to torment her with wine stains and brutish men. As the carriage began to jolt, Adelaide allowed a few rage-charged tears to fall down her cheek. The first she had ever shed for her dead husband.

Their marriage had not been for love, nor for convenience. Instead, it had been a business transaction. A distant cousin that Adelaide's father had forced her to marry to keep their fortune, and her name, within the family. Graham, like all the men that she had ever known, was cold. The kind of man who spent too much time and thought on work. When he wasn't in the office, he was analysing the days ahead. He had an activity for each day, each hour, and sometimes each minute. Very rarely did Adelaide enter into his planning. She was alone for most of their marriage, save for Friday nights when Graham would routinely sleep with her. Regimented, passionless, sex which would eventually procure the result Graham wanted – a son, James.

Despite all of Graham's calculations, he had not prepared for illness. Neither of them did. Adelaide had a mere six months of motherhood before her child was taken by scarlet fever. Graham shortly followed the month after. At just 26, Adelaide had amassed enough grief and fortune to be left alone for the rest of her life. She moved back to her family home and had spent a year in a dejection that her sisters and mother could not awaken her from.

Staring out the window of her carriage, that familiar pang of despondency echoed in her chest. She clenched her fingers tightly, keen to dispel the darkness rising slowly in her. She had promised herself not to bring this grief away with her, but it tainted the beautiful sights of London. A black cloud as thick as the city's smog was descending, twisting her into knots. After taking a deep breath, she dispelled the fog with a calm breath.

Over a year ago, a newspaper article on Russian cosmopolitan traveller Aleko Konstantinov had caught her eye. What an inspired way to live – bouncing from city to city, immersed in the cultures they had to offer. Chicago had become a tomb and America had become broken, filled with enough torment and traditions to stifle Adelaide. She was sparked alive again by the thought of Parisian Bohemians, the hot beaches of Spain, and London's social life.

For once, Adelaide was thankful that she was a widow because it meant she could travel without a companion. Though her younger sister Rosie had been eager to join, Adelaide was insistent that she took the journey alone and promised, when she was ready, she would send for the young girl. This was a new feeling for Adelaide, and she could not squander it on someone else and, for the first time, Adelaide could see in herself new prospects in her future, and she was excited to be looking forward.

Pulling up at her hotel, Adelaide wondered if she was taken by foolishness instead. The dizzying ideals of these new countries and cities clouded her judgement. Maybe she wasn't made for the loud and loutish life of London. It was her second day here and already she had been drenched and insulted by an oaf of a man. Walking up the stairs to her room, she was doomed to be miserable forever. So, she wasted no time in opening the door, and collapsing on her bed, ready to sob eternally.

However, as she lay there, no more tears arrived. She huffed loudly and threw herself on her back instead. Staring at the ceiling, her stomach twisted again. It was not the anxiety she was used to – the gnarling grief that had consumed her for years. It was a fresh exhilaration that was pulsing through her body. One that glided down her skin so delicately that it intrigued and excited her all at once. She blushed and suddenly burst into ripples of laughter.

For now, as she was alone, covered in baby blue and red wine stains, all Adelaide could think about was his bright green eyes.

New Year's Eve 1891

London burned with many different types of incandescence. The flames of the past rippled upon the skyline with the electricity of the future. There was an inescapable buzz to this city, bounding through the air and winding through everyone. The chatter of the people was turning into a roar. They loudly hung their promises upon the hooks of the new year. This decade was trembling already with change and the city was shedding its tradition. Its new skin glistened in this darkness, spotted with history's fires that still burned.

What a thrill it must be to be caught in such an evolution. The excitement of the unknown, constantly changing, so fast and ferocious, and never really knowing its final form. If a final form truly existed, that is. One could spend a whole lifetime without settling on the person they were meant to be. Maybe that was the same for places. Especially one as vast and plentiful as London. Adelaide was certain that London would never become one singular thing and perhaps that is why she found herself back here.

Standing on the roof of the Piccadilly Theatre, she stared out at the city she had left almost a year ago. The different types of lights flickered within the night. She was certain that there were new ones here. The orange spots upon the horizon illuminated windows and buildings. As her sights reached out as far as they could go, she thought about each person behind the flame. A never-ending life as bountiful as the stars above them. London was most beautiful within the dark. She shivered with its possibilities.

Adelaide's sojourn around Europe had ended yesterday and had been perfectly pleasant. She had promenaded around pretty Paris, sizzled in the Spanish sun, took a gander at Germany's grandeur, and intimately investigated inspirational Italy's cities. She was awash with experience – her soul now knew colours and sights and sounds that she never thought possible in the confines of Chicago's social circles. The world was now within her and, as she made her way back home, she promised herself that she would venture out again. Her mind was alive with adventure and the ends of the Earth called her.

She smiled, rubbing her arms from the cold, and wondered why, then, she found herself standing within London's skyline once more. She couldn't quite place the series of events that took her here. One minute she was sitting by a great ship in France, watching the puffs pillow out of the funnels. Man-made clouds entering the blue without thought. She bit her lip, trying to find the faces of her family in those clouds. Gripping tightly to her handbag, Adelaide stared but could not find anyone of note in the plumes.

Suddenly, an odious horn blared out causing Adelaide to jump and gasp. The next thing she knew she was at the ticket office, then she was boarding a different boat, and then she was sailing across the channel. Then a train, then a cab, and then she was back in the heart of the city. It was almost as if she had mistaken the call. It wasn't the ends of the Earth calling.

It was London. Calling her home.

The realisation made her shiver. She gripped onto herself and couldn't help smiling, despite the cold. She would've gone inside, out from the freezing weather, but she had found herself trapped on the roof, having accidentally closed the door behind her. The revels of the party were raging on and after slamming her fists for a long time, she realised it was too loud for anyone to hear and help. She settled on the fact that she might be up here for a while. Sighing, she held herself close and started to count the lights to distract herself from the cold.

Adelaide had reached thirty-six when the door violently swung open. It slammed loudly against the wall and let out the screech of the hubbub. As she turned around, she heard a voice say, "This isn't the gentlemen's parlour."

When Michael Jenkins had first set foot in the Piccadilly Theatre last year, he had immediately sworn to himself that he'd never return. The common crowd had leered around him, swilling his stomach with a disgust he couldn't sate. Even though he had tried, sipping furiously at his red wine to quell the abject horror of being thrust into this popular place, he simply had not been able to assimilate to his peers. He had clutched his glass with an ever-growing rage. Both at the carnage surrounding him and at himself, for his inability to blend with the masses.

It had all changed when he had spilled that same wine onto an unsuspecting woman.

Now a year later, he found himself stepping back into the place he vowed never to return to. Everything had changed. It was as though he suddenly had fresh eyes. He now viewed the crowd with a different perspective. All these lovers drenched in an array of colours as they entwined their words and bodies. The electricity in the air charged his stomach with promise. This rose-tinted atmosphere, so heavenly in riches, was sparking a small chaos within him.

For he was most certain that he would find her here.

Michael would be the first to admit that the idea sounded preposterous at best. That somehow in a city of thousands, he'd collide once more with the same woman. The same brightly blonde haired, hazel eyed woman, dripping with the scarlet remnants of his beverage. Michael did not care for grand romances or fairy tales. Yet now he was the Prince searching for his Cinderella after the ball.

He had, in fact, spent the past year figuratively slipping on glass slippers to every blonde woman he'd happen to meet. Sometimes he'd be shopping around London and catch a glimpse of yellow hair and rush forward expectantly. Almost always Michael was met with a gasp of shock, and sometimes, a hard hit of a handbag. Once again, Michael's pernicious nature had garnered a few more bruises. His reputation was similarly getting hit.

As Michael had not confided in anyone as to why he was approaching random women on the street, he was starting to look crazed. Yet perhaps the most damning evidence against his character was his sudden excitement at another New Year's Eve jaunt to the Piccadilly Theatre. He had not been formally invited by Damon who had heard most of Michael's gripes last year and made a note to never invite the man again. However, when Damon was talking to others about the event, he was surprised to be met with nothing but enthusiasm from Michael Jenkins, and reluctantly invited the man.

Damon watched this overtly proud and traditional man dissolve into nerves and excitement like a giddy child. Michael said few words as they travelled in the carriage, and he quickly skipped through the doors of the theatre. When Damon suggested that the group get a drink first, he was bemused to find that Michael had gone. He had all but disappeared into the crowd, so Michael did not see Damon's shrewd smile.

Instead, he scoured the venue like a police detective searching for clues of a precedent murder case. He peered into the faces of everyone there but couldn't find anyone who so much as resembled the woman he had seen last year. Every step he took, his excitement dissipated, and he feared this frantic year of searching had been for nothing.

Exhausted, Michael finally made his way up the final set of stairs. Breathless, he squeezed through the loud crowd and his annoyance built up again. The world was mocking him for having such frivolous feelings. There was no way he would find this woman. Perhaps, this American had journeyed back to her hometown. Yes, that made more sense to Michael. All was lost, romantically, and he sternly told himself to stop, turn around, and at the earliest convenience, ask his parents to set him up with someone plain and ordinary.

Resigning in his endeavour, he barely made it up to the top of the theatre before he turned around to make the trek back down the stairs. Unfortunately, as he spun around, he collided with another reveller and their red wine spilled down his white shirt and waistcoat. Apologising profusely, the unknown assailant soon disappeared into the night. Michael sighed, looking down at the purple-red stain on his suit.

"Well," he said to no one at all, "that's what you get, Michael."

Scanning the building, he saw a solitary door that he assumed was the bathroom. He grabbed hold of the doorknob and pushed it open, falling outside.

"This isn't the gentlemen's parlour," he said, blinking as the cool breeze hit his face. As he looked out onto the night, he found a woman looking back. Michael tightened the grip on the door handle. "Oh! It's you!"

Adelaide had yet to pay attention to the figure in the doorway. The heat of the theatre was already extending its arms and calling to her. She rushed forward the minute she heard the door click open, muttering her gratitude. But this exclamation caused Adelaide to stall in her tracks. In fact, she took an unexpected step back and found herself staring at someone very familiar. Someone who had drenched her in wine exactly a year ago today. She twisted her lips and, in an entirely different manner, replied, "Oh, it's you."

She hadn't entirely meant to be so sullen in response. She was trying to ignore the fact that her stomach flipped the minute she locked eyes with him. Those green eyes that had followed her all-around Europe.

Michael barely noted her inference. He was too excited to see her – the girl with the ringlet blonde hair and hazel eyes. His Cinderella. She was standing right in front of him and all of that anxiety rushed through him. His heart thudded in her throat. He smiled wildly and stepped forward, speaking rather quickly as he did. "I have wanted to see you since last year…" As he moved towards her, Michael let the door go and it began to swing shut.

"No! Wait!" she gasped and ran but it was too late. The door slipped back into the slot, mocking the woman with an impertinent click. "Oh, you absolute oaf!" she shouted, half to the man, and half to herself. She wriggled at the handle and knocked on the door to no avail. "We are trapped."

Michael's face fell. He ran to the door and similarly tried to pull it open. He tried to prise it with his fingertips, he pushed against it with the door, and then began slamming his fists against the metal door. To no avail. Breathless, he stood back and simply went, "Ah, yes. It would appear we are trapped." He swallowed, realising how close he now was to the girl. He turned to her and in a small gasp said. "I am truly very sorry."

"Whatever for?" Adelaide said as a sly smile appeared on her face. They caught each other's eye in a sudden second of knowing. A beat of wondrous harmony, where the world slots its puzzle pieces together and one can see the brilliant picture forming. As if all of life's mysteries had unfolded and this pair, at this precise moment, could see all the secrets at last. They stayed locked in this stare for a while, wondering whether the other could feel it too. Could they sense the sweetening of the atmosphere?

It was Adelaide who broke the hold. She looked away, shuddering with the cold and the way this strange man made her feel.

"Here, allow me." Michael removed his jacket and wrapped it around her.

Adelaide took hold of the jacket daintily and offered a small smile of thanks. She then glanced at his shirt, seeing a familiar red stain upon him. It echoed of last year. His gaze hadn't entirely left her, so she stayed fixated on the spot, embarrassed to look upwards and catch his eye again. She gestured up and down. "It seems you have the worst of luck when it comes to red wine. Might I suggest a clearer liquid next time?"

Michael turned the same colour as the stain. He looked down at his shirt and let out a small sigh. "Yes, I am almost persuaded to swear off the drink entirely. Then again, if one stops taking something because of the stains, then one would have little to consume. I am frightfully clumsy, I am afraid. I am told, however, that it is a family trait haphazardly passed down through generations. Though I am still sorry that you were on the receiving end of such a trait last year. And it seems this year I have unwittingly trapped you outside in the cold. You are an innocent bystander surrounding my calamity."

The way Michael spoke was pacy and plentiful. Adelaide watched this mouth motor on and nodded her head politely with it. When he stopped to take a breath, she simply replied, "Speaking candidly, I was trapped long before you arrived."

"Well, at least you have company now."

"Quite."

They caught each other's eyes again. There was something mesmerising about the glint in Michael's green sights. It sent a wave of unsure emotions through her. The minute the ripple cascaded down her arms, she pulled his jacket closer to her and smelled a puff of musk and cinnamon aftershave. It caused her to inadvertently sigh. She turned around away from him and looked at the London skyline once more.

"Wow," he said enthusiastically, "that certainly is a beautiful view of the city." She heard him take a few steps forward and suddenly he was beside her. The warmth of his body charged within her. They stayed that way for a few silent beats, until Michael coughed and said, "May I inquire your name?"

Adelaide did not turn to him as she said quietly, "Jenkins. Adelaide Jenkins."

"Good Lord, it can't be!" Michael said excitedly. He practically jumped next to her, clapping his hands as he laughed. Adelaide cocked her head, confused. "I might've known. What a hilarious coincidence. It truly can't be!" There was a beat as he waited for her to catch on. "Oh, forgive me, but I don't suppose you are related to *the* Christopher Jenkins – the finest purveyor of gin in Chicago?"

In a quiver of a breath, Adelaide replied, "He's my father."

"The Ginkins!" Michael smiled. Adelaide bristled at hearing the garish nickname that had dogged her most of her life. Seeing how her face soured caused Michael to launch into another tirade of words. "Oh, I am truly sorry. It is just, well, your family's name does precede you. Well, more that it comes up in conversation around my family most of the time. I've always wanted to meet someone from the infamous Ginkins family. Oh, forgive me, again, it seems I cannot help but say it." There was a pause as he studied her puzzled face. "Oh! I am also a Jenkins. Michael Jenkins."

"Good God, I hope we aren't related," Adelaide replied, it came out more cutting than she would've liked. She hadn't meant it as an insult, it was simply because she was already having sordid thoughts about this man and couldn't bear it if they were distant cousins.

"No, no, we are not." Michael's face broke out into a brilliant smile. "Trust me, if anyone were to find a relationship between our families then it would have been my mother. One does not wish to speak ill of a parent, but she has a knack of sniffing out a fortune whenever it is nearby like one of those truffle pigs. Oh! Not that I am calling my mother a pig. Nothing of the sort. It is somewhat admirable how she has scrutinised her entire heritage and bloodline, and my father's, to try and find—"

"Mr Jenkins—"

"Michael, please."

"Michael, are you always this loquacious?"

"Yes. Another family trait, I'm afraid. Does it offend you?"

"Not at all. I quite like it."

Adelaide grinned at him brightly as she meant every word. Her family were well known for their silent demeanour, believing words to be so charged with meaning that they must only be uttered when completely necessary. It unfortunately meant that they only spoke to give a scathing retort or a cold business decision. Growing as a child, Adelaide had known best how to hold her tongue and she had then taken that skill into her short-lived marriage. Widowhood was like a living death. Travelling alone hadn't inspired much conversation either. She had grown tired of being on her own, listening to her own thoughts go round and around and around with no one to utter them to.

How refreshing it was to find someone who seemingly found joy in speaking. The way Michael spoke was like a babbling brook. His stream of sentences skimmed stones with absolutely no thought behind their intention. Every time he opened his mouth it was as though the dam within his mind had burst and he could not hold his thoughts back. It was clumsy, sure, but riveting to watch.

However, her last sentence seemed to have stunned him, finally into silence. Michael moved closer towards her gently as they both turned outwards to the night sky again. Adelaide gripped onto the railing, fearful that these big emotions within her would cause her to tumble away. Michael had the same apprehension and similarly clung onto the cold metal. His hand brushed up against hers.

The chime of Big Ben rang out across the night. In several places, fireworks hit the dark in a dazzling array of colour. The pair gasped at the beauty of it, as though they were the only two people in the world. Alone upon this rooftop it certainly felt that way. The sole people in the whole of London who were witness to such a marvellous sight. A set of clumsy circumstances bringing them to this exact point. Dare they question the fate of it all? It was impossible yet standing here, side by side, it charged through them.

"Happy New Year, Michael Jenkins." Adelaide said, within a puff of gasping steam as her warm words hit the freezing weather.

"And to you, Adelaide Jenkins." Michael turned towards her. "May I… May I kiss you?"

Adelaide was finally brave enough to meet his eyes again. "Yes, you may."

The year was turning new again. Upon the rooftop of the Piccadilly Theatre, miles away from the braying crowd, and the rest of the world with all its secrets, Michael and Adelaide wrapped their arms around one another and kissed for the first time.

New Year's Eve 1892

It wasn't like Michael to be so quiet.

He hadn't suddenly started the day that way. Adelaide had noticed this at the beginning of December. She had chalked up the humorous change in character to nerves. After all, she hadn't expected her family to visit suddenly. She had spent many letters telling them that it wasn't entirely necessary. Adelaide was a grown woman and if she wanted to live her life in London, then she had every right to do so without their permission. She had not mentioned Michael.

Well, not to her mother or father. There had been some correspondence with her little sister Rosie about the man whom she was courting. Adelaide wasn't entirely sure whether Rosie had accidentally let slip about Michael, or her father had stumbled upon the letters. Still, upon the doorstep of her new home near Regent's Park, on a crisp, cold December evening, she had found herself staring at her mother, father, and a very red-faced Rosie.

Whilst their arrival was certainly a shock to Adelaide, it was much worse for Michael. After he heard Adelaide exclaim their names out loud, he scrambled up from the chaise lounge in her drawing room – buttoning his waist coat and straightening his trousers up. He took his handkerchief, rushed to the nearest reflective service – the metal of a dish cover – and rubbed the lipstick from his cheeks and lips. Even when it was gone, his face was red with remnants of their tryst.

He hesitated in the drawing room, terrified to move an inch for fear of alerting people to his presence. Though he tried hard, the task seemed impossible for a man who had a natural magnetism towards calamity. He wasn't even sure how he did it. One moment he was stood perfectly still, the next he was toppling into a table, sending a rather lovely pink speckled vase crashing to the ground. The smash was the loudest sound he ever heard. It was followed by the gravest of silences.

"Michael, please come into the front room," Adelaide beckoned, breaking the deathly quiet with a shrill and embarrassed voice. Michael's cheeks burned further, like a reprimanded child at school. He waited a few more seconds before he sheepishly made his way to Adelaide's family: The famous Jenkins clan that he had known so much about. He was sure that tonight was going to end disastrously.

Yet despite the clashing personalities, the night itself moved pleasantly enough, and quickly. At first, Michael had tried to rouse the Americans with conversation but soon reverted into their very quiet sense of being. Adelaide ate little food, nervously watching this man she had been courting bite his cheeks to stop the river of words spilling out all over the dinner table. Her parents had said so few words, and it made her worried, frightful of the letter of disapproval she'd receive once they left.

Her little sister Rosie, however, was the only one who listened to Michael whenever he spoke and looked disappointed when he soon acclimated to the American Jenkinses' manner. She flashed knowing and approving glances and smiles over at Adelaide whenever she could.

The night was drawing to a close and Adelaide found herself holding her breath, for fear of upsetting the noiseless evening entirely. She held it further when Adelaide's father Christopher invited Michael to the parlour room for a cigar. Instead of enjoying tea with her mother and sister in the front room, she paced the doorway and bit her nails until the two men emerged – both in some sort of quiet musing. Her family left with no recriminations and no frightful letter that she was conjuring in her mind had appeared on her doorstep.

Michael left Adelaide shortly after, with just a small, gentle peck on the cheek. He sighed and looked on the cusp of saying something but for once, he was mute. It was as though her father had stolen all the wind and words from Michael. Confused, Adelaide bid him good night and wondered whether it was the last she would ever see of Michael Jenkins. That cold thought sent daggers into her stomach. She had become so used to his being. She didn't want it to end so suddenly and without good reason. As he walked into the night, quiet as the winter's frost, it was as though she were saying goodbye forever.

Adelaide closed the door on him and ran upstairs. She threw herself on her bed again and this time, bawled unjustly, wondering why her family hated her so much to deny her such happiness. She grew angry with their torment, having had most of her life dictated by her parents. Screaming into the pillow, she grew enraged by Michael's sudden change in demeanour. Did he not feel as strong about her as she did him? Did he not ache with the same love and adoration that she had for him? Did he not want to spend the rest of his life together with her? If he walked away so lowly after one meeting with her family, then he was a lesser man than she thought. She cried and screamed into her pillow until she fell asleep.

Their meetings over December were scarce. The winter's chill spread illness around like the plague and Michael was busy at the hospital. Though he'd send her letters, lamenting that he could not see her, she was disappointed. This was evidence that he was pulling away from their courtship. She was further dismayed when Christmas came, and went, and Michael could not make it to her planned dinner. He had told her in advance of such a snub, but it still bruised her spirit to spend the holiday alone in a house that somehow was hollow without him, though he did not live there.

In the week that followed, Adelaide decided to compose her own letter ending their courtship. She could not stand the silences any longer, living decades in the shadow of her family. In neat, flowing handwriting, she demanded that Michael be a man and break her heart fairly for she could no longer stand this uncertainty. *Please*, she wrote in desperate nouns and pained verbs, *release me from your love so I can move on.*

Adelaide tore each letter she wrote and threw it into the fireplace.

As they turned into cinder and ash before her, Adelaide understood why Michael hadn't the constitution to say goodbye.

On the morning of New Year's Eve, however, Adelaide was surprised to hear a series of knocks upon her door. Sitting in the front room and cross-stitching the skyline of Paris as a gift for her sister, the interruption caused her to jump. The pin went straight through her index finger, causing a small trickle of blood to splash out. Flushed with irritation, she stormed to the front door only to find a smartly dressed messenger. He bowed to her and handed her a somewhat large box, wrapped in a yellow bow. Before she could ask any questions, he was already walking away with a glint of knowing in his eyes.

By the time she got it in, the brown package was covered in splodges of her blood. Removing the bow, she wrapped it around her finger delicately. The first item that caught her eye in the box was a silver brooch. It was intricately shaped like a glass shoe and shone with fine diamonds. On top was a yellow envelope and inside that was a note:

My dearest Cinderella (Adelaide Jenkins.)
You are cordially invited to the New Year's Ball at the Piccadilly Theatre.
Your carriage will arrive at 9pm promptly.
There I shall be waiting.
Your Prince Charming.
(Michael Jenkins.)

Underneath the note, and layers of fine tissue paper, was a burgundy dress. The colour immediately made her laugh in a loud, obnoxious honk, as she thought about a similar shade of stain. There was a label from her favourite boutique. *Clever man*, she thought to herself, knowing the shop would have her measurements. Adelaide simultaneously picked up the dress and stood up, letting the box clatter to the floor. She pressed the dress against her and admired its decolletage. It had short sleeves, and a plunging neckline, with black lace along the side. It was dark, delicious, and utterly decadent. Her cheeks flushed the same colour as the dress at the prospect of the somewhat conventional Michael choosing something so devilish. She wondered what deeds he was concocting.

"Well, Adelaide," she muttered to herself, with a grin, "this is the most lavish way a man has broken a courtship."

At exactly 9pm, the carriage appeared on her doorstep. It was an unassuming cab. Deep dark brown wood panelling with a plush red velvet interior. There were two black horses pulling it along with a smartly dressed driver aloft the cab. The same man who delivered the parcel was there to guide her into the carriage.

It was unassuming, yes, but the minute Adelaide stepped into the carriage, the earth moved. A cloud of anticipation filled the carriage as the horses started trotting along the London streets. It took most of the oxygen, making it hard for her to catch her breath. This air of knowing caused her heart to beat wildly. Her face grew hot, and she was positive that she had turned the same colour as her gown. Taking a small fan out of her pearl-coloured clutch, she tried to cool down her cheeks. What was causing such a commotion within her was the knowledge that as she was pulling closer and closer to the Piccadilly Theatre, her life was about to change dramatically.

Michael was caught in a similar commotion as he waited on the steps inside the theatre. He wore a deep burgundy suit which matched the dress which he had selected for Adelaide. As a man who had never deviated from browns and blacks for suits, the colour felt at odds upon his skin. The more time that passed waiting for Adelaide to arrive, the more foolish he felt. As crowds of people began their ascent around him, the throng as intoxicated and loud as they had always been, Michael was a peacock who had entered the lion enclosure. He swallowed his nerves and waited for her arrival.

If she ever would arrive, that is. He hadn't entirely meant to pull away from her these past few weeks. It's just he had a secret, one that he wished to keep from her until this precise moment. As a man who would, more often than not, find words unexpectedly falling from his lips, he was ever so frightened of ruining such a special night. So, instead of lavishing her with all the love and attention he had wished to do over the holidays, he had kept himself busy.

It didn't help that her family had scared him completely. Of course, that was not something he blamed Adelaide for. When they had first met, he knew that she was a quiet creature that hid an extremely passionate nature under the few, albeit scathing, words that she'd deliver. Over the course of the past year, she had unfolded like rose petals before him and showed her wit and intelligence. Gradually she had told him about her life in America, the grief she had suffered, and, eventually, her family's cold nature.

To find himself surprisingly in their presence had been a massive shock to Michael. He wasn't so used to such quiet dinners, having come from a family that debated heavily at the kitchen table (which, also happened whenever he was having dinner, owing to his spectacular ability to put his foot in it.) The evening in December, however, had been a learning experience. His garrulous way of speaking had been grounded to a halt for the first time in his life. He had sipped soup silently, munched meat mutely, and chomped cake calmy. When her father had invited him to the parlour for a cigar, they had puffed out few words, though they were charged with importance.

The biggest surprise was how the evening had cemented everything he was feeling about Adelaide. That knowledge powered a tremendous fear and excitement throughout him. It shocked through his limbs as he clutched his hands together and tried not to pace upon the steps of the theatre.

To try and alleviate his nerves, he dove into his pocket to retrieve his watch, and stared at the time. It was half past nine. By his calculation, she should be here now. He frowned and tutted loudly.

"I hope I have not kept you waiting for long," Adelaide muttered, causing Michael to jump erratically. His heel collided with the step, causing him to topple backwards, his bum landing sharply on the ground. He grimaced with pain and embarrassment. However, in that moment, they shared a similar gratitude as both were thankful that he hadn't opted for a wine.

Adelaide could not help but grin widely down at this man. She leaned her hand down to help him back up again. Michael stared up in avid admiration. She looked divine, as though God had graced him. This angel from America who had blessed his life in more ways than one. He practically trembled before her.

As Michael stood back up again, he was overcome with all the words he wanted to say. He reached into his inside pocket, pulling out a little black box, and spurted out a long continuous sentence. It would've been indecipherable, but Adelaide was already fluent in his language. "Adelaide Jenkins, I have been meaning to ask you. Well, first of all I must apologise for my absence in the past couple of weeks, I had rather hoped that this would be a special night and… Oh by the way… may I say that you look most handsome tonight? Impossibly perfect. As you always are. Oh yes, anyway, I must profusely ask your forgiveness, if I have offended you in some manner, it was not my intention. I needed to get it all right. I even asked your father and I think he gave me his approval. At least, that is what I have surmised. Perhaps, then… I should say it… ha ha.. anyway. Years ago, on these very steps. I think. Perhaps a little bit up from here. This is all getting away from me a bit. What I mean to say is that Adelaide Jenkins, will you do me the honour of marrying me?"

"Oh," Adelaide replied with a response that neither of them had been expecting. As Michael's eyes widened in dismay at her utterance, Adelaide smiled. For all at once, she saw him entirely. From the moment they had collided, Michael had changed her. The green of his eyes had moved through her like spring, colouring her world in a vibrancy she had not known existed. When they had kissed for the first time, her soul had bloomed and unfurled into different flowers, each as spectacular as the last.

The years between their encounters had laid down fertile soil. Her trip abroad had allowed Adelaide to be free. She had grown and branched away from her family, finally knowing her true foliage. Her year with Michael had rooted her down in a home and had helped her grow in different ways. She had opened up more from her quiet existence whilst Michael settled down somewhat from his oafish ways. Though their views collided now and then, they learned together, and a garden was beginning to grow between them.

Yet now, before him, despite being ready to give him her earth, she hesitated.

She sighed, swallowing the seedling of the true answer. She stepped up to meet him, she kissed him softly on the cheek, and grabbed his hand. "Come with me."

There was an air of knowing inside that unassuming carriage again. Michael could sense it the minute he slid in opposite Adelaide. It permeated the cab like her floral perfume. His cheeks began to flush, and he tried to calm his breathing to no avail. Each breath he took was more jagged than the last. Against his better judgement, he took his hat off and gripped tightly to the rim to steady his nerves. He looked out upon the night-time scenes that trotted past, trying hard not to look at Adelaide. Every time he glanced at her, he'd catch a glint in her eyes so entrancing that he very nearly forgot himself, wishing to dive over to her and anoint her with a thousand kisses. The way her eyes burned, the way her mouth crooked in a secret smile, and the way she stayed silent made it all too clear her intentions.

They were about to have sex.

And the very notion terrified Michael more than anything.

As they arrived back at Adelaide's home, they abandoned any formalities. Adelaide dismissed her housekeeping staff immediately. Before anyone had the chance to leave, and despite knowing the implications, she took Michael's hand and guided him upstairs to her bedroom. He too was forgetting the traditions and societal rules that had fuelled him. Each day with Adelaide, the rigidity that he was raised in was melting happily away. As they reached the bedroom, he had all but forgotten his father's voice in the back of his mind, urging him to find a nice, quiet, upstanding woman of society.

It was one of the few rooms in her home that he had yet to enter. As she calmly strolled in, he found himself caught in the doorframe. An invisible barrier of social convention froze him whilst desire tempted him to cross. The wooden panelling loomed over him, mocking the very fear that kept him frozen on the threshold. Here he was at the point of no return. His whole world was shifting beneath him, and if he stayed here, gripping onto his top hat, he could steady himself.

"Close the door, please, Michael," Adelaide said in a dull roar of heat and passion. The tone matched the crackle of the fireplace that illuminated the whole room.

He nodded dutifully but was dizzy with anticipation as he stepped through the barrier and closed the door. Michael placed his top hat on her dresser by the door, and instantly regretted it. Without the distraction, he was restless and fidgety. The nerves electrified him as Adelaide walked over to her bed and sat down upon it. The springs rang out in the silence, and he desperately wanted to fill the void. Another clutter of words threatened to come. "Adelaide I—"

"Michael, you know that I adore you. More than anything..." she interrupted, as she lifted her legs to lay down on the bed. She shifted up to her pillows and cared not that her legs were now on show. It was an invitation after all. She watched his eyes glide over her and ached for his hands to do the same. Instead, Michael clutched them into a worried ball. She let out a hot steam of air, tinged with frustration and desire. "… but I cannot live a passionless marriage. Not again."

The sentence paled Michael and his face fell. Adelaide felt guilty in ambushing him like this. By his own accounts, he was passionate. He kissed her, albeit mostly in private, with an absolute unbridled, loving manner. He held her in his arms with all the warmth that he could muster. In their courting, he showered her with so much love that it made her heart swell and swoon all at once.

Yet whenever she tried to push him further. When she tried to guide his wandering hands to the intimate places of her body, he would freeze in fright and stop everything. One lowly night, after she had sighed from frustration, he admitted to her, quite quietly, that it was because he was a virgin and had been saving himself for marriage. This had not phase her in the moment, but the more she dwelled on it, the more she had been afraid. She had promised herself unlimited desire since the death of her callous husband, and though she understood Michael's hesitation, she couldn't bear the thought of entering a similar situation, no matter how much she loved the man who stood before her.

Michael had not blinked since her admission, trying to decipher a response as her words landed upon him. After an agonising minute, he closed his eyes briefly and settled on a small nod in response.

Adelaide mirrored the action. She placed her hands in her lap and twiddled with her thumbs, not quite sure where the night was going to go. "I do not need you to do anything now. But I must know. I need some assurance."

Michael sat on the edge of the bed and sighed. Adelaide was right, he was traditional to a fault. What had started as an admirable notion, chastity before marriage, had turned into crippling anxiety. The more he had gone without ever knowing sex, the more he had realised he was too nervous to even try. The minute he had met Adelaide, he had wished to throw the very notion out of the window, but it had become his armour. Knowing that she had some experience in the matter didn't sour his feelings for her but made him lament his own shortcomings. So, he pulled away from such things. He couldn't disappoint her if he asked her to wait. He desperately wanted to never disappoint her.

Gripping his hands together, Michael looked at her now, lying upon the bed. She still looked as angelic as she did in the theatre, yet there was something devilish about her now. The colour of the dress contrasted with the pale of her skin. Her breasts heaved slowly in the tight corset. Ringlets cascaded down her chest, framing her bosom perfectly. As the candlelight flickered in her hazel eyes, blazing with all her desires, he found himself overcome. Trembling again at the very feet of her temple, the wish to cradle her, covet her, and caress her was too powerful to deny.

"Show me," he said quietly, "show me what a husband should do."

"Very well," she whispered and tapped the bed next to her.

Michael shuffled up the bed, half-hoping that his slow movements would come across as seductive, instead of conveying how cripplingly shy he was. When he reached her, he turned his body to face her and leaned one hand across Adelaide to the other side. Michael leaned down to kiss her ardently, though his lips were quaking, and his breath was uneven. The very taste of her, all that sweetness and tenderness, brought him to his senses.

How foolish he was to deny himself of her.

He scooped his arm beneath her to bring her petite body closer to his, hoping that she could feel how wildly his heart beat for her. The very action caused her to giggle which he mirrored. They broke apart from their kiss and leaned their foreheads against one another, allowing the laughter to flow into the evening air like seedlings caught on a spring breeze.

"What happens now?" Michael said earnestly, laying her back down on the bed.

She gave him a soft nod and sat up against the cushions. She paused for a while, her mind racing with so many different thoughts. Up until this point, sex had been cold and violent. There was work to be done undoing such memories and finally her fantasies lay at her feet. This was the moment where everything would come together in rhyme, and she was scared. Terrified. What if it wasn't everything she dreamed?

Adelaide breathed in, somewhat shakily, and reached over, taking his hand. She pulled him close to her, kissing him deeply again, as she guided his hand to her body. First she placed it on her neck, and she gasped at its touch, then she pushed it gently down her chest. When they had found her breasts, she gave his hand a squeeze so that he would mimic the movement. He grabbed them carefully, but the very motion caused her to moan against his mouth.

After a short while, she took his hand again and brushed it down her dress. As they skimmed the black lace and burgundy silk, she shuddered suddenly, knowing how close their hands were getting to her sex. The anticipation was almost unbearable, and her privates began to tingle from the excitement. With her free hand, she pulled her skirts slowly up, every single layer pulled up to her thigh until she was almost exposed.

She kept his face close to hers, kissing him every few seconds, but the minute he touched the bare flesh of her thigh, the pair both let out a sound – a gulp and a sigh. Carefully, she caressed his face and smiled then guided his hand to her sex. There was a pause as they crossed the line, changing their relationship for the better. Michael drew a sharp breath inwards as he touched her warmth.

Their eyes met, their souls gazing into one another's, as she began to move his hand on her clitoris: Slowly, unhurriedly, and in circles upon her aching spot. She bit her lips at how sweet it was and how lightheaded his touch had made her already. It made her breath stall in her throat. She sighed alongside the shades and shadows, stoked by the firelight. This tender way he was appreciating her bound through her spirits. With each stroke, his confidence grew, but his eyes never left her face as he watched her start to moan with the motions.

When Adelaide was assured enough that Michael would continue on his own, she removed her hand from his and grabbed his arm as it moved. This was unparalleled. These secret sensations that she had kept to herself were being shared with someone else. They rippled through her, storming her senses with need and desire so fiercely that she wanted, more than anything, for him to bring her to completion. Just so they could share this moment together. He moved somewhat haphazardly but kept his finger still on her spot as directed. She moaned loudly.

"Faster," she whispered, as she began to gyrate upon him.

Michael did as she obliged and watched as she threw her head back, puffing and panting as her body moved. Her sex was soft and wet. She was so tremendously striking as he pleasured her this way. Though his hand began to ache from speeding up as per her instructions, he couldn't help but wish to do this again and again. She deserved someone who could. With every circle of her hips on his hand, his cold contempt for this modern world eased away. Adelaide dug her nails into his arms as he moved and started to cry out louder. Suddenly she tensed and begged him not to stop.

The orgasm showered over her. She tried to keep quiet, frightful that someone somewhere in the whole of London would hear her. Yet it was so good to be pleased by another. She let go of his arm and fell back down to the bed. As she did, Michael slowed his motions down to a stop, admiring her form.

"Yes, Michael Jenkins," she said through breaths and giggles as she spread her arms against the bedding as she laid back. "Yes I will marry you."

Taking his hand back, Michael smiled broadly at Adelaide. There was a circle of red on both cheeks, a peel of sweat on her brow, and she was gradually calming down from her excursion.

She looked most beautiful, his now soon-to-be wife. All at once he wanted to see every inch of her. Every pale inch of skin in its naked excellence. He throbbed for her, now hardened more than he had ever been before in his life. At once, he knew what he wanted to do. In a breathless urgency, he said, "May I take you?"

"Are you positive?"

"Oh God, yes!" Michael said, removing his jacket and discarding it across the room. He picked her up again and furiously kissed her.

"Quick, get me out of this divine dress, which I never truly thanked you for. It is magnificent." Adelaide wriggled out of his grasp. Without waiting for a response, she turned around, signalling for him to unhook the clasps. As he began fiddling with the back, she said, "Quicker."

Sometimes you've imagined how delectable a piece of cake is and, upon finally having a slice, you are satisfied with your lot. You savour that sliver until the next time. Sometimes, a slice is not enough, and the taste sparks a hunger long dormant within you. You are eager for your next bite, ravenous to the core.

The pair wasted no time. They fumbled at each other's clothes until the garments lay strewn on her bedroom floor. Now naked both Adelaide and Michael paused to admire each other's striking nudity. Their hands quickly coveted whatever flesh they could find. They twisted their arms around one another, their mouths anointing their skin in a need too urgent to deny.

Then it was time, Michael climbed between her legs. He hesitated, his nerves trying to push through the yearning he had for her. Adelaide smiled and nodded softly to him, reaching down to guide him to her entrance. Then he thrust into her slowly.

Once inside, he held onto her for a moment, kissing her lips so tenderly that Adelaide almost cried. How glorious this man was. Clumsy, an oaf at times, and yet so sweet and steadfast in his affections for her. She began to rock him slowly, coaxing him into movement.

Both knew that this wasn't going to last long. Michael groaned in her ear as he pounded into her. He wanted to hold on as much as possible but the way she felt inside was so delectable that he was close to releasing himself. He squeezed his eyes closed and tried to tell himself to hold on and keep going, for her. To please her. His Adelaide.

"Let go Michael," Adelaide whispered as soft as a petal upon the water.

Oh God," he mumbled repeatedly before he climaxed. He collapsed on top of her in an exalted heap.

There were a few beats before Michael fell out of her and landed on his back. They both stared at the ceiling, paired with equal heavy breaths. Then quite unexpectedly, they burst into fits of raucous laughter, as bright and brilliant as before, bursting into the atmosphere, as fireworks broke and banged in the distance.

New Year's Eve 1894

It had been five minutes since the crowd had filtered back out into the foyer and bar areas of the Piccadilly Theatre. It was eleven-thirty and the on-stage performances had paused for an interval as the people grabbed whatever drink they could to usher in the new year. There was an undeniable momentous feeling in the air, and everyone could sense it. Half-way through any decade was always exciting but the turn of the century was indeed upon them. How lucky they all were to witness such a turning point in time. Unlike the more hedonistic and suffocating celebrations of years before, this was a quieter and more ticketed event. However, almost everyone in the theatre was profoundly alive – awake with the youthful promise that was laid out in front of them.

Most, that is, but not all. Two men loitered on the middle banister, at the foot of the main stairwell. Both wore gold yet garish masks representing two different animals – a cockerel and a fox. To anyone who passed, it would seem they were in a big debate. The cockerel was flapping his wings wildly, squawking into the ear of the fox who focused on his glass of champagne, and nodded as politely as he could. It seemed like an argument, but on closer inspection, the fox had yet to say anything since they entered the foyer. He just listened politely.

"And then she has the gall to come waltzing into these meetings," the cockerel flailed furiously at the fox, "looking like a dishevelled mad woman, I must add, as she always does, and demanding we all kowtow to her ridiculous suffragette dogma." The man in the golden beaked mask then pitched his voice higher, "'Oh gentlemen, please will you stop being so pig-headed and think about the women in my care.'" The fox took a breath and went to protest this but thought better of it. Instead, he closed his mouth in irritation. The cockerel, not noticing, sighed, lifting his drink to take a sip. "Honestly, John, the audacity of this woman is unparalleled. And we must suffer through it because she's the chairman's daughter!"

There was a distinct pause, before the fox began to laugh. "Michael, if I did not know any better, I would say you were smitten with the girl."

"Who is my husband smitten with?" Adelaide said as she glided into the conversation. Her appearance made both men jump to attention. They stood up straight, both turning red underneath their masks. Adelaide was struggling to hold three glasses in her hand, and she carefully handed one other to each of the men. Neither of the men replied, not knowing how to continue. Adelaide scrutinised their reaction. The parts of her husband's face that were uncovered were a deep shade of burgundy. He was tightly clutching onto the glass she had just handed him. Adelaide had seen that colour and expression on him before. She chuckled. "Oh, I see, we are talking about Miriam Clayton once more."

Michael broke the glass in his hand, spilling the contents down his black suit and sending fragments of glass all over. Adelaide gasped and reached out her hand to help him, but he shook his head dismissively at her. Dropping the remains to the floor, Michael mumbled, "I'll go clean-up," and rushed away from the scene altogether, leaving a bemused Adelaide and John in his wake.

After trotting down a flight of stairs, Michael peered around to make sure that neither his wife nor friend had followed him. When he was adamant he was alone, as alone as one could be in a crowd of thousands, he found a small bit of wall to lean against and breathed out. He thought about the way his agitated fingers got the better of him. He wiggled them fast to dry them from the wine cascading down.

Truthfully, Michael was surprised by his own reaction. By all accounts, he loathed Miriam Clayton. She represented all the ideals that he was staunchly against. Even if his wife had tried to usher him into the new times, there was something about Miriam Clayton that enraged his sensibilities. They came to blows at nearly all of their meetings. He spent many nights talking about his contempt for the woman. He was furious that anyone could think there were ulterior motives to his anger. How could anyone believe, for a single second, that he was smitten with Miriam Bloody Clayton?

Michael grimaced. The idea wasn't far from ludicrous. He'd be foolish not to admit, to himself at least, that he had pondered on the notion. Sometimes he'd be watching Miriam shout in the board meetings, incensed at her impudence, and think about showing her who was boss. In their arguments, Michael would imagine rushing forward and putting his tongue down her throat. Would her vile words then taste sweet? Michael would love to, just once, bend Miriam Clayton over the dark brown table of the boardroom and give her biggest fucking of her life.

All of this only added to his frustration with Miriam.

What's worse, he thought to himself, is that Adelaide knew him so very well. Enough to provoke him about Miriam. He wondered if she knew the extent of his attraction towards the girl and the details of his imagination. Did his new wife look into his eyes and see this sexual fantasy with another woman? The very idea seemed impossible to bear. He loved Adelaide more than anything, and all these thoughts seemed like a great betrayal. They had only been married a year. In fact, exactly a year today. He should still be enthralled entirely with his beautiful wife. Michael sighed loudly and leaned his head gently against the wall in a soft bang.

Miriam Bloody Clayton.

"Excuse me, I believe you are bleeding on my dress."

The vaguely familiar voice made Michael jump somewhat. Instead of looking at the woman, to confirm his suspicions, he looked down at his hand. In the sudden breakage, glass had clearly cut into his flesh. He hadn't noticed, in all the fear and embarrassment. Now he was bleeding directly onto someone else. He followed the trail of red that cascaded from his wound and saw his blood dotting a light, lilac gown.

Michael was thankful that he was wearing his mask as he was practically green from the mishap, standing dumbfounded before the woman. He was even more thankful to be wearing a mask when he followed the skirt of light purple dress upwards and found himself face to face with Miriam Clayton. He closed his eyes and opened them, hoping that it was merely a mirage. But sure enough, there stood the woman he had just been moaning about on the steps of the theatre. The woman who had entered his mind without invitation. The woman who loathed him so. *That* woman was standing next to him.

In one hand, she held a silver wolf-shaped mask on a stick. The other hand was pawing at the dress he had besmirched with his blood. She twisted her lips and waited for an answer from him. Quietly, and in a voice he had never spoken with before, Michael said, "I am sorry."

"No matter. I am more concerned about this wound," she said, breaking out into a smile. Before Michael knew it, she was grabbing his hand. "Here, allow me to take a look, I am a doctor."

Michael thought about making his identity known but he held his tongue. He couldn't pass up such a rare opportunity. Miriam was, for the first time since they had started working with one another, being nice to him. He knew if he were to announce his true identity, she would immediately scowl and verbally abuse him. Instead, he allowed her to take care of him. Without asking, she removed his pocket square from his jacket pocket and began to brush away the blood and flecks of glass from his hand. She tended to his wound like it was second nature.

"Ah, luckily it is just superficial. I fear you are going to have to keep this hand after all, no matter how hard you may try to lose it."

She winked at him which caused a slight swoop in his stomach. Then, Miriam reached down into her cleavage and pulled out her own purple paisley handkerchief. Bemused at this unbecoming parlour trick, Michael used this time to inspect her. The way her plump body curved, the deep blue of her eyes, and the scent of lemons began to cloud his judgement. He tried to swallow all the dark and sordid thoughts that were rushing within him. As Miriam Clayton wrapped her handkerchief around his hand tightly, she gave him a slight squeeze. "There. You best be careful around glasses. Tricky creatures."

There was a jovial glint in her eyes which Michael had never seen before. The very presence of it caused a small commotion within him. He tried to splutter out a thank you, but it came out as a honking, gasping sound. Panicked, he ran away from Miriam, hoping that he could dispel the image of her still burning in the back of his mind.

"You are welcome, I suppose," Miriam called out after him.

Adelaide and John stood silently together, awaiting Michael's return. Unlike the clumsy man they knew, both were happy in that manner. They were sufficiently content in their own thoughts to feel the need to make idle conversation. Occasionally, they would smile politely at one another then go back to surveying the crowd of people. It was no big shame to either of them – the pair had yet to establish their relationship. John Bennett was a relatively new friend of Michael's, having joined the latter's cricket team in August. She had seen him at matches, and he had been to dinner at the Jenkins' only once by himself. Even then Michael had done most of the talking.

After a short while without Michael, John was the one who stirred the silence, "If I have yet to say, you look very beautiful, Adelaide."

"Why thank you John," she said, instinctively grabbing her skirt and swaying from side to side in glee. She too was wearing a mask – an owl – and had an extravagant gold feathered dress to match. Within her bright blonde hair, regimented into ringlets again, sat the most precious gold-coloured feathers. Both men had delivered their compliments to her, and in their sights, she was divine. She beamed underneath the mask - a goddess amongst men.

There was a small, stilted sigh as John took off his mask to readjust it. At that moment, Adelaide was struck by how handsome he was. How strange, she thought to herself, to have not noticed this before. Then again it was hard to discern John's attractiveness when he was playing a sport, or when she was trying to quell her husband's stream of words over dinner.

As this evening drew closer to midnight, Adelaide could see how desperately gorgeous Doctor John Bennett was. The way the new electric lights caught his light blue eyes, the perfect way his dark brown hair waved, and the plumpness of his lips where a neat handlebar moustache sat - all of these things started a slight chaos within her. It caused her cheeks to burn.

What are you doing? she chastised herself. She tried to think of, instead, her new husband; how they were only married a year and how happy she was with him. However, in this quiet moment, her thoughts turned to how greatly paired she would be with John. She wondered if beneath his pleasant and peaceful persona, he had a passionate power like she did. What greatness could his surgeon's hands do if given half a chance?

"Forgive me if I upset you Adelaide," John said, snapping her out of her musings, and misconstruing her daydreaming. There was a twinge of disappointment as he slipped the mask back on his face. John continued, "It was all in good jest. Michael does love you very much."

"Oh, do not fret John, I know how easy it is to wind up my husband," she said with a laugh that was a little bit too loud. She took a large slip of wine to drown whatever sordid thoughts were springing to her mind. "And I, too, love him dearly." It was a very true statement, but she still nervously finished the remnants of her glass, hoping it was also the last remnants of her fantasies with John. "Between you and me, it is awfully fun to see how Miss Clayton riles him up. Riles them *all* up. I believe she is somewhat marvellous."

"Have you met her?"

Adelaide shook her head fiercely, causing one of the feathers to fall delicately to the floor. "I've seen her at hospital functions, but I believe Michael keeps me purposely away from her." She gave a small fluttering wink at John. He flashed an arresting smile at her. She tried not to dither too much.

She was grateful when Michael appeared carrying a new set of drinks for the trio. Taking the glass from him, she noted the new purple paisley bandage that had appeared, wrapped neatly around his palm.

"Oh!" Michael chose not to say anything about his collision with Miriam. "A steward aided. Seems I also cut myself."

"Silly," she said softly and kissed him on the cheek tenderly. Adelaide slithered her arm into Michael's and pressed her body close to his, allowing the warmth of him to wrap around her spirit. She looked up at him. A set of hazel eyes met a set of green. Soul gazed into soul. The very action caused them both to sigh contentedly. It dispelled any thoughts of anyone else. They were happy together – newly-wed and ready for their marriage to truly begin with the new year. What a fine time to be alive, they thought, unknowingly, together. They gave each other a gentle squeeze, caring not that John stood awkwardly beside them.

"Happy New Year," screamed the crowd suddenly. They had all but forgotten about why they were in the theatre.

The trio of animals lifted their glasses up in toast to one another. The married pair went to take a sip in celebration. John paused and, lifting his glass again, said loudly with a beaming smile, "And I suppose Happy New Year to Miriam Clayton! Whomever and wherever she may be!"

Both Adelaide and Michael choked on their wine.

New Year's Eve 1895

Adelaide had awoken in a miserable mood.

The minute Michael opened the curtains, and the winter's sun hit her face, Adelaide grimaced. She hid herself underneath the blanket and groaned softly. Though the minute she squeezed her eyes shut, she wasn't entirely sure if she wanted to go to sleep again. The night had left her disjointed – a series of images that tickled the crevices of her grief, pouring out her sadness from wounds she believed were long healed. She opened her eyes, and it was as though she were drowning. The water of her past filled her lungs and made her chest heavy.

"Adelaide?" Michael whispered gently as she curled up underneath the sheets. "Adelaide, are you quite alright?" She drew a sharp intake of breath, as though she were trying to disappear from view. If she stayed deathly still, it was almost as though she wasn't there. There was a brief pause before the sheet lifted up and Michael's face was staring right at her. The way he looked, concerned, and caring, nearly made her dissolve into tears. She blinked to stop them coming, but a solitary tear escaped and dragged down her face. Michael sighed. "Unwell again?" She nodded gently. "Do you wish for me to stay at home?" She shook her head. "Very well. I shall be back as soon as possible. Call for me if need be." Another nod.

Adelaide listened to her husband get bathed and dressed for work before he left her alone. Once the front door closed, she removed the blanket from herself and lay there in the maudlin morning. She waited to cry, the tears that had moved within her since she woke up, yet they failed to come. The sorrow remained curled up on her chest like an unwelcome cat. She allowed it to purr for an hour, caught between the wish to sleep again and the need to be proactive and shoo away this burden.

What was most annoying about this bout of sadness was that it wasn't new to her. In fact, she had carried around this weight for so long that she had grown accustomed to it. Adelaide had built up so much strength to pick it up as though it was nothing and carry on with her day. However, every so often, it would change its shape and she became unable to lift it as usual. Today was unequivocally sad and intangible. A day where she thought of nothing but her son – James.

He'd be seven by now, nearly eight. The image of who he would be by now filtered through her senses. A little gentleman who was developing his own personality and sense of being. She couldn't help picturing him walking into the morning with his latest drawing, jumping on the bed between her and Michael, and listening to him chatter about his day, his wishes, and all the funny things that children say. They'd laugh and plan picnics in the park, and trips to the zoo, and spend time reading books.

Except, as Adelaide pondered on this, she realised that this wouldn't be the case at all. If James were still alive, it would stand to reason that Graham would be too. Adelaide would be trapped in that loveless marriage. Her thoughts turned sour, and she agonised over the possibility that James would've grown up just as cold and bitter as his father. At the right time, her son would be turned against her, following in her family's tradition of being silent, still, money making machines. She'd grow old, abandoned in this societal jail, having never known love and passion.

If James was still alive, Adelaide would have never met Michael.

The notion struck her heart like ice. She threw her hands up onto her face and waited to cry again. Yet still she could not shed a tear. She screamed into her fingers out of frustration.

Some say the worst type of sadness is the one you don't see coming. The day that's fractured for no discernible reason. You are just broken as you try to piece yourself together. That kind of sadness you can try to chase away with tasks and activities until it is displaced from your mind.

Adelaide always thought that was wrong – the worst type of sadness is the one that you can trace back. You can follow the threads and find the ball of yarn from which it came. It's worse because you know why and yet you cannot stop yourself being so desperately despondent. Adelaide knew exactly why the memory of James came to her that very day, and she couldn't do a single thing about it.

Sighing, and flopping her hands to the bed. "Enough," she whispered to herself, before unwillingly climbing out of bed. "Enough of this."

When Michael walked through the front door, he nearly dropped the bouquet of fresh yellow tulips on the floor. There was something strange afoot in his quiet townhouse near Regent's Park. This was a day without housekeepers, as Adelaide has started to give them the holidays off, and yet his house was practically sparkling clean. He peered around the hallway; everything had been wiped and dusted. Even the picture frames on the tallest part of the walls looked brand new. The whole house glowed in the candlelight with picturesque perfection.

There was the smell of baking, and he could hear Adelaide humming and clattering in the kitchen. Placing his bag on the floor, he followed the sound through to the dining room. The scene before him bewildered him further. The table had been set up for two people, as usual, but it was as though they were hosting a lavish dinner party. Upon their finest tablecloth sat their most expensive china, gleaming alongside the household.

Michael stood dumbfounded until Adelaide came out of the kitchen, carrying a silver bowl of fresh vegetables. She saw him and yelped loudly, "Michael! My goodness you scared me." She placed the bowl down on the table as she regained her breath. Then she rushed forward and threw her arms around her husband and pulled him into a warm embrace and a deep kiss.

"I believed that you were unwell Adelaide," Michael said as he held her with his one free hand. He brought her closer to him and held onto her to give her some comfort. He then chuckled, "I'd rather resigned myself to a bread-and-butter supper."

"Well, if you wish to have that instead of the pie I've been baking all evening, then be my guest." Adelaide gave him a cheeky wink, and another meaningful kiss. She wriggled out of his embrace, talking faster than she had ever spoken before. "But I would prefer it if you joined me for dinner tonight. I have been working all day, did you notice? The house is positively new. Well,

I thought it ought to look nice for tonight. It is, after all, a night of celebration. Are those flowers for me?"

"Oh, of course," he said, handing the bouquet over to her, wondering what had sparked such energy in his wife who was ghost-like this morning. He smiled weakly. "Happy anniversary, darling."

The words fell into the atmosphere clunkily, landing on Adelaide with a heft. She breathed in shakily, smiling in an attempt to stop the frightfulness rising in her. She took the flowers and examined them closely. She grabbed each petal between her fingers as though she were about to pull them off. Quietly, she said, "They are lovely."

"Are you sure you are quite alright Adelaide?" Michael said, noting how her face suddenly turned into the night. The shades of light danced within the distance that stretched out in her eyes. The red from her face had faded. Michael tried to discern what was making her act so oddly, drifting between emotions so easily. One such theory popped into his mind again and suddenly he blushed, as though he was stealing the colour from his wife. He tried desperately to dismiss the memory.

Not noticing Michael's worried eyes, Adelaide shook her head furiously before busying herself with the dinner again. "Yes, quite alright. Now let us eat. The Piccadilly Theatre awaits."

The Piccadilly Theatre opted for an even quieter affair this year, and, instead of a party for New Year's Eve, they were putting on a play. It had rather excited Michael. Even though he had attended celebrations there since 1890, he had always found them far too unbecoming. He found it amusing that the theatre was becoming more muted, slipping into a more refined nature. It went against the tide of an ever-changing decade and Michael deemed it more respectable. He smiled with unparalleled content the minute the pair glided into the room. There was no room for accidents tonight, he could keep hold of his wife and keep her safe from the crowd.

Adelaide was also thankful for the change in pace. She had busied herself for the whole day but now out of the house, she was possessed by herself again. She clung onto Michael's arm tightly, as though she were afraid if he were to let go of her, she would tumble away from this existence and drown in her grief forever. It seemed he noticed, because he clutched onto her hand as well as he took them to their seats in the stalls. Every so often, he'd give her a gentle squeeze.

As they settled down, Adelaide happily unlocked herself from his grasp. Michael nodded and then flicked through the programme handed to them upon entrance. For the first time for that whole day, Adelaide breathed out, expelling a little bit of grief. In a few short moments, the show would start and offer yet another distraction. Another distraction meant that the night was drawing to a close, and Adelaide could awake a new day, and a new year, anew.

She looked around the theatre admiring its beauty in a way she had never done before, noting the gilded edging and painted ceiling. She counted the amount of crystals on the chandelier before she turned her sights to the crowd. Her gaze peered into the faces before them. The night had certainly attracted a more traditional theatre crowd. The old and weathered faces of the elite all stared blankly ahead of themselves. Some were craning their necks, examining the people in the room whilst trying to discern any gossip. Their eyes picked at the bodies before them, hoping to gain some sustenance for their daily chit-chats. Adelaide grimaced at the sight, knowing how easy it was to fall into this behaviour.

In the boxes sat, usually, the wealthiest of these vultures. Except, in one of them, Adelaide found a familiar face fixated on the empty stage before them. "My goodness, look Michael, it's Miriam!" Adelaide elbowed Michael before pointing wildly at Box Three.

Michael jumped and followed her finger. Sure enough, there was Miriam Bennett, sat in the regal box, as still as a portrait, and just as pretty. Suddenly, he took a sharp intake of breath, his face burning red, as he mumbled, "Indeed." He then buried his head back into his programme, slinking down in his chair.

"Odd, is it not? I had never guessed Miriam to be the Box type of person." Adelaide had seemingly not noticed the change in demeanour of her husband. Instead, she furrowed her brow. "And there seems to be no sign of John."

"He was in surgery most of today. Perhaps he has been held up," Michael said with a wave of his hand. He did not turn back to where Miriam was sitting.

"Perhaps. Do you suppose there is time to say hello?" Adelaide asked though she had already started to rise from her chair.

Michael looked at his pocket watch. "Yes I believe so." He then hesitated. "If you'll permit me, I'd rather stay here."

Once again, Adelaide did not notice that her husband's face was glowing red as she was already walking down the aisle. The minute she had seen Miriam, Adelaide had become awash with urgency. She was certain that speaking to her closest friend would help dissipate the feelings that clung deep to her. There were things she wished to discuss that she couldn't bring herself to tell her husband.

As she left the auditorium doors, Adelaide noted it was strange. After all, she had known Miriam for merely a handful of months whilst she had known Michael for five years. But the moment Adelaide had been finally introduced to Miriam at the engagement dinner, Adelaide knew that they were going to be close. Miriam had an uncanny ability to envelop you in her world immediately – with the same love and devotion she would give her family. *Just look at John,* Adelaide thought to herself as she climbed the stairs, *and how quickly he fell.* Miriam had accepted him into her life immediately and whole-heartedly. They were a divine pairing. Miriam was a whirlwind of a woman, and Adelaide was similarly thrown into the fray.

When she reached the door of Miriam's box, Adelaide hesitated. Perhaps this wasn't the time. Perhaps this wasn't the place. Perhaps she should tell Michael first. But before she had time to turn around, she was already knocking on the door. There was a long silence. Adelaide knocked again. And then again. There was a small sound of a scuffle before Miriam called for Adelaide to come in.

Nervously, Adelaide pushed the door open and was greeted with the warmth of her friend. "Oh Adelaide, hello!" Miriam sat on the stiff, gold, and red chair. She did not rise but turned her head around and offered, instead, a beaming smile. There was a brief pause as Adelaide looked confused – usually Miriam would wrap her in a welcoming embrace. Miriam noted the funny circumstance. "Oh, forgive me if I remain seated. It's… erm… this silly corset and huge skirt. It is rather tight, and it took me forever to get comfortably sat down."

There was no reason to question this: Miriam was wearing an extravagant orange dress, with the largest sleeves, and gold trimming along the hems. The crinoline was large enough to house two people and Miriam was cinched so tightly that her breasts were gorgeously accentuated. Adelaide wondered how Miriam made it out of the house without fainting. Nodding, Adelaide took a step forward, stumbling over her words. They came out meekly. "Well, I'm ever so glad I saw you, Miriam. I needed to talk to you. I—"

Unexpectedly, Miriam interrupted Adelaide with a soft moan and a giggle, as she gently shushed someone. Though she tried to be quiet, Adelaide sure enough heard Miriam whisper John's name sternly. There was another scuffling sound before a foot appeared from underneath Miriam's large skirt. Adelaide took a step back. At first, she thought Miriam had somehow twisted her ankle as the foot was at a strange, impossible angle for how Miriam was seated.

After a beat, Adelaide noted that the shoe was a man's black brogue. As soon as the realisation settled in, it disappeared from view. Adelaide was both incredulous and impressed. One half of her mouth cocked into a knowing smile though she wanted to cry at the same time. Miriam's eyes were wide with surprise and mischief.

"I best leave you to it. I shall call on you tomorrow Miriam," Adelaide said quickly and left before Miriam could respond. She could hear her friend calling one last time but as Adelaide closed the door, there was a succession of giggles coming from the newlyweds.

The further she moved away from the scene; the more the agony twisted in Adelaide's stomach. The mortification curled up on her cheeks, as vivid and vibrant as her husband's usually did. She grew sicker with each step she took. When she returned to Michael, she asked if they could leave immediately.

Adelaide was propped in bed again, as though the day had not happened. Michael watched her stare at the end of the bed as he removed his clothes and pulled his pyjamas on. It had yet to turn midnight but there was no reason to celebrate in this household. Adelaide had returned to their seats in a strange panic. There were beads of sweat on her forehead and her face was flushed. The manner in which she had arrived caused Michael to leap out of his seat and whisk her away from the theatre immediately. He had asked no questions.

Now at home, Adelaide had grown into the silence again that had struck her this morning. He would like to say that it was sudden, but Adelaide had grown quieter in the past couple of days. At first, it did not seem unusual. Adelaide was quite content with saying little to no words at all for hours at a time. Sometimes she could go a whole day without saying anything, as Michael spoke wildly for the both of them.

Yesterday, Adelaide was not just quiet, she was also sick. She was pale, clammy, and nauseous. It was perfectly acceptable for one to be sick, but as Adelaide withdrew from him into a sleep filled day Michael's mind started concocting wild theories. The succession of possibilities seemed more ludicrous than the last and it was easy to dismiss them as quickly as they arrived.

All except one. He fixated on it for the whole day. When they awoke this very morning, and Adelaide was sick again, the notion sprung to his mind with a ferocious intent. He spent his entire workday stupidly mixing up medications because he was elsewhere. Adelaide's strange behaviour at dinner did not help. Nor did her sudden pleading at the theatre. After all, the last time Adelaide had acted so bizarrely was Christmas day. Michael buttoned up his nightshirt right to the top, and it immediately constricted around his throat. Still, he did not take his wary eyes from his wife. He shuffled awkwardly by their wardrobe before he mumbled, "Are you quite alright Adelaide?"

"Yes, quite alright…" She did not turn to her husband. "… Quite alright."

"It is just that you seem rather spooked after your conversation with Miriam." He wiggled his fingers. "I hope she did not say anything untoward."

"What?" Adelaide turned her head quickly towards Michael. Then she started to laugh. "Oh heavens no. Nothing of the sort. I…" She lifted her fingers to her lips as though she needed them to help her speak the words. "Well, if you must know, I caught Miriam and John in a rather salacious position."

"Oh." Michael stopped wiggling his fingers. He was paled by the admission. For there it was again. The memory that had started to embarrass Michael. The notion that had followed him around all evening. The suggestion that had teased his fears out. Christmas Day. It had stalked him for a week, and he was unable to escape the images of the tryst.

The proposition was initially met with a lot of scorn from Michael. It took Adelaide the whole of the day to convince him to join in. It helped that she slipped him a drink, a kind word, and a loving hand to prime him for such activities. Tipsy and aroused enough, Michael gave his consent and suddenly, found himself in the bedroom of his best friend, and by his accounts, the women he loathed most in the world. Naked. As they all enjoyed and shared one another.

He would be foolish to say that the act the four of them committed wasn't exciting as it was happening. The whole affair blurred by in a moment of booze and laughter. He was carried away in the whirlwind that was John and Miriam. Yet when Adelaide and Michael awoke the next day, they were pained by the alcohol, and panged by the memory of it. They moved around their home timidly, struggling to readjust back to their ordinary married life. Before Miriam and John had entered their lives.

The image of them all nude and undone burned in the back of his mind. He was afraid it would forever.

Michael closed his eyes as Adelaide watched him, and he shook his head. He was terrified to ask her what his mind was suggesting. But he had to say the niggling notion that had been plaguing him for days. "Adelaide, are you quite satisfied?"

"I am most satisfied."

The lack of hesitation pleased him, yet he pressed further, taking a step towards the bed in which she lay. "You would tell me if you weren't? If I was not fulfilling your needs as a husband."

Adelaide blinked before she laughed loudly. Except she did not really mean to, and when his face fell into a grimace, she abruptly stopped. "Michael, why do you ask?"

Michael sighed and sat down on the edge of the bed. Turning away from her, he could finally say his deepest concern, but he was at a loss for words. A rare occurrence. "That whole business on Christmas Day…. with Miriam and John… I…" He breathed out.

"Oh that! As fun as that evening was, I have no desire for it to happen again." It was the truth. Adelaide had nearly forgotten about Christmas Day. Despite the nervousness the next day, it soon frittered away as other worries nestled into her bones. Sometimes, when one has a taste of something, one is ravenous for more and more and more. Sometimes, a simple taste is all it takes. Adelaide had promised herself passion, Miriam had teased out her darkest fantasies, and it had reached a rather brilliant conclusion. For Adelaide, it was easy to place it back in the box, content at the completion. It hadn't crossed her mind that it had had a different effect on her husband. Now she started to worry the same as he did. "Michael." She reached forward and placed her hand on his back, stroking it out of comfort. "Are you yourself satisfied?"

Michael spun around. "Unequivocally, yes." He grabbed her hand, shuffling upwards towards her. "Adelaide, I could die happily tomorrow knowing that I have lived a fulfilled life with your love."

"And I you." She smiled, taking him into her arms as he laid upon her chest. With his weight upon her, as she kissed his forehead, her chest lightened as though he had untethered the sadness from her, and they were floating away. How foolish, she thought, to deny herself this man who had a magical way of making her feel most like herself.

"That being said," he muttered, against her, his words skimming her skin like a soothing balm. "I'd rather like to grow old with you and have lots of children."

That was all Adelaide needed to hear. She inhaled. "That is most excellent news, Michael, for Dr Jones told me yesterday that I am with child."

Michael sprung upwards from her grasp, staring at her with wide eyes as a smile danced upon his lips. He was practically trembling as he said, "You jest?" When she shook her head profusely, Michael let out an unexpected squeal and clapped his hands, causing Adelaide to giggle at him, though a few unexpected tears came tumbling down her cheek. Michael kissed her. "This is truly wonderful!"

"Do you truly mean it Michael Jenkins?" she replied. He nodded wildly. She watched the glee dance splendiferously in her husband's eyes and tried to match his enthusiasm. Yet something else gripped her spirit and she found herself awash with grief again. She tried to shakily control herself, frightful that bursting into tears would ruin such a special moment.

Michael had spotted this, however, and stopped smiling as a tentative realisation spread across his mind. He took her hand, and he couldn't help the words tumbling out of his mouth, "Adelaide, as marvellous as this news is, please know that this child could never replace James. Nor will he be forgotten."

"Oh," she said softly. Then the tears she had been holding back came. The rush of unexpected emotions caused her to dissolve into unrelentless sobs. She brought her hands to her face to try and hide them, crying out into her hand. There was no stopping the dam that had burst in her very spirit.

Michael looked dumbfounded. "My goodness, I am sorry."

"Oh Michael, whatever for?" Adelaide said before throwing her arms around him and pulling him close again. Michael Jenkins was a man prone to accidents. In both action and speech. Yet with Adelaide, in such special moments, he could say the absolute right thing to make her feel loved. Those were absolutely the correct words she needed to hear. In that moment, his green eyes met her hazel ones as their souls and hearts beat in time. In that moment, he had read her mind and soul, perfectly surmised her thoughts and feelings. In that moment, it was the most warmth she had ever felt in her entire life.

They lay there in each other's arms, thinking of the blisses that had been bestowed on them. Joys that had begun with an unusual collision – the first of many for the pair. As they melted into these memories and mused on the months that lay ahead, their hearts beat as one with excitement and affection. Though Adelaide was keen to enjoy the silence, Michael soon started fervently, whispering fast his expectations for the child. She did not mind, meeting his words with nods and smiles. As foolish as some of his words were, it only added to her own exhilarated anticipation. 1896 had yet to begin and yet it held such promise.

Suddenly, the clocks chimed wildly, and the sounds of the fireworks broke their heat as the sky was illuminated. Michael lifted his head from her chest and kissed her. "Happy New Year, Adelaide Jenkins."

"And to you, Michael Jenkins," she replied with a beaming smile, "Happy New Year."

Valentine's Day

Friday 14th February 1896

Miriam Bennett had never been one for Valentine's Day. It wasn't through her own volition; she had just never had a regular suitor to indulge in the whims of a holiday she deemed silly at best. She'd scoff at the lace-trimmed cards or roll her eyes at couples who would make an enormous fuss over one another just because society said they should. Coolly, she would moan that the idea of lavishing attention on one's lover just for one day was ridiculous at best, before swiftly reminding people that St Valentine was murdered. Brutally.

Of course, that's not to say that Miriam did not make use of some of the day's traditions. In fact, she had a particular proclivity for sending vinegar valentines. She would spend a large chunk of her spare time doodling caricatures and making jokes at the expense of the board members.

For the entire year beforehand, she would collate the greatest insults she could muster and pour them into these cards. Though they were sent anonymously, the men would all know it was Miriam who delivered the abuses their way. Their faces at the next board meeting would be beetroot red, huffing and puffing but without recriminations. Miriam would be brimming with delight – at least there was something of the dreaded day that could fill her with glee.

Alas, whilst some traditions endure, some often have to break.

This year, Miriam had no time at all to plan vinegar valentines at all. The men on the board were safe, at last, without vulgar pictures of themselves and they were bemused when their cards did not arrive that morning. After all, anyone could see that Miriam's thoughts and attentions were centred on one man. And she was planning greater games to play with him.

It was all she could think about whilst working on the wards. The way his touch slid down her skin, the way his lips caressed her body, and the way he felt inside of her. She agonised over the memories of their trysts and tonight's plans for more filth. The thought of him gliding over her flesh so deftly and dangerously made her insides roar for him. At a few points in the day, she excused herself to her office in the basement, and pleasured herself fast and ferociously with her own fingers, releasing the agonising tension that had built up within her. She'd then glance at the clock, hoping it was time to leave for this evening's activities. Each passing second added another wave of excitement to her, building up that tension once more…

A few levels up from her ward, John was similarly fantasising over the same possibilities that the night could unfurl. Though he had no idea what Miriam was concocting, he knew that her surprises were sensational. He resigned himself to paperwork in his office because the titillation and teasing of merely the idea of the evening caused him to harden at inopportune moments. There wasn't much that the words on the page could do anyway. By the time the afternoon rolled forward, he realised that he had, in fact, just drawn crude visions of his wife. He sighed and wondered whether there were parts of her body that he hadn't touched yet. The thought sent goosebumps down his spine. There was nothing but glorious chaos in his mind.

John had spent so long willing the clock to turn quickly that when the desired time finally rolled around, he was hesitant to move. Suddenly a cavern opened up in his gullet and his heart tumbled within. Rarely does life match your expectations, especially when they soar so high. With Miriam, most of his aching and furtive yearnings had been met. For a split second, John wondered when they were bound for a fall, like Icarus did when he flew too close to the sun. He admonished himself quickly though. After all, would he deny himself pleasure for fear of his wings burning? Even if they were, wasn't the pain beautiful enough to endure?

The soft sound of paper gliding across the wood slid into his mind and interrupted his musings. He smiled. Without glancing, he knew that the game had begun. Closing his journal defiantly, he stood up to see a note on the floor. He paced himself and walked slowly over to the folded piece of paper, taking his time to pick it up and read it. He did this to keep his composure and to not show too much glee at the very thought of her and her fiendish schemes just in case her beady eyes were watching him somehow. The note gave few clues to her plots. It simply read:

Dearest J,

Come home quickly...
    A surprise awaits...

        One rule, however,
            no touching

unless explicitly instructed otherwise.

        Love, M.

After reading the note, John wasted little time in his office. He bounded out of the hospital as quickly as possible.

The door glowed orange as though a fiery hound of hell lay behind it. As John rushed up the steps of his home, he stopped at the top of the steps and tried to peer through the frosted glass to see if he could glimpse her. There was a giddiness sparking electricity throughout him. He was afraid that if he touched the ornate metallic doorknob that he'd illuminate the whole house and then it would explode into flames. He waited for a little bit longer to temper the exhilarating nerves throughout him, knowing that his shadow would be looming in the doorway, and send shivers throughout Miriam's body. John relished what little control he could have over the situation.

With a glass of red wine in her hand, Miriam lounged at the fireplace. As she warmed by the flames, she tried to steady her breathing – having rushed all the way home, cleaned up, and gotten dressed so lavishly before her husband could arrive. She wanted to come across cool and collected.

From this angle in the living room, she could see his figure hovering through the windows of the front door and Miriam chuckled. *Foolish man*, she thought to herself. John often relinquished himself to her bidding, but at times would try and tease her back. Whether it is with choice words during sex or lingering just outside of the door, John tried to rile her sexually – especially as he knew that her teasing and dominating ways would arouse her as much as it did him. This time, however, Miriam knew that whatever tricks he was trying to play would be useless the moment he saw her in the dress.

The click of the door caused her heart to race.

Tonight was about to begin.

John adored crossing this threshold every time Miriam had an exciting experience for them to both enjoy. As he stepped into his own home, he would marvel at how he blossomed repeatedly in their marriage with fresh and, at times, frightening feelings. A wild beat thundered in his chest as he stepped into the hallway. From the corner of his eye, he saw her figure standing at the fireplace of the living room. He took a deep breath as he turned to see her.

The dress she was wearing was extravagant and unusually unique for Miriam who had a penchant for colours. Her wardrobe was always a vivid array of oranges, pinks, and blues, which was also the case for her corsets and underwear. This dress was different and so richly decadent. It was a silk and lace, black garment with deep red trimmings on the skirt and big puffy sleeves, which sat off her shoulder. She was cinched tightly, and her large breasts were barely contained in the bodice. As Miriam sipped at her wine, with silky black gloves trailing all the way up to her elbow, she knew that John was staring at her cleavage and smiled with the utmost happiness.

With the glow of the flames illuminating her figure, Miriam looked otherworldly. It reminded him of the first time they had made love but in a different way. She had evolved; she stood stronger and more determined in the wake of their marriage. John felt that way too, constantly shaping into the person he was born to be. They were forged in the same fire and were spending their lives trying to reunite – over and over again. There was an urge to forgo whatever Miriam had planned. John wished to ravage her right there. He stayed deathly still, however.

"Remember, John, no touching. Not until I instruct otherwise," Miriam said, reading his mind once more. The way John looked at her made Miriam want to leave her body. Never has a person gazed at her with such love and adoration. She quietly reminded herself to show him the same attention, in her own ways, of course.

"Oh Miriam, what torture!" he said in a soft, breathless way.

A flash of gleeful darkness streaked across her face. "Yes. Exquisite, isn't it?" Miriam smiled. She nodded to the banister. "Your outfit for this evening is upstairs."

He wasted no time in getting changed, fearful of taking his eyes off of her for too long. As he rushed upstairs, there was an excruciating need to see her again, standing with all the flames of lust draped across her skin. He bounced like a child eager to play with his new toy.

Upstairs she had picked out an evening suit that matched her dress, the shirt and pocket square was silky red, whilst his waistcoat, tie, jacket, and trousers were black. There was a matching laced mask that covered the upper part of his face – to keep himself anonymous in whatever activity they were pursuing tonight. He held onto it as he made his way downstairs, eager to see her drenched in black and red again. Walking slowly down the staircase, he found her waiting for him at the bottom. The look on her face was ravenous as she drank in every inch of him. The scene reminded him of the ball at Lady Gray's only this time he was the debutante, ready to dance with his devil.

"Quick, put the mask on," she said, tying a matching mask around her face. "The Piccadilly Club awaits."

He froze as he was putting the mask on, unable to conceal his disappointment. As enjoyable as The Piccadilly Club was, it had become requisite for their depraved ways. The private members' club sat storeys up from a theatre, hilariously mere metres away from the hospital. The entrance was shrouded in secret shadows behind the building. There were little to no rules. The ones they had were strictly enforced: no touching without permission; no speaking of the club in civilised conversations; and absolutely no revelations of your identity. All nights were a masquerade. It made people conduct their wickedness with ease.

Only high-end clientele were permitted to use it. John and Miriam did not consider themselves particularly wealthy people as they had little need for fancy things. They spent their money, however, on their indulgent hobbies – outfits, toys, and now this club which they had frequented for a few weeks now. The way Miriam was speaking on this night John had expected something new for their evening of activities. So, when she said, "The Piccadilly Club," John couldn't help but let out a dissatisfied, "Oh."

Miriam blinked at him then burst out into raucous laughter "John, fear not, all is not as it appears."

In the carriage ride over, Miriam sat opposite him, fearful that she might neglect her own rule and touch him all over. Her hands often found their way into his trousers whenever they were journeying together. Even in the early morning ride to work, getting him hot and heavy before departing for a day from one another. Tonight, Miriam could only tease by keeping herself silent and still. She peered out of the window and watched the London sights roll by, anxious that her plan was unfolding. She tenderly dragged her hands across her chest to calm down the excitement and the feat that was burgeoning within.

John watched her paw at her neckline, knowing that she was grappling with the same heated agitation that he was, whilst also dangling herself in front of him. Dastardly thoughts emerged in his mind. He wished for nothing more than to bury himself in her chest, and he bit his lip to stop himself.

Often John would find himself milling with the men of the hospital at societal functions. In cigar rooms after dinner, they would bemoan all sorts – and often that source of grumbling was about their wives. John said nothing, letting his reputation for being quiet take over. Even if they asked questions about Miriam, John would politely nod or shake his head.

Truthfully, every time the topic of conversation fell onto the sanctity and imprisonment of marriage, John would be enraged. Of course, he knew some marriages were made for social preservation, himself having been betrothed to a marriage almost entirely passionless. Yet he couldn't fathom how anyone could live with someone they actively hated. What was worse, John loathed how these men of his station would encourage him to blather on about how rotten being married to Miriam was. He was quite happy, thank you, and would say as much. His answer was often met with the usual ribbing and laughter. But the world was full of these leering men wishing to dominate women. *Did they not know how rousing the other way could be?*

As Piccadilly came into view, John was gripped with an unexpected nervousness. The Piccadilly Club seemed busier than usual, and they had to wait in their carriage for some time before being ushered into the building. The longer it took for their cab to arrive at the doorway, the more unrest spread through him. It didn't help that as they entered the club and Miriam led them up the staircases, they were met with a sea of over-excited bodies.

"May I take your hand?" he said unexpectedly, as he followed her through the crowd. It was infantile to ask but John was afraid of losing her in the hubbub. There was a dull roar of chatter as they walked up the stairs, and the sea of unfamiliar masked faces made him nervous. He had been here a handful of times, on his own and with his wife, yet every time he ascended that staircase, he'd be instantly weak-willed. It was though he was fearful that he was about to be exposed to a tide of disapproval and discernment. He didn't want to break the rules, but he also didn't want to be left adrift here. He wanted to be grounded to someone familiar and to know he wasn't alone.

"Did I not instruct…" Miriam began sternly, turning to him with eyes filled with sex and sin. However, when she caught his worried gaze, she softened and smiled. "Yes, John, you may. But touch nothing else."

He nodded as she slid her hand into his, grateful for the anchor. Allowing her to guide him up the stairs, John became more confident with each stride. As long as Miriam led, he'd happily explore whatever carnality she had in store.

The façade of the Piccadilly Club was a theatre and music hall, where most of society could watch entertainment for a few pounds. Way above the rafters lay its sordid secret – a haven for the deliciously debauched. The club itself was a set of four huge rooms for performances. Each had its own colour that denoted what was on show there: Blue was meant for stripteases and cabaret dancers; red was for ropes and whips, black was for penetrative toys, and pink was for queer performers. Miriam and John knew each colour well. There were hidden places, too, where couples could fuck – privately or with other people. This club of theirs was a den of the depraved that Miriam and John adored.

John let go of her hand as they reached the Red Room entrance - safe in the sanctity of this refuge - the pair's favourite room. He was much more confident now, especially as anonymous waiters along the way presented them champagne. The pair would take whenever they were offered, both needing the courage of fine alcohol. Merry, John held the door politely for her. Miriam laughed and said, "John, we are not going in there."

He cocked his head out of confusion. "Really?"

"Well, we are, but not that side," Miriam said lustfully, tapping her side as one would do in command of a dog. "Come now, follow me."

Dutifully, if albeit, perplexed, John followed her through a seemingly secret corridor that was hidden behind a red curtain. John had never noticed the winding, undecorated, wooden, passageway. Miriam navigated the curves with ease, like a snake leading a mouse to its utmost ruin. Every so often she would look back and smile at him, lapping up his bewilderment. *What game are you playing, Miriam?* John thought to himself. He decided to study the bare flesh between her shoulders and wished to decorate her back with caresses.

Miriam took them through a small door and led them to a room. It was similar to the red room – the walls were covered in swirls and patterns of the colour. The floorboards were dark brown wood. There was a familiar red velvet curtain, except it was closer to them, curving around them in a semicircle. She stopped still in the centre as John sheepishly entered the room. Watching the way John was figuring out their surroundings elated her. She kept herself very still so as to not give the game away too soon, though she was acutely aware that there was a time limit here. The night could wait for no man, and neither could Miriam. She flashed a mischievous grin. "Have you not figured where you are?"

"I haven't the slightest," he said, his tone filled with intrigue and slight concern.

Miriam stepped as closely as she could without touching him. She uttered in his ear, quickly but steadily. "Do you not recall John? How often we would talk after the red room? We would speak on what we would do if we were up there. The wanton deeds we would commit if given the chance to spread ourselves on this very stage."

"Yes but…" Then the realisation dawned on him. "Good Lord, Miriam!"

"I have paid for half an hour. The stage is under our control, but you know as well as I, that there is a hungry crowd practically salivating for entertainment and we must oblige. So, in actual fact, you have mere seconds to decide John."

"But Miriam…" John said in half-protest as he hesitated over the idea. The couple had indulged in a lot of acts in this very club, some beyond their wildest of dreams. However, to unveil themselves so brazenly in front of a crowd, become a pawn in their scrutiny, scared him beyond belief. He shook on the spot in the centre of the stage. "Miriam I don't…"

Miriam didn't say a word, but her eyes interrupted him. Those deep blues scrutinised him as she tried to decipher his decision. A lightning bolt thundered through her sights and struck him fiercely. The storm shifted within him. There was no denying that he was terrified. It gripped tightly. The thing about absolute fear though, is that it comes with exhilaration. John cocked a smile and soon enough, he submitted to her will with a short, swift nod.

"We can leave anytime. Roses to stop, remember?" she whispered, heedless of the nerves that were also coursing through her. Miriam leaped into action. From the side of the stage, she brought out a chair and placed it in the centre of the room. She ushered John to stand in front of the chair, trying desperately not to caress him in order to comfort his consternation. Beneath his mask, his eyes stared straight ahead, as though he were already assuming the position. Miriam caught herself in the reflection of his eyes. "Are you positive you wish to do this?"

"I am," he said, winking at her with a big, broad grin. "Ravage me, miss."

Miriam squealed, leaning down to produce an old favourite weapon of choice, a long wooden cane like they use in schools. She then stood inches away from him, posing as she readied herself for the show. After a couple of beats to steel herself, Miriam leaned over and pulled the rope of the curtains.

As the blinding spotlights and clapping audience startled John, Miriam said loudly, "Ladies and gentlemen, this student must abide by one rule and one rule only. He mustn't touch. No matter how much he wills it. If he does touch…" Miriam signified to John to touch her. His hand comically touched her breast. She pouted and batted it away from her. "Then he is punished."

Miriam then had John bend over. In no time, she rapped him on the buttocks. There was a ripple of joy across the crowd.

And so, they played out the act that they had always envisioned together. John stayed as still as possible whilst, to cheeky, uproarious music Miriam began to strip. At first, she started slowly; a glove and then another, riling and bating the crowd. John stood completely still until she would do something, such as sliding off his jacket. When she did, leaning close to his face, John would cheekily kiss her. Then she would exclaim loudly, bend him over, and whip him giddily, getting harder with each infraction. A stroke down her arm. A kiss on her shoulder. There was even a squeeze on the bum. Every time he did, in well versed moments, Miriam would punish him, striking his behind with an almighty whack of the wooden stick. "Oh!" she gasped and said exaggeratedly, egging on the crowd to laugh and jeer at them, "bad boy!"

The act wasn't perfect, and the performers were sloppy – tipsy from wine and one another. However, Miriam was a fine hostess. She knew how to tease and entertain, stirring the audience into an almighty furore. With a mask covering her face, a cane in her hand, and John by her side, Miriam was free.

The music was ending. Miriam strutted around in stockings, small black drawers, and a corset that barely covered her nipples. John was in just his drawers and his mask, standing in front of the chair and covering his yearning. She gently pushed him onto the chair. Turning away from the crowd, Miriam then straddled him, pulling at the clasps of her bondage. She released her breasts but only to John, though the crowd knew she was near naked and there was a cheer as she discarded the girdle across the room. She knew that John wanted nothing more than to fondle her bosom. He throbbed against her. Still his hands didn't move. Teasing further, she bent forward to kiss him but stopped – letting the air between them do the work. When he stayed deathly still, she laughed loudly. "Good boy!"

The music met its crescendo, and Miriam flung her arms up as a magician's assistant would do to signify its finale. *Look at my trick,* she thought, *look at how I have this man under my every whim.*

There was an applause from the crowd. Miriam leaned to the left and pulled the rope. The curtains began to slowly close. Miriam sat still on John for seemingly the longest time, his agonisingly hard dick against her. There was a wetness from her naked crotch, through the slit of her drawers, as she sat on his leg. In a growl, so only his heated words touched her flesh, he whispered, "You are positively dripping."

A sweet gasp fell from her lips. "Fuck me, John."

"Now? Here?" he giggled, acutely aware that there was still a hoard of people on the other side of the curtain, clapping wildly and loudly. He was also aware that someone else might want to take the stage. He was waiting to be ushered off by an angry manager. "Is there time?"

"Yes." She grinded up against him and his stiff member which was protruding from his underwear. "I need you inside me. I implore you."

"Very well." Unsheathing his penis entirely from his underwear, he lifted her over him, pushed aside the material of her drawers, and guided himself to her entrance. With one very quick and deep thrust, he was inside her. She groaned, not caring who may hear her. They stayed in that position for a little while until Miriam began to circle her hips on him. She started slow and steady, pressing her hands on his legs to help lift herself up and down in a drawling, cyclic movement.

Now with absolute permission to touch her, John wasted no time in dragging his fingers across her flesh. His fingers adored her; every slight touch of his soft, sweet hands made her skin quiver. The way he skimmed over her indentions and scars was as though he had never touched her before. She was like marble, come to life with his caress, and she was afraid that if he stopped, she might crumble to dust and stone. The thought made her scared and excited, so she pressed herself closer into him.

As her breasts pushed up against him, John buried his head into her cleavage. He dripped kisses along her neckline. Her skin was now hot and sweaty. She tasted of bergamot and lemon, a scent that was popular with most women of the time. Yet tangled with the salt of her heated pleasure, she tasted purely like Miriam. These were fragrances which no manufacturer could replicate. He loved every sense of her.

Cradled in her chest, he could hear her heavy panting and random squeaks as she tried not to be too loud. It reminded him that the world was just a breath away. If they listened carefully, they'd be able to hear the clutter and chatter of the crowd that they had entertained just movements before. He wondered what would happen if the curtain was to rise once more. What would the world say if it saw these two beasts ravenously taking one another?

Miriam could sense it too: The red velvet barrier that kept their voracious ways secret from beady watching eyes. She thought on the faces of those watching before, hankering over her naked body. Oh, how they'd like to see someone take her in such a passionate manner and how they'd like their own grubby mitts on her skin.

The very thought of being exposed in such a manner caused Miriam to gyrate faster on John's cock. The pair could hear footsteps. The fear and excitement caused a familiar sensation to rise within them. Miriam looked for home. She reached down, taking his chin, and leaning it upwards. Their eyes met each other's in a similar, worshipping gaze. It had a terribly instant effect on John who, after a few, fast, ferocious thrusts, ejaculated into his wife. Miriam let out a soft stilted sigh. They slowed to a complete stop, giggling together before they scooped up their clothes and exited the stage.

The pair stepped back into the night with their clothes slightly askew from their activities on stage. The exultations in which they had participated were coursing through them alongside the wine. Standing, waiting for their horse-drawn cab, Miriam bristled at the cool wind. Though the night was somewhat chilly, there was more of a disjointed emotion ebbing through her. Whilst she enjoyed herself and their act, she was left slightly unsatisfied, and she couldn't shake the disappointment from her bones. After all she had planned every detail and built up the tension all throughout her mind.

As someone who indulged in pleasure more than most, Miriam Clayton was never under the illusion that all sexual encounters would end in an orgasm, especially from a woman's perspective. But it was rare that John would leave her this wanting.

As their carriage pulled up, John guided her into the cab before heading over to the driver. After he said their address in St James' Park, he slipped folded notes into the driver's hand and said loudly, "Cabbie, the night is as young and as beautiful as my dear wife. May we take a more scenic route home?"

The driver nodded with a faint smile as though he knew that John had a cunning plan. John then climbed into the carriage, removing his mask as Miriam removed hers. She cocked her head at him, trying to decipher both the words she had heard and the gleeful expression on her husband's face. Confused, Miriam laughed. "John? What the devil are you up to?"

John leaned over her and kissed her passionately. The carriage started suddenly causing them both to fall back. His hand reached for the hems of her skirt as he started pulling them up. Breaking from her lips, he smiled profusely and stroked her nose with his. "I posit to you, Miriam Bennett, that as satisfactory as our evening was, you did not reach completion."

"I had the most wonderful time," Miriam replied but could not hide a streak of disappointment that rushed across her face. The thought of not climaxing in the club, however, was soon melting away as he slid his fingers up her legs as studiously as he did the first time that he had laid his hands on her.

"Hmmm, let me examine you. I am a doctor after all," John whispered as his fingers found their way to her privates. She gasped at the touch as he gently glided over her wet and sticky spot. For a few minutes, he stroked her deftly; alternating between up and down, or circles upon her clitoris. She bit her lip but couldn't stop little squeaks of enjoyment coming from her.

Then John's index finger slipped into her, and he groaned in admiration, as though it were the first time that he had ever entered such a place. Miriam thought he looked the most attractive in these moments. Whether it would be drinking his favourite whisky or gazing at a beloved painting over and over again, John always showed his appreciation as though he were a thirsty man trying his first drop of water. It sent waves throughout her. Placing her hand on his chest to steady herself, Miriam said in a breathless whisper, "What is the prognosis doctor?"

"Oh my, this is graver than I first thought." His eyes were alit with mischief as he slipped another finger inside of her. Pushing them in and out of her, John used his thumb to start circling her spot. She groaned against her closed lips, trying to not alert anyone to their activities. London strolled merrily by, seemingly unaware of the sordid acts that were happening in the unassuming carriage. Turning away from the incandescence of the city, Miriam placed a foot onto the seat across from them so that she could writhe better on her husband's hand. His hot heated words fell on her cheek. "I prescribe several lashings at once." John's gaze did not leave her face as he eagerly studied the way pleasure rolled over her features. "May I administer your treatment Madam?"

Miriam nodded enthusiastically. "Yes, doctor, you may."

"Very well." John then took his hand from her as he knelt on the carriage floor underneath her. He wasted no time in burying himself underneath her skirts and dragging her drawers from her legs, discarding them on the floor. Miriam giggled gleefully.

John quickly found her sex. The air moved before him and delighted her before his mouth did. When his tongue followed, she seethed out through her teeth, wishing that she could cry out loudly in delight. He chuckled against her before he started in slow motions. With just the tip of his appendage, he flicked up and down her slit, tasting every inch of her privates. Then he used his whole tongue, licking her wholly.

As they pulled down Pall Mall, with Buckingham Palace bobbing by, John changed his motion and set his actions on her throbbing spot. Miriam groaned unwillingly. By all accounts he was an expert in this – almost surgical in his movements. He'd start in the same perpendicular movements then he'd circle before sucking. Sometimes Miriam swore he was spelling out words upon her. Occasionally, she could hear him moan in enjoyment and it would cause her to whimper in delight.

Miriam pawed her neckline as it grew hot with beads of sweat. She marvelled at the manner in which John had read her mind and body completely and would bestow such incredible attention on her so that they would both be satisfied. For a moment, she wondered about all the women that knew so little about pleasure. All those wives who allowed their husbands to fuck them and leave them frustrated in all sorts of passionless trysts. Though she tried to avoid it, Miriam would find herself in parlour rooms after dinner with the women of society who talked about their boring, almost sexless, marriages. Did they not know how rousing the other way could be? To be stimulated in every aspect by someone who wanted to shower you with utmost attention.

John wrapped his arms around her thighs and pulled her as close as possible, lapping at her tenderness with an eager and plentiful hunger. She placed her other foot against the seat opposite to stop herself slipping off from where she was sitting. Gripping onto the leather cushion, Miriam tried to focus on the pleasure that was turning within her. Her cheeks flushed and her toes curled. She huffed and puffed, stopping cries in her throat. As she could hear him lapping her up, she couldn't help but wonder how she tasted with the remnants of him still inside her. The thought had a terribly instant effect on her.

As they turned into their street, Miriam found herself similarly arriving.

Back at home, Miriam cradled John in her bosom as he gazed lovingly up at her. She tenderly tucked his dark-brown wavy hair behind his ear as she always did to comfort him from their busy nights. Though he'd give anything to stay awake and watch her for the whole evening, the gesture was soothing him into a much-needed slumber. They breathed in and out together, inhaling with the starlight and exhaling with satisfaction. There was no peace on earth quite like the one right now – curled up in each other wonderfully and wholly.

"Oh John, how silly of me, I almost forgot," she said, disturbing the silence and causing him to stir from his impending sleep. Reaching over to her drawer, she rummaged for a little while and pulled out a small postcard. She handed it over to him with a snickering breath. He took it and forcefully opened one eye to find a doodle of the pair of them. In this crude drawing, John was on all fours, following a voluptuous Miriam who had him tied around the collar. In her messy cursive writing, she had written "Lovesick as a Dog." The drawing was crass, but it amused him to no end. He sighed with a tired laugh before snuggling back into her arms, allowing the vinegar valentine to fall beside them.

Alas, some traditions endure.

The Anniversary

Wednesday 4th March 1896

8.00am – Miriam

The two doctors were locked in concentration.

The day had barely begun but there they were caught in a problem that they were both struggling to solve. All other matters were stripped of attention. A spillway had formed and the rolling river of thoughts that tumbled through their minds were directed for this one purpose. Time was against the pair of them as well. A clock on the desk ticked away the seconds with increasing anxiety. It would be the only sound in the room if it weren't for these two doctors tutting away at different times: One at every tick; one at every tock.

Doctor Miriam Bennett leaned back in her chair with a hefty sigh. She stared at the page in front of her and furrowed her brow. In one hand, she wiggled a pen violently back and forth between two fingers. Occasionally black ink flecks would land on the page, her hands, and even her white blouse. Every so often, her eyes would dart to the clock, and then to her father, and then back to the page.

Sir Fredric Clayton kept his hand on his mouth, rubbing his index finger across the bare skin beneath his nose and above his bare upper lip. The terrain was unmanned and unfamiliar, he regretted shaving his moustache from his face. Though he kept his signature mutton chops, there was an exposed feeling that made him more anxious about solving this conundrum. It didn't help that his daughter kept flicking her eyes over at him, scrutinising how he was thinking or the new lack of facial hair upon his face. He coughed authoritatively and turned back to the problem at hand, certain an answer would unfold in a m—

"Ah-ha! Finished!" Miriam said, slamming her hand on the clock and placing her bit of card on the down on the table. She leaned back, trying to quell the smug smile forming on her face as she rolled her tongue on the inside of her cheek.

"Blast it!" Sir Fredric replied, equally chucking his paper down on the table. He sighed heavily but watched his daughter's celebratory smile with admiration. There was a bright glint in her eyes. With a slight chuckle, he leaned back in his office chair. "Unbelievable, I had two left to decipher!"

Miriam shook her head in disbelief, twiddling her pen between her fingers and absentmindedly dotting them with ink. "Two? Father, if I didn't know any better, I'd say you were letting me win."

"Alas Miriam, you do know me better, and are privy to the absolute monster I am when I lose." Sir Fredric contorted his face to look grotesque as if he were a gargoyle. He even made shuffling, moaning sounds.

"Indeed, I know it well," Miriam said with a playful tut to hide her childlike giggles, having seen this face many times in her life. She leaned over and looked at the clock on the table before picking up the metal pot. "I believe I have time for one more coffee?"

Sir Fredric nodded as Miriam poured the warm brown liquid into the white ceramic cups on his office desk. This had been a morning routine since Miriam had learned to read and write. It had started off small – a trivia puzzle or riddle for the child to solve as they had breakfast together. As Miriam reached adolescence, Sir Fredric would set wordplay challenges to see who could come up with the best. When she had turned twenty, Miriam was setting her own and starting a long-standing competition between the pair.

Their latest hobby was rebuses. Though they no longer lived with one another, Miriam would call upon her father most mornings at his office and they'd share a cup of coffee, exchanging their hand-drawn puzzles with one another. Pictures that denote a special phrase or saying. Sir Fredric was extremely fond of these times before they got swept up in the hospital mayhem. Today he clung onto the morning desperately. Truthfully, he was less concerned that Miriam had beaten him but that in doing so, she was certain to leave any minute. He was desperate for her to stay longer this morning.

"So, proceed Miriam, what do mine say?" Sir Fredric gruffly muttered, taking a sip of the bitter coffee with a grimace – it was too cold to be enjoyable.

"Right well, the first one was far too easy - Bang up to the Elephant."

"Yes I guessed the elephant would give that one away."

"Second is slightly tricker, the letters threw me, but is it 'Son of a Gun?'" Sir Fredric nodded gleefully. "And finally, you went rogue," Miriam frowned, picking up the mug, and tapping the ceramic accusatory. "Took me a while to figure out the presence of the goat, however, is it 'Butter upon Bacon?'"

"Very good, Miriam, very good." Sir Fredric let out an exasperated sigh but smiled, nonetheless. "You best put me out of my misery. For number one I had 'Bags of Mystery?'" Miriam enthusiastically nodded in response, a brand-new smug smile forming slyly on her face. "Well, yes, I suppose that was quite simple. Now my dear daughter – what on earth is that?"

Miriam leaned over and inspected her paper, frowning at her own scratchy drawing. "A dog. For 'Bow wow mutton.'"

"A dog?" Sir Fredric exclaimed with a faux anger, his deep booming voice reverberating throughout the office so loudly that he was fearful the whole hospital would hear. "How on earth is that a dog? It is a horse, surely!"

"A horse, father?" Miriam was unphased by the fake rage that bounced gleefully against the walls. She leaned once more back into her chair, placed her legs carefully on the table, trapping her deep red skirt with her legs. "My goodness, it is time for spectacles?"

"The nerve! I should've disciplined you more as a child."

"As if you could ever." They partook in a succession of gleeful giggles until Miriam glanced at the clock on the table. "Quickly, this hospital waits for no man."

Miriam had said the sentence with urgency and yet it halted all sound. Sir Fredric's jovial manner fell as though his soul was being pulled into a deep, dark cavern. She did not see that his eyes had started glistening as though sacred light frittered down into that abyss and caught a pool of water, shimmering with sorrow. He looked down into the recollections of the day that filled his mind. "Yes, well, I was truly stumped for this one. I have no idea."

His daughter did not note his drastic change in demeanour. Instead, Miriam tutted and leaped up into action. She bounded around the table and leaned over her father like a schoolteacher would her naughtiest child. "See the clock. Now observe what time it is? Yes, it is one minute past-twelve, which means it is past noon. Or? Yes, well done, after-noon. Add the if, and the eye. Afternoonified!"

"Quite right, you clever thing, you have truly bested me this time," he said in a low rocky rumble. Then, certain she would not hear, he whispered, "I still think it is a horse."

"Do not sound too disappointed." Miriam chuckled. As she began to walk away from the desk, she leaned over and grabbed her cup of coffee, and threw down the cold dregs with a grimace not dissimilar from his own. With a gasp, she continued, relishing her win. "It stumped John also."

Sir Fredric suddenly looked up from the piece of card and watched his daughter. There was something so congenial about how she moved, lighter than the air around them. A picture of contentment, complete in herself and the world around her. She showed it in the way she walked nimbly around the room, she radiated it in the permanent glint that now resided in her bright blue eyes, and she illustrated it in the sunny way she now spoke. All at once she seemed like herself and brand new to him.

Miriam rebuttoned the fern-green waistcoat around her white blouse, covering up the splotches of ink now on her shirt. When she stopped buttoning at the chest, too small to fit around her completely, Sir Fredric realised that she had stolen it from her husband. The realisation struck her father hard as an echo wormed throughout in mind.

You'll be all she has.

Curled in his cheeks was a flush of disappointment. The upset crawled across his now bare-face and made him hot. He watched as she straightened herself up as she always did. It was like watching a boxer in a ring. Miriam psyched herself up for battle, unafraid to throw her punches. Yet in the middle of this routine, she looked up and caught his wine-red wistful expression. Her face fell into immediate concern. "Father, are you quite alright?"

This did nothing to alleviate his melancholic state. In fact, it added waves to the tide turning within that cavernous gullet of his. Sir Fredric was wounded by the very question. All at once it had become clear to him: Miriam had forgotten.

She grew more concerned as she looked to him for an answer. Instead of telling her the truth, Sir Fredric hesitated and settled on, "Just a spot of indigestion. And an incurable case of being still sore from losing."

Miriam sighed with a smatter of a smile, she walked around and kissed his cheek to say goodbye. He cherished the small touch before he playfully dismissed her.

You'll be all she has.

As Miriam walked out of the door, Sir Fredric realised that wasn't true anymore.

11.30am – Doctor Michael Jenkins

The minute Doctor Jenkins stepped into Sir Fredric's office; he began to speak fast. The words poured out of him in indistinct and incoherent sentences. Sir Fredric had barely had a chance to say 'hello' before Jenkins dissolved into a flurry of excuses. The chairman sighed the minute Jenkins had begun, watching the dark blonde-haired man pace back and forth, gesticulating crazily. Sir Fredric was almost lulled into a hypnotic state, zoning out of the scene right in front of him. As Jenkins was running out of words, he grabbed the back of the chair, and shook it violently. "Sir Fredric, please, it has been almost three months without a medicine mix-up, and I haven't broken any equipment in, well, almost a year."

With that sentence, Sir Fredric was broken out of his fugue state. He shook his head with a snicker. "Well, that is certainly good news, Jenkins. Very good news indeed. But that is not why I called you into my office today."

There was a sigh of relief as Jenkins sat down in the chair. He wrung his fingers to stop his nerves from jangling throughout him, but his shoulders were still tense. "Well, if it is about Miriam…" Jenkins turned beetroot at the mere mention of Sir Fredric's daughter's name. Suddenly, Jenkins' eyes widened from shock. "I erm I mean Miss Clay— Doctor Clay— Doctor Bennett, then I can assure you that there is no ill-will between us."

Sir Fredric glanced over Michael, curiously picking at the bewildered and strained expression on Jenkins face. After a couple of beats, he snorted and replied, "Jenkins, you and I both know that my daughter is more than capable of defending herself."

"Oh, quite right." Jenkins shoulders dropped. There were a few moments of silence before he continued, "Then why did you call me here?"

"Ah yes, well, the reason is much more commemorative." Sir Fredric leaned down, opened his drawer, and removed a bottle of champagne that had a blue bow around it. He placed it on the table between them. "I believe congratulations are in order." Jenkins looked perplexed, causing Sir Fredric to roll his eyes and slide it closer to the pharmacist. "You are going to be a father, are you not?"

Jenkins' eyes lit up like a child in a candy store. He grabbed the bottle with an awe-filled expression. It was expensive – Perrier-Jouet, no less – and it practically glistened as the sunshine of early spring fell into the office. Jenkins carefully pawed at the bottle before flying into another flurry, "Oh why yes, sir, yes I am. This is incredible, thank you sir. Thank you. This is such an honour and I—" Jenkins unexpectedly, and somewhat violently, threw his hands into the air, forgetting that he was holding the bottle. It soared across the room and smashed against the wall. Jenkins winced and looked down to the ground apologetically.

"Fear not Jenkins," Sir Fredric exhaled, then reached into his drawer again, pulling out another bottle with another blue bow attached. "I bought another, just in case." The chairman placed it on the table, but Jenkins did not dare pick it up again, not until he had to, though he nodded his thanks gently. Sir Fredric smiled brightly. "There's another reason why I called you in here, Jenkins. If I may, I wish to impart some advice. From one father to another?"

"Certainly sir."

"By all accounts, you are a traditional man, are you not Jenkins?" The younger man nodded. "So, I assume that you wish for a boy?" There was a hesitation before Jenkins conceded and bowed his head in agreement. "I see, well, I must profess that I was much the same until Miriam came along. If you do happen to have a daughter, Jenkins, all I want to ask of you is that you treat her with the same reverence as you would a son. Do not be like other men. Do not distance yourself. A daughter is a gift."

"I understand," Jenkins said, his cheeks growing scarlet as though he had been reprimanded. His green eyes burned with shame at the notion.

Sir Fredric looked at him with an unclear countenance. Though he lowered his brow, there was a glint in his eye and a smirk on his face. He gave an almighty sigh before he began in his usual booming voice. "I say this from experience. If anything, God forbid, were to happen to your dear wife – Adelaide? – Yes, Adelaide, then you'll have to stay strong." Then suddenly there was a shake in his voice, he tried to cover it with a cough. "You'll be all she has."

And then...

Then the office was filled with a dreadful pain. Sir Fredric began mulling over the very words he just said, reaching his hand up to his mouth as though he regretted uttering them. Michael looked up at him, cocking his head out of confusion as he tried to decipher why the air in the room had suddenly disappeared. His jittery tongue wriggled as questions bubbled within – ready to pop. Jenkins thought better of it, fearing that whatever he was going to say would come flying out his mouth and smash against Sir Fredric heavily. Instead, Michael let out a hot agitated breath from his nose.

The sound caused Sir Fredric to look up and chuckle, waving his hands to not only dismiss the moment, but dismiss Jenkins from his office. Jenkins smiled, cautiously scooping up the champagne, and left Sir Fredric alone in the office.

2.30pm - Deputy Chair Gerard Phipps

Gerard Phipps was not a man of medicine. He was a shrewd man of business. Short and stout, he spent more time in calculation, than he did caring. Even now he looked at the sheet before him with a frown: There were not enough numbers here for his brain to infer clear, concise information. Sir Fredric did nothing to help Phipps decipher the report; in fact, he relished the one aspect of this hospital that Phipps had no knowledge of.

Despite the fact that they had been working closely together for the past three years, and that they were both fifty-two, they had never developed a fondness for one another. Their views on the world were vastly different in many different ways: Phipps was forward thinking when it came to money and technology, whilst Sir Fredric was more charitable and amiable. It did not help their relationship that Sir Fredric assumed a dual role at the hospital – appointing himself in charge of business and medicine. Phipps was always deputy. This strained their working relationship and they argued more than they agreed.

Their latest heated debate was on installing electricity for the hospital. For once, Phipps was charged with the idea – knowing that the extravagant cost of doing so would ultimately save money for them in the long run. Sir Fredric baulked at the idea, fearing that oil lamps would suffice and refused to divert spending from patient care. It took several months of convincing. The entire board, including Miriam and John, were excited about the prospect. So, Sir Fredric relented, and the hospital was slowly transformed, ward by ward, over December and January.

Phipps had triumphed. Even this morning, he smugly walked into the Chairman's office and pulled on the toggle to illuminate the office. In retaliation, Sir Fredric removed the medical report, and handed it over without giving Phipps a single clue as to why he was doing so in the first place.

A few minutes had passed until Phipps shook his head. In a light, Scottish accent, he grumbled, "You know as well as I do that I know not what you have handed me."

"What you are holding, Gerard, are the records of a patient from another hospital. After a thorough examination, and an x-ray, it has been concluded that the patient is showing early signs of cancer."

"Ah I see," Phipps said, though the state of his brow had not changed. In fact, it furrowed deeper than before.

"Phipps, those are my records."

The admission curdled the air immediately. Phipps looked up from the sheets and went as pale as one. His eyes-widened suddenly. There was an eerie silence as though the sound had been sucked out of the room. Even the lights above them seemed to react, causing a momentary flicker. Phipps' eyes darted over Sir Fredric as he searched for a satisfactory reaction. "Sir Fredric…you have my condolences."

"No need." Sir Fredric immediately shook his head to dismiss whatever pity Phipps might dare to show. "It is an early prognosis. No one else knows, not even Miriam, and I wish to keep it that way."

The second admission washed over Phipps with unease. There was an uncertain emotion on his round, grey-bearded face, as he attempted to decipher the very words Sir Fredric had said. Perhaps Phipps was reassessing their relationship. Perhaps they were friends after all. There were friends that still disliked each other, mind, but friends, nonetheless. Phipps looked back down at the records – they still made no sense to him, but they were now weighted with terrible meaning. "Then why tell me?"

"A formality, Gerard, that is all." Sir Fredric gesticulated his hands dismissively, as though he were merely announcing that he had a bad cold. "I was told I must rest immediately which, I must admit, goes against my better judgement."

"Ah. If you were to retire because of this illness, then naturally I would assume the Chairman role." Sir Fredric nodded at him. The final piece of the puzzle had slotted into place and Phipps finally understood what was being asked of him. Gerard finally placed the records back on the office desk. "We'd have to appoint a man of medicine as the Director?" Sir Fredric nodded. "Whom do you have in mind?" Sir Fredric's eyes were illuminated with the utmost glee. "Oh God, please don't say her name again."

"If you have a problem with my daughter…"

"It just isn't the done thing, Sir Fredric."

"I find it risible Phipps that you are willing to promote this new-fangled electricity and yet are so close-minded to true progression." Sir Fredric laughed a little bit too much, causing an ache and a cough to follow the sound. He covered his mouth, hoping Phipps had not seen a grimace of pain. He stroked the empty space above his lips. "Miriam is a very accomplished doctor but truthfully, the role is beyond her years and experience." There was another deep sigh. "This is all moot, of course, I have yet to decide whether I wish to retire or not."

With that air of finality, Phipps nodded and began to rise from his chair, buttoning his black jacket over his yellow waistcoat. "Well, whatever you decide Sir Fredric, I am sure this hospital will move forward in your absence."

More words again to turn the atmosphere. Only this time, their meeting ended on such a sour note. Phipps had meant it as a kindness, but it angered Sir Fredric somewhat. There was no doubt that the hospital would continue to thrive without him, but he didn't want it to. Not really. He wanted the building to fall apart at the very thought of his retirement.

The senior gentlemen nodded their goodbyes and Phipps left the room, taking with him a grave secret. The Deputy Chairman was right, of course. The hospital would continue and progress long after Sir Fredric.

As the lights above him gleamed, Sir Fredric was suddenly at odds with this electric environment.

5.30pm – Doctor John Bennett

Sir Fredric held the leaflet cautiously in his hands, as though it were a fragile thing set to disintegrate between his fingers. There was no denying that the paper was already in a precarious state. The sheet had been clearly unfolded and folded repeatedly, falling apart at one of the seams. The tatty manner in which the document was presented to the chairman did not faze him. It was almost as though the owner had worn away the material from mere excitement alone. There was care in the creases, tenderness in the tears, and love lining this entire leaflet.

The older man was acutely aware that he was being watched. He hadn't said anything since being handed the paper and it had created a stilted silence Sir Fredric looked up to see his Deputy Head of Surgery in a dizzying heap of stress. John Bennett moved his gaze between the leaflet and his father-in-law whilst biting his nails. If Sir Fredric was a lesser man, he would make things harder for her daughter's husband. He'd glower with grievous intentions to make the doctor squirm under his gaze. Instead, he tried to hide a smirk and turned his attention back to the leaflet.

It was a single sheet of paper, emblazoned with a striking cartoon of a train and huge colourful lettering – both in English and in French. It was filled with all-types of information, including times, prices, and cities such as Istanbul, Vienna, and—

"Paris?" Sir Fredric finally said, breaking the quiet with his bouncing, booming rumbly voice.

"Yes," John muttered, taking a sharp intake of air suddenly. There were a few beats. Sir Fredric could see that one of his son-in-law's knees was bouncing up and down. "Do you think she'll like it?"

"Bennett..." Sir Fredric purposely paused again. He may not be a lesser man, but he did take some pleasure in holding someone perilously between his fingertips, frayed and practically falling apart. Suddenly, Sir Fredric broke the hold and grinned. He stood up, and leaned over to pass the leaflet back, before saying with absolute warmth, "I think it is a marvellous idea, Miriam will adore it."

"Really?" John smiled proudly, taking the page, and glancing at it for the millionth time.

"Truly." Sir Fredric sat back down, scooping up his glass of brandy and a cigar from the table. He leaned back in his chair, lit the cigar, and took several puffs.

John slipped the leaflet into the inner linings of his jacket then mirrored Sir Fredric's very action. The small office was soon filled with their usual Thursday evening smoke. Since John married Miriam, this routine had become requisite for the two men. Often they would share stories, musings over work, and the latest sporting scores. A lot of the time, they'd speak about Miriam in safe yet doting anecdotes. Sometimes, they just sat in quiet rumination, nursing a brandy and cigar after a long day of work. Since John's first visit to the Manor, the two doctors had developed this fondness and friendship.

Still, they were keen to not to let the whole hospital aware of this relationship, fearing Sir Fredric may be seen as having another favourite. Both men had reputations to withhold within these corridors, and John did not want anyone speaking badly about Sir Fredric. To not arouse suspicion, then, almost always, at the end of their meeting, they would start an angry argument, and make sure those nearby could hear.

"Would it also be possible for Miriam to be relieved of her hospital duties? And myself, of course. Just for those two weeks?" John said, punctuating his puffing with the words, causing loops of smoke to unexpectedly come out of his mouth.

"I don't see why not." Sir Fredric stubbed out the remnants of his cigar into the thick glass ashtray on the table. As he did this, he tried to ignore the pain filling his chest. Instead, he took a sip of brandy, savouring the way the light-tasting earthy ash balanced with the floral, golden liquid. He relished the mouthful as though it were the last thing he would ever drink. Flicking his eyes back to John, he continued with almost laugh, "Though I suppose you will have a hard time trying to convince Miriam of it."

"Oh, I have my ways of convincing Miriam," said John in a quiet manner, a smug smile forming slyly on his face. He too had finished his cigar but swallowed his brandy quicker than usual. He quickly stood up and buttoned his jacket. "Speaking of which, I best be going as she will be waiting for me."

Sir Fredric said nothing in response but watched John as he gathered his things. There was that burning sensation again, bounding through his whole face. A familiar sensation with new spikes. John moved lightly; as though he were a young man again; as though the world were alive with incandescence, as though there were no more worries to be had. Sir Fredric remembered being that way – so jubilantly in love that the earth shifted without care and time passed by with utter joviality.

You'll be all she has.

Except now Miriam had John. A perfect couple, most would say. The pair were so well suited to one another that Sir Fredric didn't mind that people scorned their quick engagement. In many ways, he was thrilled that his daughter was now married and truly happy. Doctor John Bennett was a fine man. indeed. In that moment, however, as John rushed to see Miriam, leaving Sir Fredric alone, the older doctor was suddenly marred with jealousy.

"Perhaps before I go, we should…" John waved a hand between the two of them, gesturing wildly, with a glimmer of glee in his eyes.

Sir Fredric snapped out of his musing, but his cheek's still flushed red. He was momentarily bemused until he cottoned onto the scheme, laughing somewhat as he exclaimed, "Ah yes, how should we proceed?"

"I know just the thing," John tried to stifle a smile and arrange his face to be more serious. His attempt to be stern was strained. "Bow wow mutton?"

"Oh ha-ha – are you talking about the horse?"

"I thought it was a cow!" John raised his voice, enraged. "It is absolutely ludicrous to believe that it was a dog!"

"Positively absurd!"

"Preposterous!"

John turned to leave and walked straight into Matron. The action caused both of them to yelp loudly.

6.30pm – Matron Lockett

As John skirted by Matron, whispering his apologies fast, she raised an eyebrow. Then, rolling her eyes she turned to Sir Fredric and said sternly as she closed the door gently behind her, "I hope you know that no one believes this ruse."

Sir Fredric chuckled and gestured to her to sit down. "Matron, what a pleasure it is to see you. Though…" Sir Fredric reached down to the diary in front of him and skirted his fingers down the page. "… I do not believe we had an appointment today."

"You say that every year." Matron reprimanded him with a fond smile. She walked into the office, taking the seat that so many had done throughout the entire day. She reached up to her hair and removed the white bonnet from her head, placing it down on the table without caring that strands of her grey hair now stood in alarming attention. There was a pause as the pair stared at one another. After a minute, Matron gestured to Sir Fredric, "Come on man, am I to do the honours this time?"

Shaking his head, Sir Fredric took the two glasses that he and John had been drinking from. He wiped the rim of John's with a light red handkerchief that he pulled from his inside jacket pocket. Then he poured more brandy into the glass and handed it over to Matron before he poured himself another. "Thank you for remembering." There was a beat. "Miriam had forgotten."

Matron's face fell into an expression that was both sincere and aghast at this admission. Instead of taking a sip of the drink, she slowly spun the glass in her palm and stared at the light-brown contents. "Oh Fredric, I am sorry."

"It's OK. Her mind is occupied with other things nowadays."

"A folly of youth, I am afraid. I am sure once she remembers, she will be apologetic."

"Indeed."

Matron swiftly nodded then lifted her glass to the air. "To Anna."

"To Anna." Sir Fredric mirrored the action, but the pair drank in silence. Sir Fredric sensed Matron's eyes as they moved over him as she tried to assess his state. For twenty-eight years, Sir Fredric was used to this from nearly everyone that he had known. It was a kind of pitying appraisal that came with being widowed – people skirted their eyes over you as they tried to discern what kind of mood that you were in and how to act accordingly. As well-meaning as the action was, and no matter how much he loved the person doing it, Sir Fredric loathed it entirely.

When the quiet had stretched out far too thinly, Matron said: "Fredric? Are you quite alright?"

"Oh yes, I am fine. Nothing that a fine brandy and your company cannot fix, Elizabeth." Sir Fredric reached over and gently placed his hands hers. The very touch caused him to sigh. Matron Elizabeth Lockett and Sir Fredric Clayton had known each other for twenty years and worked in several hospitals together. There was a kinship between them and, at different times for the pair, it would develop into something more. A love that neither could ignore entirely, nor would they ever act upon it. Not again.

This motion, as simple as a kindly hand, then, had crossed somewhat of a line, but Elizabeth allowed it. The sullen silence seeped through the scattering smoke. Elizabeth decided to place a kindly hand upon the one Sir Fredric laid on hers, giving him a gentle squeeze. "Do you wish to speak on what is vexing you?"

"The things I wish to say to you Lizzie… are the things I dare not to."

"*Freddie…*" Matron took back both of her hands and placed them in her lap. She looked down as she fiddled with the hems of her white apron. "I thought I made my position clear."

"Indeed, you did." Sir Fredric leaned back in his chair, bringing his hand to his bare face, and smoothing out his skin. He tried in vain to ignore the sensations that were still upon it. He could not deny that he was trembling at the very thought of her, remembering the time that he had explored her body. Just once. Ten years ago. On this very night. In an office not too dissimilar from this one. In a moment just as evocative as this one. Two people sharing drinks and moments and then each other. As Sir Fredric mused, he felt her all around him: The warmth of her touch caressed his skin, the taste of her lips were suddenly upon him, and the way her body felt as he was finally inside of her. Sir Fredric was nearly overcome by the memories.

Elizabeth Lockett was right, however. They had had this argument many times before, often in different sparring positions. In the beginning, it was Sir Fredric who scorned Elizabeth's approaches – too invested in his daughter, too busy with his work, and too grief-stricken to open up to another love. Over time, as Miriam wriggled deftly from his grasp, Sir Fredric turned to Elizabeth, but she denied him – too independent now to want someone in her life, too busy with her own work to have time for a lover, and too sure of her needs. Ultimately, she was unwilling to become second best. Elizabeth would always be in the shadows of Anna and with a firm hand, she closed the door on their possible relationship for good.

This pained Sir Fredric even now. He exhaled with his grief, unafraid to show her a few tears that he had kept guarded from everyone today. Trying to muster a smile, it alas came out more like a grimace. "Forgive me Elizabeth, this is a dreaded day."

"Would you rather I left you alone?"

"If that is not too much bother?"

"Certainly not. I shall pop by tomorrow." Matron stood up and hesitated. She played with her fingertips. Sir Fredric gazed at her as more tears formed in his eyes. Sighing, Matron walked around the table to him, bent down and kissed him on the cheek. A kindness, Sir Fredric surmised, and he chose not to proceed further, though his heart and mind wildly told him to.

Instead, Sir Fredric watched as Matron walked out of the door, closing it behind her.

Wood slotted into wood with a small bang and click. It reverberated through him, shaking the ghosts of the day out of their hiding.

It had started so simply. A late winter walk to the lake with the perambulator had winded Anna. She had leaned against the large tree that hung over the water to catch her breath. At first the pair had dismissed the motion, chalking it simply to the overtiredness that comes with new parentage. Fredric - long before he had become Sir - pushed the pram all the way home, with Anna clutching onto him to steady her steps. Still, as a doctor, Fredric demanded that his wife rest in bed for the evening. The next day, when Anna rose at midday, having slept through the night. She seemed well and the pair laughed about the whole affair.

There was nothing to worry about. Then over the next few weeks her body began to ache, and her weight decreased rapidly.

They both insisted that she was fine. Then she could no longer walk up the stairs without losing her breath. She was going to be OK; they'd wistfully think to themselves. Then the fever had begun, and a cough rattled through her lungs with bloody admissions in her handkerchief.

Anna was strong. She could survive this. They'd say this together as she stayed in bed one day, and then the next, and then the next. Soon the bed became her nest. She had no more strength to leave it – sickened in the silk. Still, they'd insist, she would pull through.

Until one day.

The Clayton Manor was always a home of warmth and laughter, but the morning of 4th March 1868, the place was eerily silent and cold. Fredric arose from the green armchair and found his home was nearly devoid of sound. If the fireplace were crackling, or the clocks were ticking, then he did not hear it. Trepidation had drained everything from the room, his home, and his heart. Not even Miriam, their newly born child, was crying. She just gurgled silently in her crib at the foot of their bed as if she too was visited by the spectre of knowing.

Wiping the night from his eyes, and massaging a painful crick in his neck, Fredric looked towards the bed where his wife lay. She was as still as the house, and equally silent. Dread hit his stomach like a droplet of poison, devouring his happiness quickly. He rushed forward and grabbed her hand, feeling for a pulse and the rest of her warmth. Only little evidence remained, her life frittering away in soft, low beats.

Fredric clutched onto her hand, looping his fingers into her almost cold ones, and kissing each one with increasing desperation. He had a childlike wish, a hope that his lips could awaken the near dead. It almost worked. Anna fluttered her eyes open gently, giving him the smallest smile – all that she could muster. As their eyes met, Fredric thought foolishly to himself, *See, she is going to be just fine.*

"Freddie…" Anna said his name with hefty meaning. All her strength hung to these vowels and consonants. Nestled, hidden, in the indents of those letters were all of her goodbyes. She took a deep breath to say more but suddenly Miriam began to cry. Fredric, still clinging onto Anna's hand, hesitated. His wife gave him a weak smile. "Go to her."

Fredric nodded, reluctantly letting her go before he walked over to Miriam's crib, scooping up the big, bright baby into his arms. By all accounts, he was an expert at this. Miriam lay in his elbow and against his chest as he bounced her gently. The minute he began cooing at her, his deep booming voice falling around her, Miriam began to quiet, nestling into him as though that were what she really wanted. Ever since she was born, her father had been the only one able to truly quieten her from griping.

Anna was too weak to move, so she just watched the scene unfold before her. She could not remember ever meeting Fredric Clayton – he had always been there in her life. Their families bound them at a young age, but it did not matter, they were thick as thieves from childhood. As teenagers, that kinship thankfully blossomed. They were the first for everything, embracing life with unparalleled passion, and they kept correspondence whilst Fredric trained to be a doctor in London.

They were married at twenty-one and three years later, they were blessed with Miriam – their only daughter. Anna did not know what she had done to earn such blisses in her life. Now she watched Fredric pace quietly across the room and studied him. She adored his stocky figure, and his mousey brown mutton chops that he had started to grow. She liked how he made her laugh with his wild stories and dirty jokes. She thought about how tenderly he made love to her and embraced her and kissed her – as though they were the only two people on this planet. Most importantly, she loved how he cared for Miriam.

Wealth and status had meant the pair had grown up around cold, heartless men. Fredric defied what was expected of him, going beyond nature and nurture to be kind, generous, and ferocious. When Miriam was placed into his arms, he looked upon his daughter with utmost wonder and adoration. Yet even knowing this, a sudden fear gripped Anna. "Will you make me a promise, Freddie?" Anna said her voice was almost too weak to be heard.

"Anything, my sweet Anna."

"Promise me that you will not abandon our girl. Do not be like other men. Do not distance yourself. Do not cast her aside in your grief. Be strong. For Miriam… For me… For you…"

Fredric looked up from his daughter and saw tears sliding down Anna's face. The very presence of them, weighted with anguish, pulled his own to the edge of his eyes. He tried desperately not to show them to his wife. Unblinking, he stared as his mind raced with ailments and cures. Surely his education could remedy this. He blinked and a solitary tear rushed out of him, giving her his answer.

Immediately he cast his gaze back to his daughter. She was asleep in his arms, at home in his embrace. Fredric didn't know how to answer, the words he wanted to say stuck dryly to his mouth and throat. Instead, he nodded, binding the promise to both his wife and daughter.

Anna mirrored his response before rasping out a reply. "You'll be all she has."

And then.

Then that dreaded silence permeated through the home again. Only this time every sound momentarily stopped. The fireplace finished crackling; the clocks ceased to tick and tock, and Miriam was as silent as a babe could be. The quiet was thick and unrelentless.

Fredric did not look up, breathing shakily as he placed his daughter back down into her crib. Placing a cotton yellow blanket over Miriam, he kissed her tenderly on the forehead. Then, satisfied that she would not stir, Fredric walked out of his bedroom. He closed the door behind him, slid down the dark brown wooden panelling, and stifled his sobs with his hands.

7pm – Alone

Twenty-eight years later, Sir Fredric ruminated alone in his office. After some time, he finally stood up from the chair and walked around the office in which he had been hiding in all day. He stretched his back and groaned, finally noticing the pain from his backside. He removed his silver pocket watch. There was an air of finality as Sir Fredric nodded to no one at all, snapped the watch such, and gathered all his things,

"You'll be all she has."

The last words his wife ever said to him. Sir Fredric was fiercely devoted to them. For many years, he and Miriam were inseparable. Whilst he had help from Isobel, Hettie, and more, for those twenty-eight years, Sir Fredric and Miriam lived by their own rules, and in their own world. He dedicated his life and love to his daughter. Oh, the things that he had done to keep her safe and protect her from the thorns of this world. He thought of them all now as tears fell from his deep blue eyes – a mirror of Miriam's.

In all that time, Sir Fredric never realised that Miriam was all that he had. He held her close; perhaps too tightly. Over the years, he tried to find suitors for his daughter, but he knew it was a fool's errand. Miriam was so proudly independent that Sir Fredric never truly entertained the idea that he'd have to let her go. He had not once thought she would actually find a husband.

Sir Fredric put on his jacket and grabbed his cane. He walked around his office habitually. For years he had enjoyed the gasping breath of the oil lamps as they squeaked off. He admired how the shadows could fade blissfully into a room, turning from blazing ambers to pitch black. He no longer needed to do this. Instead, he pulled at a dangling switch, and his office was dramatically dark. Sir Fredric hated how strange this new way felt to him.

The smell of Matron's perfume lingered in the air as he closed the door and locked his office. He tried to ignore it, but it was no use. He regretted sending her away when he really needed some company. Even if her company was charged with so many different emotions.

What an idiot he was to never suspect that his daughter would fall in love, what naivety he possessed to not see that the hospital was changing rapidly, and what a stupid man he was to not tell Elizabeth that he loved her when she told him.

Everything was now out of his grasp: Miriam no longer needed him. The hospital no longer needed him. Matron no longer needed him.

Walking through the corridors of the institution, Sir Fredric realised that his reign here was over. With an illness now filling his lungs, Sir Fredric had to rest and retire. The truth resonated with each footstep that boomed down the hall. Each click of his cane on the wood filled him with this resolution. He mumbled his goodbyes at everyone he passed, and each of them made it clear what had been brewing in him for some time.

As Sir Fredric walked through the entrance, into the dark of the evening, he turned around and gazed at the hospital. This funny little triangle building that he had built with his wealth. It loomed over him, burning brightly with possibilities, far beyond his own capabilities. He had to let the hospital move on without him.

Miriam, this building, and Matron – he had to let them all go.

With a raise of his cane, and a tip of his hat, to no one in particular, Sir Fredric smiled and finally said, "Goodbye."

Easter

Miriam was not very well on Easter Weekend.

It hadn't come on suddenly. It had been brooding within her for a few days. Maybe even a week or so. Occasionally throughout her day, she would be flummoxed by a wave of nausea. She'd be working on the wards and there would be a sudden fresh peel of sweat on her forehead. Her cheeks would flush, and her heart rate would rise. Pausing from a grip of dizziness, Miriam would close her eyes, shake her head, and then would be perfectly normal.

At night, she'd have more vivid nightmares than usual, and wake up in a cold sweat with the wish to vomit. She initially dismissed these symptoms. After all, they were so very familiar to most women. Especially as her breasts were tender to touch. For a few days, her stomach cramped, and she'd storm into the bathroom expecting red splotches of blood in her drawers. But often there was nothing there, which was even more frustrating.

The night before Good Friday, she had thrown up several times. Miriam had tried her best to hide it from John, sneaking into the guest room to use the chamber pot there. It's not that she was worried about him seeing her all withered and woeful, though that hovered awfully in the back of her mind, it's that she knew John would demand she take time off work – something she had no intention of doing.

The third time, however, in the early hours of the day, she had found herself curled up around the ceramic pot on the bed in the spare room, unable to move. Suddenly, there was a soothing wet flannel upon her forehead, a glass of water in her hand, and someone tucking her hair behind her ear. She muttered that she was fine and did not need John to look after her. She pouted and protested until his soothing motions lulled her to sleep.

During the night, John had tucked her into the guest room bed and had slept beside her, wishing to never be alone in their marital bed. When she awoke the next day, she was initially bemused as to the change in surroundings, then a turn in her stomach made her remember how ill she was. As he washed and dressed, John watched her grimace and clutch her tummy, then insisted that she stayed at home. At first it was a light suggestion, to which Miriam clambered out of bed, protesting that she was fine. The second was a firmer instruction, as Miriam tried to steady herself with the bed frame. The third, when Miriam unwillingly moaned from another wave of cramps, was a clear order.

"Fine," she mumbled, "but I want my own bed!" John nodded and helped her back into the comfort of their own room. There was a small argument as to whether or not he should stay and tend to her. "Dammit man! I am not an invalid!"

Sighing, John nodded again and said, "I shall be back at my earliest convenience."

Miriam had insisted John worked for somewhat nefarious reasons – without him home, she could easily sneak away to the hospital, and he'd be none the wiser. After he gently wished her goodbye, and exited their home, Miriam huffed and waited a tedious hour until she could exact her plan. Carefully, she put on a plain white blouse and black skirt and snuck out of the house.

She had made it all the way to the Lady Gray Ward without suspicion. Walking through the doors with a sly smile on her face, Miriam thought she had succeeded in her task. However, before she had a chance to tend to any patients, Matron Lockett had looped her arm through Miriam's and was dragging her away. Mumbling her excuses wildly, Miriam was yanked all the way to John's office, procuring giggles from the staff as she passed them in the hallways.

"You truly do know your wife, Doctor Bennett," Matron said sternly but with a small smile on her face as they walked through his office door.

John was propped against his desk, staring at his pocket watch. As though he were rehearsing a very bad play, he snapped it shut, looked up at the pair of them, and smiled. "Over an hour though," he said with a laugh, "I believe I owe you a shilling."

"I shall collect later. She's all yours," Matron said jovially before flouncing out the office and closing the door.

For the longest time, Miriam stood there like a reprimanded schoolchild. Her cheeks flushed scarlet and not just from the illness rushing through her body. John stared at her somewhat crossly before he let out a generous sigh and gestured to his left. Miriam followed his hand to find a small cot had been laid out in his office, equipped with a pillow and a small blanket. Though shocked at first, she bowed her head and slowly made her way over to the make-shift bed.

John watched her intently yet lovingly. As she meekly sat on the edge, he said, "May I ask you a question, Miriam?"

"Yes, my dear John, anything."

"I appreciate your foremost thought is that of your patients," John said with a small pause. He then stood up from the desk and walked over to her. He knelt down and took her hand, sensing the tears that were forming in her eyes. "But we have yet to discern this illness of yours. What would've happened if it were an infection that you unknowingly passed to a woman or child in your care?"

Miriam let out a tiny gasp which caused a small tear to roll down her face. "Oh, I had not thought of that."

He hushed her tenderly and pushed her back into the cot. "Sometimes, Miriam, one has to take care of oneself first before one is able to take care of others."

Conceding defeat, Miriam nodded, lifting her legs up and lying down in his office. She reached over at the plain, dark green blanket and covered herself with its scratchy material. "Where have you been hiding this? It would've made our trysts here a lot more comfortable."

"But much less interesting."

"Indeed." As Miriam snuggled against the pillow, John began to instinctively examine her. However, she grabbed his wrist and shook her head. "Please, no more fussing. This is… well… I believe… Mother Nature returning. Very ferociously, I might add."

John raised an eyebrow at her. Not because of her mention of menstruation but because he had never seen her so sick with it. Still, he had gotten her to finally relax and rest. He wished not to push it further. He nodded and simply tucked her in, allowing her to sleep in his office whilst he did rounds at the hospital.

It had not occurred to either of them that she was pregnant.

That realisation would come Easter Sunday.

After sleeping most of the day on Saturday, Miriam was better when she awoke late Sunday morning. It had been the most slumber she had had in her entire life, and it had left her somewhat discombobulated. There was a surprising streak of sunlight that had entered their bedroom. March had been a particularly rainy month, so Miriam was thankful for the heat. It made her feel more like herself. She stretched out her hands with a gleeful groan but found the bed empty.

Confused at first, Miriam had little time to ponder on the location of her husband because she was utterly ravenous. After spending the last two days vomiting, her body craved sustenance so urgently that it made her light-headed.

As if John were magic, at that very moment of realisation, he burst through the door carrying a tray of food for her. She sat up excitedly in bed and clapped joyfully as he placed the tray on her lap. He kissed her on the cheek and lay beside her. "Happy Easter, darling. How are you feeling?"

Furtively, she was already scoffing her sausages and bread rolls. She spoke enthusiastically through puffed, food-filled cheeks. "Oh much better, thank you so ver— OH JOHN FLOWERS! THEY ARE BEAUTIFUL! THANK YOU

She lifted up the bouquet of tulips and lilacs and sniffed them before she even had a chance to swallow her breakfast. He laughed at her before taking the paper he had placed on the tray as well as a bread roll. Munching happily beside her, he read the news out loud. In between bites and titbits, they'd also started to excitedly plan their day now that Miriam was well.

It would not last long.

The new wave of biliousness came over her at lunchtime. John was preparing a picnic in the kitchen. Miriam was fixing an extravagant purple hat to her hair, one adorned with flowers and feathers, which matched the colour of the polka-dots of her big, puff-sleeved spring dress. She smiled and hummed until all the contents of her stomach – all that lush food she had been gorging on just hours before – threatened to immediately expel from her. She rushed to the pot that had been placed by her bed and miserably gave in to her body's demands.

Grimly, and dejected, Miriam flounced down the stairs. John stood at the bottom holding a note and a straw hat in his hands. He was dressed finely in a cream suit, with small reddish stripes on the jacket and trousers, with a cherry neckerchief around his collar. As the steps creaked beneath her feet, John held the letter up to her.

"How fortuitous! Adelaide and Michael wish to know if we would accompany them at St James for a spot of cricket in the park," John said excitedly. From the bottom of the stairs, Miriam watched him smile profusely and wondered how sweet it was that this nearly forty-year-old man met most good things with a childlike delight. However, when John took one look at Miriam's face which was both pale and red, that glee dissipated into worry. "I shall tell them another time."

Not wishing to be the source of disappointment, Miriam rushed forward and took his hands. "No, we shall go. I am a doctor after all." She gave him a loving squeeze but the smile on her sweaty face was uneasy. "I prescribe myself some much-needed fresh air."

"Only if you are most certain."

"Positive."

"Very well." His eyes, however, darted over her face and he was still trying to discern whether they should leave the house or not. "But if I suspect for one iota that it is too much for you, then we shall head straight home." He kissed her cheek gently, without a trace of disgust at her clammy skin. "Doctor's orders."

The way he practically growled the last words caused all sorts of chaos within her. She threw her arms around him and pulled him close to her, kissing him deeply on his lips with no qualms. But John laughed and shook his head.

He couldn't help the manner in which he dripped those words into her ear. With Miriam sick, John finally had all of the power and as tantalising as it was the other way, he couldn't resist relishing the change in dynamics. She grinded her hips against him in a pleading manner, and he tried his best not to stiffen from her actions.

"Please," she said with a whine, so pathetically out of control for once and absolutely brazen for her husband.

"You are too weak for such exertions, my dear."

Though her period would often interrupt their erotic activities, the pair had enjoyed each other's bodies for the past couple of months without so much as a breather. Up until this week, that is, when they had both realised Miriam was far too sick to get up to much mischief. They had to stop their coital explorations. Whilst the pair could enjoy one another without sex, they'd be lying if they weren't slightly frustrated when it was suddenly taken away from them.

If Miriam had thought about it harder, she would've known right there and then that she was with child. But her mind was clouded with sordid thoughts about her husband. For the first time in their relationship, he had said no, with a firm, albeit caring hand, and it bridled inside her. She scowled at him, and said in an unconvincing manner, "I am feeling much better."

"If you can survive the day, Miriam," he chuckled, bringing her into an embrace, and grabbing her buttocks in a playful squeeze. He kissed her before grinning wildly at her. "Then later I shall have my wicked way with you."

"Oh John, what torture!"

"Yes, exquisite, isn't it?"

St James' Park was busy as the blaze of a sunny afternoon cascaded violently down. Miriam grimaced at the sight of the populous park as people promenaded or picnicked. Though she was bored of the confines of her bedroom, she was quickly regretting their decision to head out. She felt groggy and grotesque as her stomach was bilious and bloated. As they walked, Miriam clung pitifully to John, umming and ahhing over whether or not to return home.

Luckily, it took only a handful of minutes for the Bennetts to find their friends in a spot beside the lake. Michael and Adelaide were already laying down a huge, blue blanket on the floor. After their polite yet jovial greetings, John guided Miriam immediately to the comfort of the ground, beneath the shade of a tree.

The husbands - John and Michael - had left the women to picnic alone and looked for a place to play. Miriam was somewhat thankful because Michael could never meet her eyes following the quartet's tryst last year. He'd flush as red as he did when she insulted him in the boardroom and never answered her questions directly. It always made her laugh and roll her eyes at how sex could send a man into a tither. Besides, she wanted Adelaide all to herself.

"My little chuckaboo," Miriam said fondly as she helped guide the pregnant Adelaide down to the ground. She propped up a cushion behind her expectant friend for comfort. "How the blazes are you?"

"Oh, I am fine," Adelaide replied somewhat dismissively as though she were at her limit with fussing. "I am humongous, but I am fine."

"You are no less beautiful," Miriam enthused, thinking on how bright and beaming Adelaide looked whilst six months pregnant. The woman was always a picture of sophistication and radiance. Even now as she wore a big blue maternity dress, Adelaide had perfect ringlet hair and make-up as well as an expensive blue bonnet. Miriam both envied and admired her all at once – grotesque with her simple sickness. Pull yourself together, she thought to herself as Adelaide laid back with her big belly, you are not carrying life.

Of course, she should've realised there and then that she very much was.

The two men had found a clear spot a few metres away from them and had started to practise cricket. It started with them batting and throwing the ball between themselves. However, soon after, other gentlemen had joined them, and it had turned into a whole unexpected game in the park with onlookers turning into a small cheering crowd.

For a short while Adelaide unpacked the food. Miriam was unable to look at the sandwiches as her stomach gurgled and lurched every so often. She tried to pay it no mind and watched John play instead. To most people, John was a shy, unassuming man. It was easy to mistake him as such. After all, unless he was talking with her or his father, John didn't say much and was very happy in silence. However, he was an extremely self-assured man. He met most things with an arresting confidence. There were three things in which he truly excelled and shined at: Surgery, sport, and, of course, sex.

Playing cricket was a great example of this, especially when he was bowling. Miriam watched as he coolly focused on the wicket behind the batsman, he'd run and throw the ball, and then knock the wooden peg from the top of it. Each time, he'd grin slyly but walk away as though it were nothing. Each time, he looked back to her to see if she was watching. Each time, she'd clap happily at him.

Leaning backwards again, Adelaide groaned causing Miriam to snap into action, taking over service duties. As Adelaide puffed out, she said, "John mentioned that you were unwell Miriam?"

"Oh. I am just not up to dick. I'll live…" Miriam said dismissively, pouring the pair of them a glass of lemon cordial and placing sandwiches on a plate. "… My husband worries too much."

"That's because that man…" Adelaide replied, taking the food from her friend, and instantly taking a huge bite. "… loves you more than anything."

"What of your husband?" The pair both looked over right as Michael slipped and fell face first into the ground. There was a small gasp and Miriam twisted her mouth, trying not to titter.

"You may think him risible, Miriam, but he is steadfast in his affections." Adelaide prodded Miriam indignantly. "And I love him nonetheless."

The way Adelaide's hazel eyes softened told Miriam all she needed to know. For a small moment, she thought about how her friend's secret places tasted, and wondered if Adelaide ever pondered on that memory as well. A breeze suddenly bristled through her in admonishment. Miriam lifted her knees and clung to them for warmth. With a huge sigh, Miriam muttered, "And how is my future godchild? Any names?"

"Oh, Lucifer most definitely, the way this babe is wreaking havoc on my insides," Adelaide said in a large huff. Miriam raised an eyebrow and Adelaide batted the joke aside with her hands. "If you must know, I am thinking of Eloise. For a girl. Of course, if it is a boy, he'll be named after his father."

"I always found it unfair for sons to not get a wholly unique name."

"Traditions dictate, I'm afraid. You'll grow to love it."

"Yes, I am sure I will. Little baby… Michael." The manner in which Miriam said his name, as though it were a slug worming out of her mouth, caused both of the women to burst into a fit of giggles that erupted loudly. Adelaide was most definitely the most refined of the pair when it came to societal outings but what Miriam adored most about her friend was her uncontrollable laughter. It was noisy and almost honking as she threw her head back without a care in the world. It was beautiful. Plus, it matched Miriam's cackle very well. Neither of them paid any mind to the tuts from people around them

As the ripples of their laughter subsided, Miriam was overcome with sickness again. She froze as a way of steadying herself and closed her eyes to stop the dizziness. There was a stabbing pain in her bosom. Adelaide furrowed her brow out of concern. "You look flushed Miriam. Are you sure you are quite alright?"

"I fear my monthly is upon me," she groaned, not afraid to soothe her breasts in front of her friend or, indeed, the general public. "It has been an age, after all."

Adelaide cocked her head. "An age?"

"Yes," Miriam replied nonchalantly through a big puff of air. She leaned backwards to stifle the painful bloating as a wave of nausea came over her. "I have been free from the turn since January."

"Oh Miriam…" Adelaide then burst out into raucous laughter again.

This time Miriam didn't understand the joke though she chuckled nervously along. "What is it, Adelaide?" Her face the picture of puzzlement.

"Must I spell it out for you?" Adelaide smiled brightly, exaggeratingly running her hand over her protruding belly.

The realisation hit Miriam hard. "No," she said with a loud scoff, shaking her head in disbelief. Adelaide nodded enthusiastically at Miriam who kept repeating the word with new tones and inflictions.

"How the hell did it take you this long to realise?" Adelaide reached over and grabbed Miriam's hand to give her a congratulatory squeeze. "You are both *doctors*!"

"We were simply enjoying our uninterrupted dalliances!" She tried to be quiet, but she wildly gesticulated with her hands. Everything was slotting into place. All those classic signs that she had missed. She was foolish for not recognising it sooner. She wailed into the day: "Oh this all makes sense now!"

"If I may say so, I half-expected this sooner…" Adelaide stopped chuckling and in a soft murmur, she whispered, "…knowing how the pair of you carry on."

"ARGH!" Miriam said far too loudly before throwing her head into her hands and collapsing into tears. Each one that fell was charged with a different undecipherable emotion. Miriam did not know how to feel about the possible, impending motherhood.

If John had put his medical training to use, then he would've also realised Miriam was pregnant a few weeks ago. Alas, the naked outline of her body and the delectable fruits it offered had clouded his mind. Even now as she was ill, his train of thoughts had broken into two tracks: concern for Miriam's wellbeing and the contours and crevices of hers that he regularly inhabited. He smiled surreptitiously to himself as he aimed the ball at the wicket.

"Our wives best not be concocting anything again," Michael muttered unexpectedly as he tapped his cricket bat on the grass. The men suddenly, at the same time, remembered what had transpired at Christmas and couldn't maintain eye contact with one another. Polishing the cricket ball against his trouser whilst blushing the same colour red, John thought of his friend's uncanny ability to say whatever popped into his mind, and how that often led to his own ridicule or other people's embarrassment. If anyone were ever to ask John why he was a man of few words, he would use Michael as a prime example.

Attempting to dismiss the couples' yuletide tryst that was scorching his brain like the sunlight that licked at his cheeks, John assumed his bowler stance. He leaned his body backwards and was ready to bowl the ball when he glanced over to where the wives sat. There was a calamitous scene in front of him. Miriam had her head buried in her hands, her shoulders were shaking violently, whilst Adelaide was cooing her gently and stroking her back. A pang of guilt resided in his stomach, and he regretted dragging her out when she was so ill. Even if she was so utterly insistent on leaving the house.

There was another tap of the bat that snapped John back to his senses somewhat. Whilst still looking over at Miriam in concern, he bowled the ball with an unanticipated gusto. It bounced off Michael's cheek painfully. "Ow blast it man!"

But John was not paying great attention to the injury he may have caused, although he quickly mumbled an apology. He was already walking back up the park.

Miriam did not notice. Her head was still buried in her hands. Adelaide caressed her back the best she could. "I insist you see my doctor tomorrow. She is rather good – even if she isn't you."

The kind words caused movement. Miriam threw her arms around Adelaide and squeezed her tight. "Thank you," Miriam whispered before bursting into uncontrollable sobs again.

"My word!" Adelaide was flummoxed by the tight grip in which her friend had wrapped her arms around her. She tried to steady the crying by hushing her gently. "Miriam has this upset you terribly?"

"Quite the contrary." Miriam finally let go of her friend as her heart swelled. The shock was finally dissipating throughout her, and a joyful feeling replaced the dawning of a new chapter for her, and John billowed through her soul. "I could not be happier." And she wanted nothing more than to be alone with her husband.

As if by magic, John's shadow fell upon the pair of them. Miriam sniffed profusely, as though if she breathed in hard enough, then all the crying and emotions would be erased from her face. She gazed up at her loving, doting husband and tried to smile through the snot and blotchiness. Her face must've looked monstrous.

Instead of disgust, John smiled so lovingly, though albeit concerned, that it caused her heart to beat wildly. How lucky she was to have ensnared his angel who gazed upon her as though she were God, no matter what form. He would make a fine father, she thought to herself, seeing him in such a caring manner. John reached down. "Come, let us get you home."

Miriam nodded vigorously and took his hand. John directed her miserable heap off the ground. As she clung to him desperately and muttered her fond goodbyes to Adelaide, whose own husband was pacing his way over, grumbling with each step.

So, Miriam finally let John take care of her. Leaning against him, they walked calmly out of the park, ignoring Michael's moans of a sore cheek. The Bennetts grinned together as they heard Adelaide calmly yet sternly tell her husband to grow up in a series of tuts.

When they arrived home, John placed Miriam in the chair by the fireplace before fixing her a pot of tea – a soothing chamomile. As she mused on the day and the life growing inside of her, he pottered around boiling water for a bath upstairs.

As soon as she had finished her drink, John led her to their bedroom, There he gently took off her clothes until she was nude. She climbed into the metal tub of hot water – enhanced with lavender oils. Surprising Miriam, John then stripped himself of clothes and climbed in behind her. Immediately, he started taking out her hair pins. Taking a jug from the table beside them, he then poured the water softy over her head before he started cleaning her with leisurely and thoughtful actions. After she was scrubbed from the stickiness of the day and the snot from her crying, Miriam let out a raged yet contented sigh. He coaxed her back into his arms for a little while. They lay there until the water grew lukewarm.

After their bath, John lay Miriam naked on the bed, letting the heat from the remaining rays of light dry her. He tucked her straggly wet hair behind her ears to soothe her. There was a part of Miriam that wanted to be coaxed into a slumber, and she nearly let him do so. But she also wanted to share herself entirely with him and bask in the love that they had created. Before he could reach for her nightgown, she kissed him deeply and passionately with all the strength she could muster. He had always been so godlike to her, but in this moment, he was a pillar and a refuge. She wanted nothing more than to blossom beneath him.

John could never resist her when she was so eager for him. The way Miriam was looking at him made him lightheaded and goofy. Whatever spell she was casting over him was working. He sighed happily and climbed on top of her, already hardened by the very thought of her. In spite of her sickness, Miriam had never been more beautiful – positively glowing below him. She was always otherworldly to him but in this moment, she was grounded and earthly. He wanted nothing more than to take root in her.

The way John entered her was light and gentle as he restored her blisses. The way Miriam groaned his name was full of adoration and greatly strengthened his ecstasies. It was slow and somewhat sloppy, but they were both thankful for it, gasping into the afternoon's finality. When he quickened his pace, he was still tender in his touches, and constantly checked if she was OK. When she wrapped her legs around his hips, she was still caring, and met his concern with the biggest smile. The whole time, their eyes never left one another's. In all their games, and all their dark plays, they both knew that there was nothing as divine as this. This… sweetness.

They fumbled for a release. Yet despite their haphazard motions, they were honest and earnest. It was no surprise that they climaxed together. When they were done and they were spent, they lay together naked and utterly satisfied. The last remnants of the spring sun glided slowly across their white bed sheets. Laying back, John wrapped his arms around her and played with her hair, twisting strands between his fingers as he had done a million times over. Miriam lay upon his chest and counted the freckles under her touch, though by now she had the number memorised.

Miriam chose not to tell him about the suspected news right away, although she wanted to more than anything. She had resolved to leave it until after she had seen Adelaide's physician in the morning, just so she could be absolutely sure. Truthfully, there was a part of her that wanted to keep John all for herself for just a little bit longer. She knew that they were on the precipice of a big change. However, in the back of her mind, she was already concocting a devilish and cheeky plan to tell him.

John was none the wiser. Yet as he watched the day fade away before him, there was a peculiar sensation swirling around in his stomach. Taking care of Miriam as he had done today had only reinforced their relationship. Whatever people may say about their fast courtship and marriage, they knew that their love went beyond the animalistic need for sex. After all, what lust ever bathed their sickly lover? Their relationship may have started in a whirlwind, but it grew stronger with each passing day. In the back of his mind, he was concocting so many different ways in which he could shower her with love over their coming years. He resolved to start in the morning.

As night descended on the Sunday 5th April 1896, it signified that Easter was over. John and Miriam Bennett were too wrapped up in one another to be sad that another holiday had ended. After all, they both lay excitedly in the crevices of the same thought:

Tomorrow could not come soon enough.

The Interview

Thursday 30th April 1896

The name of the hospital had loomed over Polly Richards long before the building did.

Polly walked up Haymarket, with a sense of trepidation. Her chatelaine, dangling down from her white apron, jingled as ferociously as her nerves did. A spring breeze coaxed out her mahogany hair from underneath her hat. Every minute she tried desperately to hide the tangled mess away. The wind whipped around her, and she brought her navy cape closer around her shoulders, wishing she had had the time to go home and change into a warmer and more respectable outfit. Especially as there were dots of dried blood on her light blue skirt. The uniform, for once, made her feel garishly out of place.

The closer she got to the building, the harder the name of it hammered in her skull. She wondered on the astonishing power of names. Some simply slipped through your life without any note, washed away by ale after a supper. Yet some stick to the roof of your mouth, like a cut that you couldn't help but tongue. From an early age, Polly couldn't help but allow the name to roll over her tongue in different waves and with different tastes. Each with a memory clinging desperately to them.

As The Clayton Hospital came into view, her mouth became dry.

Walking up to the entrance, she curled the letter of recommendation into her hand. She tried desperately not to show her nerves though they jangled through her, causing her to suddenly scrunch up the paper. Tutting, she tried to uncrumple the note, desperately trying to smooth the creases. Polly took a deep breath.

Placing her hand on the door, she was charged with excitement. Even if the name hadn't already followed her for years, the prospect of working at The Clayton Hospital would have filled her with nauseating nerves. With the wood underneath her palms, she could practically sense the exhilarating energy that the hospital was charged with. Though the building had been built nearly four years ago, its reputation already reached out to trainee nurses and lured them through the doors. Polly wondered if she was going to make an impression, knowing how eager her fellow students were to work in this famed building.

Polly was confident in her chances.

Especially when she was so familiar with the name Clayton.

As she pushed the door open, she expected to see that same energy she had known and heard about – the charge of true progress and the power of tremendous charity. An alluring combination of ferociousness and generosity. She anticipated to see a bustling hospital. However, when she stepped through the doorway, she was shocked to see how quiet the hospital was.

There were people and patients, doctors, and nurses, but there was barely any noise. They moved slowly and silently, like a funeral procession. Polly held her breath, hesitant to make any sound so as to not stir this sombre scene before her. She looked curiously around, wondering if she was in the right place. Was it possible that she had stepped into The Clayton Hospital and crossed a threshold into a different plane? Shaking her head, Polly steeled her nerves and walked up to the reception desk.

"I have an appointment," Polly said in barely a whisper. The receptionist looked up curiously, cocking her head and leaning forward to hear her. Polly coughed and with a louder voice said, "I have an appointment with Head Nurse Lockett. At four o'clock?"

The receptionist scrunched up her nose, then turned to the books, dragging her fingers down the paper. "Ah, Polly Richards?"

"Yes."

The receptionist smiled politely. "You are early, which will work in your favour. Matron likes punctuality. Please sit. She will be here at exactly four."

Polly nodded, trying to hide a disappointing grimace as she sat patiently on a wooden chair. She wasn't entirely expecting fanfares and cheering. Yet this was not the hospital that she envisioned in her mind. This was not the building she had conjured. This was not the place she had dreamed about for so long.

Head Nurse Lockett, however, was exactly the person Polly had expected.

The stern, older woman with thin features scrutinised the letter of recommendation as though she had splayed Polly on the table and was examining her insides. It caused Polly's heart to beat wildly in her throat. She had duly warned about Matron's harsh and strict tone from her mentor – Nurse Williamson – but caution could not have prepared her for the weight of such scrutiny. Polly swallowed; the air unfortunately trundled awkwardly down, tickling at her throat. She tried desperately not to cough but it made the scratching worse. Red-faced, and bloated, she finally gave in, and spluttered out a cough.

Nurse Lockett said nothing, raising an eyebrow at her before she gently pushed over the glass of water she had poured for Polly at the beginning of the interview. Polly nodded and took small sips, cursing her own body for betraying her in such a fiendish manner. When the itching had been quelled by the cool, clear liquid, Polly sighed – annoyed and thankful all at once.

There was no clear expression on Lockett's face as she watched Polly struggle. She grew increasingly dismayed. She thought for sure that the cough had scuppered her chances. She wanted to frown indignantly but tried to force out a simple smile. It looked more like a grimace.

Head Nurse Lockett said, in a matter-of-fact manner, "You certainly come highly recommended, Polly Richards. Williamson is a dear friend of mine and, if you do not mind me saying, an utter curmudgeon. This reference speaks highly. As do your credentials. And you are dressed for the part."

The grimace softened into an actual smile this time. Polly breathed out a sigh of relief. "Thank you."

"I do have one question, however." Lockett passed Polly back her letter of recommendation and leaned backwards. The wooden chair squeaked. Though Lockett had a petite, frail frame, it was as though the years of respect weighted her, causing such an audible reaction from the furniture. "If you will permit me to say, you are considerably older than most of the freshly qualified nurses we take on."

Ouch, Polly thought to herself, gripping the letter tightly again. "My educational endeavours were… postponed… shall we say? My parents had different prospects for me."

"Marriage?"

"Marriage."

Lockett laughed, which took Polly by surprise. The younger of the two chuckled politely but feared where the conversation was leading. As if Lockett knew this hesitation, she sighed. "I take it you are not the marrying sort?"

The phrase wormed through Polly's brain in an accusatory fashion. Her chest constricted in panic as if she had been exposed entirely. Matron was making one too many incisions and Polly was incredibly afraid of the truth spilling out. Quickly, in a frightful mumble, Polly said, "I much prefer to work, Ma'am."

"Matron, please. Everyone calls me Matron." Then she drew a breath as though she were a gentleman puffing on a rich cigar. "More good women have been lost to marriage than disease, Polly. I, myself, have yet to meet a man to steer me away from my independence. We unmarried are not all lonely spinsters or hags."

"Indeed," Polly said with a firm nod as a short hot breath of relief funnelled out of her nose. She looked down and found that her finger had perforated the letter from holding it too tight. She stuffed it into her pocket quickly to hide the evidence.

"Do you wish to progress further in the field? To become a doctor?" Matron asked lightly.

"Is that possible?" Polly leaned forward excitedly, placing her hands upon the rim of the dark brown wooden desk.

"Of course, it is! We have the most wonderful Doctor Bennett in charge of the Women's Wards. If you are keen to progress, I am certain that she would be thrilled… to…" Matron trailed off. An unexpectant sadness crept onto her face, as though a dreadful memory had wriggled out of the walls. She brought her hand to her lips to stop herself from continuing. Polly could see fresh tears in Nurse Lockett's eyes and tried her best to ignore them. "Oh, well, she is indisposed at the moment. Sick. But when she is better, I have no doubt she would be happy to take you on board."

The conversation had hit a strange finality and neither woman knew how to continue. As Matron reached up to wipe the sadness from her eyes, Polly decided to look down at her chatelaine and play with the objects on her keychain. As she pressed her house keys against her index finger, she tried to picture this elusive Doctor Bennett – a woman, no less, charging this hospital with true progress. She considered the tenacity one must have to lead a department in a world of men. Polly imagined this woman both wild and free, yet intelligent and reserved. As the image flowed through her, Polly softly said, "She sounds incredible."

"Oh, she was." Matron then took a sharp intake of breath. "She *is*." Matron sat up suddenly, hitting her hand on the wood of the table to abruptly change the conversation. "Well, Polly, I would love to have you on my staff. I take new recruits twice a year, however. I am afraid you just missed January. Can you wait until September?"

Polly nodded furiously. It would be disappointing to wait five months, but she was thrilled to be offered her dream job. She bristled with happiness at the idea of joining the fray at The Clayton Hospital. "I would be honoured."

The two women smiled happily at one another then stood up to formally shake on the deal. As they spoke about dates and contracts, Polly's current employment at the Elizabeth Garrett Hospital, and any minor details, a question reemerged in Polly. She had it stuck to the roof of her mouth since she walked quietly through the door. She looked for the answer in the faces of people strolling through the corridor. As she sat with Head Nurse Lockett, the question loomed over her with the name and the building. As they spoke of most ordinary things, Polly wondered if she had the gall to ask it.

Yet as she was ushered out of the office, Polly thought better of it. The question hung over her, however, as Matron walked her back through the corridors of the Women's Building. The older nurse spoke about the many different features of the building, but Polly did not properly listen. Instead, she once again looked at the faces of each person they passed, scanning their features for someone familiar, hoping to see a pair of navy-blue eyes. The question burned on her tongue.

By the time they reached the entrance, Polly resigned to swallow the inquiry whole.

After all, it did not seem like the time nor the place to enquire about an old friend.

Not when Polly could find her in September.

The prospect almost dizzied her.

There were just two sips left of Polly's tea. The last of a cup that had been gently drunk over the past hour or so. They stewed, growing colder by the second. Polly had not the heart to drink them. The sooner she did, the sooner she would be ushered out. They had to stay so that Polly could stay. Every so often, she would pick up the cup, and pretend to take a sip but the remnants would stay untouched.

Polly did not have the money to waste on more beverages – or food for that matter. Often, she would pause reading her book, and remove her coin bag from her skirt pocket. She'd count the coins, hoping that in the spaces between this routine, the money had magically doubled in size so she could grab a bun or roll to satisfy the growing hunger within. When no such miracle happened, she resigned herself to starve until she was home.

There were only twenty minutes left before the tearoom closed anyhow. Then Polly could walk home and enjoy whatever food she had left in the pantry. She dared not leave a second sooner, despite the lack of food or funds. Polly's stomach growled loudly in protest.

Perhaps it was just Polly's imagination, but the sound of hunger roared throughout the small, silent shop. She flushed from embarrassment, despite being one of the only two people in the tearoom. The other was the waitress, who was busying herself behind the counter. Polly darted her eyes over and swallowed nervously. There was no reaction to her guttural moans. She breathed out of relief and turned back to her book.

As with the tea, the novel had yet to progress from the pages Polly had started with when she sat down over an hour ago. She had read the same lines and paragraphs over and over again, unable to take the words properly. If she was honest with herself, she hadn't really read much of the book. She had just sat with it open on the same page, at the same time, in the same seat, of the same tearoom. Every day for the past fortnight. Taking another fake sip, she pretended to fake read again.

"The Sorrows of Satan?" came a low estuary voice from above her. Polly jumped suddenly, closing the book as if she had been caught reading the most salacious story. Looking up, the waitress was suddenly looming over her. Polly's eyes glazed over the woman's full-figured frame that she hid in a simple, black skirt, and a dark-purple blouse. Around her collar was a red bowtie. Her jet-black hair was fashionably styled like a Gibson girl. In one hand, the waitress held a white teapot that was patterned with blue flowers and butterflies. In the other, she held two matching cups. The waitress gestured to the book. "Any good?"

Polly looked at the cover, smiled, and nodded. "Oh, yes," she lied, "engrossing."

"What's it about?"

"Oh erm… it is about an artist… and the devil and…"

"Some sorrows?" The waitress raised an eyebrow causing Polly's stomach to twist.

"Well, yes."

"Sounds charming."

"Indeed." The pair of women chuckled politely at one another. Polly suddenly noticed the time. It was exactly six. She scrambled her things quickly, closing the book and bending it so it could slip easily into one of her skirt pockets. Polly spoke fast, "Oh forgive me, I suppose you are here to tell me to leave."

"Nothing of the sort." The waitress then placed the two cups and the teapot on the table. "But I've been working on a special brew, and I wondered if you'd like to join me?"

"Oh, I erm…" Polly hesitated, thinking of the lowly set of coins in her possession.

"On the house. A reward for being my most-valued customer. Oh and…" The waitress rushed back to the counter, removing two cream buns from the display case and putting them on a plate. She shoved it in front of Polly, whose face twisted in horror. The waitress must've heard her wailing stomach. "They'll just go stale. Waste not, want not, and all that." The waitress did not wait for a response. Instead, there was a loud sound of scraping wood as she sat in the seat opposite Polly. She reached over and grabbed a bun, scoffing it without a care. As Polly timidly reached for her own, the pair smiled kindly at one another. Through crumbs, the waitress said, "I'm Lily. Lily Andrews."

"Polly. Polly Richards."

Lily wiped her hand and then reached out. Polly gently took it, and the pair shook. There was a stiff, formality to the beginning of the action before a warm, tingling sensation emanated through Polly. Lily's hands were somewhat coarse and tanned, but they were inviting. As was the playful glint in Lily's olive-green eyes. Polly practically dithered over it. When they broke from the handshake, she blushed and wished she hadn't tucked the book away. It would've made a great hiding spot. All at once, she felt exposed. She fidgeted with the bun in her hand, pinching small bites and swallowing them down.

"I shall play mother," Lily said with a grin as she leaned over and lifted the teapot as a magician would at the start of his trick. She even waved a hand mystically over the vessel. In a hushed tone, she continued, "Now, Polly Richards. I want you to watch very carefully. Watch closely. This mysterious liquid will certainly confound you."

Polly frowned but took the advice. She watched as Lily calmly and carefully poured the liquid from the white pot into the matching teacups. A brilliant blue colour concoction appeared which caused Polly to gasp as it hit the bottom of the pale cup. "My word, blue tea."

"Blue tea," Lily said in a chuckle as she poured her own drink, picked up the cup, and slipped back into her chair, satisfied that the trick had suitably entertained. She then noticed Polly hesitating. As Lily took a sip, showing that it wasn't poison, she said, "Aparajita flower. 'armless. Known for fighting stresses and melancholy. Useful if one were experiencing a particularly bad case of the morbs."

Taking the cup, Polly sipped. The tea was unusual but sweet. Most importantly, it was warm. Polly nodded gratefully. "I suppose I should inquire about your extensive knowledge of teas but…"

Polly gestured around the room as she swallowed the last bit of her bun. "You do work here."

Lily looked around the pokey tearoom as though it were the first time she had ever seen the place. It was a small shop with a light-pink façade. The walls were a deeper shade of pink and had many shelves with different, brightly coloured teapots and kettles on them. Behind the dark wooden counter were jars and jars of herbs and spices. Lily glided her eyes over every detail before she turned back to Polly. "My dear, I own the place."

Aghast, Polly's eyes widened. "Oh!"

"It is called Lily's Tearoom, after all."

Polly did not know how to continue. It was an unintentional swipe. After all, she had never really taken notice of the name. Just the colourful façade. The shop, which was nestled in Dean Street, Soho, was something she had stumbled upon whilst walking through the city. In need of a refreshment, she had headed into the place and immediately found a liking for it. Despite being a somewhat arduous journey from both the Elizabeth Garrett Hospital where she worked and her dorm rooms in Victoria, Polly had started to come here regularly. "Forgive me, Lily. I did not mean to offend."

"Oh, fret not." Lily beamed brightly which made Polly somewhat lightheaded and goofy. "Though I suppose this means I need a more eye-catching sign…"

The door of the tearoom slammed open causing both women to jump and yelp at the same time. Lily scrambled upwards, brushing herself down as though she were making herself presentable for whatever wayward customer had entered her business after closing hours. Polly turned around and was surprised to find a gentleman standing, breathless in the shop.

"Walter!" Lily exclaimed loudly before rushing over to him. "You're early!"

Walter smiled weakly and apologetically though he stared solely at Polly. Walter was a short, thin man whose black suit was baggy on him. He wore a red necktie that matched his pocket square. Crooked in one hand was an umbrella, though there was no rain today, and on top of his head sat a grey bowler.

Lily walked over to him, her hands outstretched to greet him, and Walter took them and squeezed them tightly. A pebble of disappointment sank in Polly's stomach. It did not help that Walter's deep-brown eyes were still scrutinising Polly. They did not leave her. Not even when he said to Lily, "I could no longer stand to be in the same room as him, Lily. The whole affair was excruciating."

"Understandable. But you are 'ere now. That is all that matters." Lily followed his gaze to Polly, who felt her face grow hot and scarlet. Lily sighed before turning back to Walter as she muttered. "Your sister Minnie is waiting downstairs."

"Are you most certain she is safe to be here?" He nodded swiftly to Polly which caused her to slip down in her chair. She wanted to turn away from this scene but thought that rude somehow.

Surprising both Walter and Polly, Lily began to laugh. She let go of his hands and slapped Walter a bit too jovially on the arm, causing him to fall to the side somewhat. "New recruit, Walt. New recruit."

"Oh?" Walter said, finally alleviating Polly from his gaze. Lily grinned goofily at him which caused Walter to exclaim, "OH! Oh, I see." He then finally tipped his hat politely to Polly. "It's a pleasure… I… erm?"

"Polly," she replied, mouse-like and afraid. The word recruit blazed in her mind dangerously. There was no discernible look on the other's faces to give Polly a clue as to what she had been recruited for. She gripped the back of the chair to steady the nerves that were shaking through her as she began to regret ever setting foot in this pink tea parlour.

"Ah. Polly. Hello." He smiled innocently enough to make Polly's fear somewhat subside. He took off his hat, showing gelled-back blonde hair, and hung it alongside his umbrella on the stand, by the door. "I best go see my sister Minnie, if that is quite alright?"

"Certainly," Lily replied.

Just as quickly as he had arrived, Walter rushed around the counter, and then he had all but disappeared. His footsteps sounded out as he walked down into an unseen basement. The waitress hesitated as she stood looking at Polly. She fiddled with her fingertips before she said quickly, "Every Thursday, Minnie, our friends, and I like to gather 'ere for our club. The Women's Fencing and Archery Society – is what we call ourselves. There's just a few of us. I thought you might like to join."

Polly stared at Lily for a while, dumbfounded by the proposition. The scene she had just witnessed busied around her mind, flipping like a kineograph. She brought her fingers to her lips and rubbed them deftly, trying to procure the right words for the situation. In a calm, collected and childlike whisper, she said, "I haven't the foggiest on how to do either of those things."

That playful glint sparkled in Lily's eyes again. "I didn't neither. You will eventually find yourself quite proficient, I am sure. At the very least, join us for this meeting? I am positive your mind will change once you me—"

The door swung open again. This time with a loud bang. It reverberated around Polly's head. She was sure a headache was about to form. Especially as the calamitous thud was followed by two, loud, squabbling voices.

"The thing is Andrea…" came the squeakier of the two.

"Smith." A stout voice.

"Yes, right, of course, *Smith*. The thing is that if you are going to parade yourself around in that attire through the streets of Soho, you are going to get gawked at. Oh, hello Lily, we nearly walked straight into you there, and OH HELLO? SOMEONE NEW!"

Two people now stood in the spot where Walter had been. Their eyes similarly fixated on Polly. Her knuckles were now white thanks to gripping the chair to steady herself. This evening had turned into a whirlwind. In front of her stood two very different people, though they had a similar height.

The woman who had wildly addressed Polly the moment she had entered the tearoom was smiling broadly. She was tall and square, from her body to her face, with light-brown hair curled in a bun atop her head, though some wayward strands had fallen down. She wore a cream and pink striped day-dress with large sleeves and a pink prairie bow around her neck. She carried a small pearl-coloured parasol that matched her earrings, bracelet, and gloves.

The other was frowning, scrutinising Polly in an unforgiving gaze. They were stocky, with a big puffy chest that strained the buttons of their suit and waistcoat. They wore an entire three-piece suit ensemble, with a yellow-gold waistcoat, a wine-red cravat, and a teal, velvet-tailed jacket. Atop their head was a grand-burgundy top-hat with a peacock feather protruding from it. Strands of their wavy blonde hair framed their face but the rest of it was gathered underneath the almighty hat. They wore tiny round glasses at the end of their small nose and had a half-smoked cigar rolling around their mouth. Judging by the conversation Polly had just witnessed, she deduced that this was Smith.

Lily was nervously silent. She extended a welcoming, introductory arm at Polly. "Ladies, this is Polly. Polly, meet Smith and Gertie."

"Hmm, charmed," Smith said, puffing smoke into the air like a steam-train. Smith then turned to Gertie and continued their conversation, "I must attest that I expected gawks and stares – especially as I am looking so devilishly dashing – I think I took offence mostly to the man calling me a freak."

"An absolute insult, yes, but no reason for you to kick him on the shin."

"It was an accident! I swear it."

"You are an absolute terror A—sorry—Smith. And bugger and blast it, you are being terribly rude to our guest." Gertie walked excitedly over to Polly again, who was dizzy from the new names and faces swimming around her head. "Are you going to be joining us tonight?"

Polly flapped open her mouth and closed it again. She was taken by a calamitous tension. She would be lying if she didn't want to gather her things and run out of this tea shop, never to darken its doorstep ever again. For a short while, she stared at no one in particular until she caught Lily's encouraging gaze. Olive eyes and a spirited smile that melted any nerves into a sudden resolve. Polly did not say anything to the trio in front of her, all expecting an answer.

Instead, she swallowed her consternation and nodded.

The basement of Lily's Tearoom was not what Polly was expecting. Instead of boxes of supplies, and more jars, the dank venue was almost completely empty. Though lit by as many lamplights as possible, there were many parts covered in shadows. Enough to make Polly squeamish entering such unknown territory. A few chairs and a table sat on one end of the room, whilst at the other end was one large, beige target – punctured from practice. As she walked down the steps behind the others, Polly was both impressed and terrified.

However, when she went to inquire about the room, she found that Lily had momentarily disappeared, slipping into the shadows of the basement.

Now standing in the middle of the room, without the comfort of her somewhat friend, she felt as exposed as she was in Matron's office. What had started as a daily visit to her favourite parlour had grown into something new and uncertain. Many beady eyes clamoured over her and made their surgical incisions, trying to deduce what sat under the skin of this wayward nurse. A worrying sweat spread across Polly's brow and her nurse's uniform felt more like a silly costume. It was as though she were a peacock entering the lion's den. She expected to be devoured instantly.

In a row of chairs in front of Polly sat Smith, Gertie, and another new face - Lady Minnie Cheatham. Walter had all but disappeared. Polly looked around the room but found only traces of him in his sister. They must've been twins. They shared everything: The same-coloured eyes, the same stature, the same dark-blonde hair. Only Lady Minnie's was more of a pompadour style atop her head. She wore a red and black evening dress with a plunging neckline though it lay flat against her chest. A silver necklace with red jewels decorated her pale skin.

Lady Minnie shuffled awkwardly under Polly's gaze. The young nurse tried to apologise by softening her features and nodding. It worked because Lady Minnie breathed out a sigh of relief and smiled back.

Stuffing tobacco into a pipe, and lighting it with a match, Smith said gruffly, "Honestly, Lily, this woman is clearly no fencer."

Polly agreed but was slighted by the tone. She tried to stand up a little stiffer, to show she wasn't bruised by the accusation. Staring straight ahead, above the heads of the glaring three, she decided she wasn't going to show a single emotion. She didn't even waver when Gertie prodded Smith sharply with her elbows. "You said the

same of me and one could say I am the finest *fencer* of them all."
She giggled wildly – in high-pitched squeals and wheezes.

"Never a truer statement Gert," Lady Minnie breathed out. She
spoke in a hushed, altered light tone.

"I weren't much of a fencer myself Smith." Lily was suddenly
beside Polly which caused her to startle once more. She wasn't sure
if her heart could take the surprises. As she took several deep
breaths, she focused her attention on the bow and arrow in Lily's
hand. Noting the curiosity, Lily winked at Polly which caused the
latter to dither somewhat on the spot. Lily took the arrow and
placed it upon the bow stretching the string widely. She took the
archer's position and aimed the arrowhead straight at Smith who
did not falter from their bemused and still somewhat stern
expression. Lily quickly spun around and shot the arrow at the
target. A bullseye. "I am much more proficient at archery."

The three seated clapped wildly.

"Good show Lily, though I would've much preferred if you
kept to your original target." It was Smith's turn to prod Gertie
with their elbow. "Ow! Lily was trained by the great P.L.
Lawrence," Gertie said to Polly then slapped her hand across her
mouth. "Oh, Goodness, I bet you don't know about Penelope
Lawrence. No matter, we'll teach you everything."

"Indeed, we will teach you everything. I'd say you're more of
an archer anyway." Lily said, stepping closer to Polly so that their
shoulders brushed up against one another. Polly could practically
hear her own pulse – it drummed in her ear so loudly that she
could barely catch what Lily said next. "I would love to have you in

our little group, Polly, but like most societies, there is an induction process. We need to see if you really are an archer."

"But I've never... I don't know... I..."

"No matter, I'll show you."

Lily thrust the bow in Polly's hand then walked across the room to retrieve the arrow from the target. When she returned, she unexpectedly spun Polly around, facing away from the eagerly prying audience. Their stares still burned. Lily then stood behind Polly, reaching around to position Polly's arms with the bow and arrow.

All of this, being instructed on the correct shooting method, should've made Polly more confident. However, as Lily's arms brushed against hers, Polly melted into the movements. The waitress she had admired for many weeks, so much so that she dragged her tired body to her tearoom every day, stood dangerously close to Polly. So close that she could smell the Lily's floral perfume. A bouquet reminiscent of her name. The warmth of her skin similarly enveloped her, making it hard for Polly to concentrate. She took a sharp intake of breath, holding it once more as Lily nestled her chin on Polly's shoulder, Lily's lips were moments away from Polly's cheek. "There, Polly," Lily cooed gently, "that's right, now all you 'ave to do is focus on the target. Very good. Stretch the string back on the bow. Yes, there we are. Now release when I say so, got it?"

"Got it."

There was an excited whinny from those behind her. Polly could hear the squeaking of the chairs as they shuffled eagerly forward. Polly tried to pay them no mind as Lily's hands settled on hers. A rush pummelled through her as she waited for the signal.

The earth seemed to turn an eternity before Lily said lowly, "Let go, Polly."

The words brushed upon Polly's cheeks.

They were followed by Lily's lips.

In a thunderous heartbeat, the world had frozen. The heat of the moment blossomed on her face and suddenly Polly thought of all the times she had found herself in the tearoom, sitting in the same chair, at the same time, reading the same book. Day after day, page after page, tea after tea – she sat and stole glances at the waitress. She remembered how quickly she had committed to the routine – how swiftly she had decided the minute she found those olive-green eyes.

Polly pondered on the astonishing power of strangers. It is amazing how someone can loom over you without ever knowing their name. Polly had pictured this woman's lips upon her in many ways – slow and ravaging, fast and rampant. Yet in all her dreaming, she never pictured how perfect it would feel – even if it was a small, soft touch gazing at her skin. Now Polly had more than just Lily's name. She had new eyes to stalk her and a new warm world to explore.

The beat unfroze. The kiss spiralled through her system. It had a devastating effect on Polly. She suddenly gasped loudly. She did, indeed, follow the instructions but released both the arrow and the bow at the same time. They clattered to the floor, neither having flown very far. The sound echoed then silenced the room.

As Polly grew red from the moment, she tried to compose herself. After all, she had failed the test. Lily stepped away from her and Polly felt like a complete fool. What was worse was that she thought Lily had tricked her cruelly. The kiss was only to undo and mortify her in front of the others. Polly couldn't help it as tears welled up in her eyes.

Suddenly, there was a thunderous applause from behind her.

"Oh, bravo Polly, well done!"

"Jolly good show!"

"That was *wonderful*!"

As Polly turned around, she saw that everyone was on their feet, clapping and smiling wildly at her. She wiped the tears away as she looked bewildered at the scene before her. The applause subsided and Polly had no idea how to react. She was scared and yet excited all at once. Somehow, she did not feel strange in this basement anymore. Quickly, Lily wrapped an arm around Polly and pulled her close, "I am dreadfully sorry for the imposition. I 'ad to make sure you were truly one of us, Polly."

"One of us?"

For once, Lily wavered on the spot. "Oh, 'ow do I put it?"

"A gentleman jack?" bellowed Smith.

"Has yet to take up a man?" replied Lady Minnie.

"Not the marrying sort?" chimed Gertie.

The realisation dawned on Polly like a soothing balm over her skin. She took an unexpected step backwards from the eagerly smiling quartet as she processed not what they were saying, but what they were offering. Polly had known she was a lesbian at a young age which meant she had flitted through life constantly hiding herself away from others. In the small town which she grew up in, Polly had shrouded herself in secrecy and shame. When she moved to London, she wondered if the city could finally be her home. It was loud and boisterous, vibrant, and vast, with lots of secret places for people to hide in.

Could home be in this dark, dank basement of a pink tearoom?

Polly realised that the room was quiet, waiting for her response. Hoarsely, she stuttered out, "So you are all... like..."

"Let's just say that the only man in my life is the one in my name," Lily said. She grabbed and shook her fiercely again, causing Polly to chuckle. "Muffin wallopers, the lot of us. This society is our safe 'aven. So, we can all be ourselves. It is marvellous that you've come on board. If you so wish to, that is." The other three had already begun to move the chairs around the table. Polly watched the scene unfold as though she were Alice at the Mad Hatter's tea party. They were suddenly setting places for the five of them. Five chairs. Five teacups. In the blur, someone was pouring a bottle of Old Tom gin into the cups in celebration. The women took their places excitedly, first Minnie, then Gertie, then Smith, and then Lily. They turned expectantly to Polly as Lily said, whilst gesturing to the empty chair beside her, "Do you wish to be?"

Polly took a deep breath. "More than anything."

Another round of applause. Polly rushed towards the table and sat in the space reserved for her. Her shoulders brushed gleefully up against Lily's. They lifted a toast to her the minute she sat down, causing her face to turn scarlet again. As she took a timid sip, Lily nudged her gently, and grinned. "Welcome home."

The chatter of the evening clung to the air with the cigarette smoke. The last laughter echoed down the streets. Three of the group – Smith, Minnie, and Gertie – had left together, merry from finding a new acquaintance, and the gin that someone had provided. Though no one could quite remember who. The two they left behind were sober – neither having the need nor inclination to drink further than the congratulatory toast. Neither wanted to spoil the evening, or their moods, with liquor.

Polly and Lily looked at one another as the group peeled off into the night. Frozen as they both thought about how the night had turned out and the sweetness of Lily's kiss. When the door slammed shut, they jumped and moved into action. Polly rushed to her cape, still draped over her chair, whilst Lily collected the cups, and moved them to the sink out back. There was a clatter of crockery before she returned with a cloth and a smile.

"Shall I call for a carriage?" Lily said. She began cleaning the tables of the tearoom, busying herself with the night-time chores as though she paid no mind at all to having changed Polly's life. She brushed away the evening with a frayed, striped cloth and a small smile.

"Oh no. It is fine." Polly wrapped the blue cape around her shoulders and tried desperately not to look Lily in the eyes again, for fear of turning completely pink and blending into the tearoom walls. Polly struggled with the strings, losing them completely as she fumbled with all the emotions she was feeling. "I only live in Victoria and could do with the walk."

"I am not altogether certain I should let you leave alone. A young woman was viciously attacked just around the corner from here a few weeks ago. It don't feel safe." Lily sighed, placing the cloth down and walking over to Polly. Suddenly she was as close as she had been during the archery lesson. Polly swallowed as Lily began to tie the strings of the cape. "I have a few errands to run 'ere but I'd gladly chaperone you to your digs."

"But where do you live?"

"Oh." There was a distinct pause. "Well, upstairs."

"So then, who will walk you home?" Polly chuckled nervously but cursed her tongue. She didn't know why she was dismissing this notion so quickly. She wondered how sweet the stroll would be, stealing glances and looks as they walked through this bustling city. Yet she was stalled – hesitating on the proposition. She half-wished that Lily had invited her to stay.

"God, you're not going to make this easy, are you?" Lily reached upwards and straightened the collar of Polly's blouse, skimming her fingertips against Polly's neck. Polly tried desperately not to shudder loudly, but a slender sigh slipped from her mouth. Lily smiled as though she had procured the exact response that she had wanted. "Very well, but I expect you back 'ere promptly tomorrow."

Then Lily kissed Polly. Gently and politely on the lips. As though they were merely friends bidding each other goodbye. But the very action caused Polly to smile brightly. The sensation pirouetted on her skin like a petal skimming down from the tallest blossom. She breathed out a soft goodbye and gave Lily a plentiful, knowing nod in return.

Polly left the tearoom, practically skipping off into the night.

Walking back down Haymarket, Polly's heart raced desperately in her chest. The night was dark and unforgiving as the dim lamp lights flickered above her. She did not care for the lonely stroll back to her dorm rooms in Victoria.

Over the course of the day, Polly had happily collected three things: A new job for September, at a hospital she had long admired; a new group of friends who shared similar likes and interests; and a possible new love – one with olive eyes and jet-black hair. Lily somehow could see more of her than anyone.

Well, almost anyone.

Polly walked around the outskirts of a now-dark St James' Park, choosing a more scenic route for her thoughts as she merrily drifted into them, intoxicated from the blissful day. She grabbed her chatelaine and played with the keys and ornaments, partly to use in self-defence, and partly to fidget with a memory. As the keys jangled, she let her mind flow backwards. She fiddled with the moment between her fingertips, pressing her keys between her fingers and picturing a hand that similarly did the same.

In that moment, she knew why she had dismissed Lily's offer. Someone else was clearly seated in the back of her mind. There was someone else that she had desperately wanted to see at the hospital. There was someone else whom she wished to walk home with.

Walking further and further from the tearoom and the hospital, Polly could only think on one name. The name that blasted building bore. That name that had stalked her so sweetly since she was fifteen. That name brought forth the memory of an old friend in a sweet blaze of navy-blue eyes.

Polly Richards smirked in the shadows of the evening.

Indeed, this day had brought so much into her life.

But what excited her most is how much closer it had brought her to Miriam Clayton.

The Birthday

John had been planning Miriam's birthday since his own last November. His wife had treated him to a whole wealth of presents. There were the ordinary gifts of expensive cigars, whisky, and fine clothes. There were theatre tickets to *The Notorious Mrs Ebbsmith* at the Garrick which both Bennetts were keen to see. She had treated him to a new cricket kit and purchased a book of Aubrey Beardsley illustrations as well as John's very first copy of The Yellow Book.

all these things, however, she had planned for mischief. The pair, sadly, had to work at the hospital. In the morning, they wandered into the building together, but Miriam followed him to his office. She pouted and told him repeatedly that she didn't want to leave him on such a special day. He laughed at her sincerity, replying that they would have the evening all to themselves.

"Another birthday gift then?" she whispered and then instructed him to sit down on his chair and from her bag, she produced a rope. John's eyes practically bulged with exhilaration. Tying his hands to the chair, Miriam began to tease him. She kissed him repeatedly, grinding her body on him. Her hands writhed over his body until he was stiff with delight. Throbbing against his trousers, John panted heavily, waiting for her to release him so they could make ardent love.

However, just when he was about to explode. Miriam stopped and walked out of the office, locking him in. For a short while, John laughed out of confusion. He watched the door, expecting her to romp back in at any minute. Then, after an hour had gone, he realised he was trapped here. At first, he tried to get himself loose from the rope, but Miriam was too good at restraining him. Her knots were unfathomable. Daring not to call out and have one of his colleagues find him in this situation, John realised he would remain stuck until she released him.

The entrapment caused a cavalcade of emotions to run through him. Anger, frustration, and most strongly, excitement.

They'd power through him in waves. Each time he thought of her return, he'd harden and groan from the anticipation.

When Miriam returned, late in the afternoon, there was a sheepishness on her face. Though she tried to keep a sultry, sexy expression as she slowly walked over, it was clear she hadn't meant to leave him in here so long. John looked at her aghast as she untied him. When free, she removed her drawers, hitched her skirts up, and bent over the desk. Though he was still eager for her, John paused. She couldn't see the slick smile on his face as he hesitated. He knew the pause would drive her wild. When Miriam let out a little gasp of frustration, John unbuckled his braces, released his member from his trousers, and then took her roughly. He released all those emotions he had been feeling as he pounded into her harder and harder, shaking the desk, the office, and practically the whole hospital. She whimpered and yelped with joy as he did. When John gleefully released himself, he gruffly asked her to do it again – having never fucked her as hard as he did right there and then.

In such a short time together, Miriam understood him empathically. There were life-long marriages who didn't know each other the way the Bennetts did. Back home, they made slow, ardent love for the entire evening of his birthday, entwined together – perfect and naked - as the day ended. Wordlessly, John vowed to show her the same amount of affection and understanding on her birthday.

From that point, John started planning it all. He noted every little thing that she grew excited about but didn't buy for herself. The necklaces that caught her eye, the really expensive teas that she'd dismiss as too indulgent, and the books she pawed at before, ultimately, saving them for another time, John would hurry out and buy. He collected all these gifts, hiding them away in parts of his office and the house.

His biggest surprise was a trip to Paris. The pair had both read about the city of love and all its sordid places in Montmartre that were perfect for these divine sinners. After their Valentine's Day performance, John was adamant that visiting the illustrious Moulin Rouge was a must. He secretly booked time off for the pair of them and purchased the tickets and hotel. By March, John could barely contain his excitement, having never left the country before nor had a wife in which he could shower this much love on.

The trip would never happen.

Miriam's birthday fell in early May.

And April had changed everything.

Instead of boarding a train to a different country, Miriam was bedridden and broken in the guest room of their home. Instead of traipsing through the streets of a new bustling city, John was tending to his wounded and woeful wife. Instead of sharing their love in a land across the sea, they were both suffering different types of heartbreak.

However, when her birthday came around, John still wanted to try for her. He wanted the day to be as special as it could, in spite of her pains. There was, after all, a pile of gifts. John could dole them out throughout the day so as to not overwhelm her. John wanted her to feel loved for the entirety of her birthday, so he would bestow these little treasures whenever she looked sad or despondent. Some presents, such as corsets and garters, were to remain unopened.

Lying fully clothed, in his best cream day suit, John watched her sleeping peacefully. Propped up on the pillow, breathing out of her nose heavily, Miriam looked angelic. It was one of her quieter slumbers, where she wasn't twitching and turning from nightmares. At that moment, John wished for her to stay this way – in this sweet, heavenly plane where the horrors of the world had not touched her. Where she remained so blissfully boisterous and exceptionally excited about everything. John lamented and trembled at the thought.

This serenity would not last long

Miriam frowned as she slept, her eyes rushing wildly beneath her eyelids. She grimaced and began moaning frantically, her breathing became faster. John froze in his quiet adulation for her as sorrow began to swell and tears formed in his eyes. He swallowed and pinched the bridge of his nose, knowing she was moments away from waking and did not wish for her to see him this way.

When Miriam snapped open her eyes, she instinctively reached for John's arm and gripped it tightly. There was a sigh of relief as she picked up his arm and wrapped it around her for comfort. He snuggled closer to her lightly as she whispered with a slight croak in her voice, "You're here."

"Always," he said and kissed her on her cheek. As Miriam held onto him tightly, her eyes opening and closing as she tried to dismiss the terror of her own mind, John stayed silent. He wanted to enjoy this moment – just the two of them, locked in a fierce and loving embrace. They almost fell asleep together, as though nothing else mattered but the sound and rhythm of one another's breathing.

Miriam moaned, however, and muttered, "What day is it?"

"Wednesday. The 13th …" There were a few beats before he whispered, "Happy birthday, darling."

"Oh!" Miriam exclaimed, struggling to sit up in bed. She winced as she moved and John helped her, placing cushions so she sat comfortably. There was an undeniable excitement that flashed in her eyes. John wished to grab it and force it to stay for the entirety of the day. As she breathed out from the pain of movement, she said, "It's my birthday?"

"Yes." He breathed in nervously. From underneath his pillow, he pulled out a small package. It was haphazardly wrapped in brown paper with a piece of red string around it. He cautiously handed it over to her and waited for her reaction.

"Oh John, you shouldn't have." Shyly, she pawed over the present as though it were the first time that she had ever received a gift. Flicking her eyes up at him in a childlike wonder, she looked for permission, to which he nodded eagerly. She unwrapped a small tin of expensive tea from Fortnum & Mason.

"The finest tea I could find," John stated as she thanked him dearly whilst clutching the tin close to her chest happily. "Therefore, I believe it deserves the finest vessel." From behind him, he removed a small box. Inside of it was an ornate porcelain tea-set. The pot and cups were white. There were delicate roses painted all over them and a gold rim.

Miriam gasped at the detail, her eyes memorising every inch of the set. John always thought Miriam looked the most beautiful in these moments – she met every new thing with a childlike wonder and most gifts with an unshakeable graciousness. Somehow seeing it in these dark days made John somewhat hopeful. He smiled warmly at her. "I shall fix us breakfast."

The pair ate in the morning in the exact same way they had done since they'd been married. Miriam would eat plentifully from a tray and John would swipe a bread roll, then read her the news from the paper in between bites. Even after the attack, they always had breakfast together as John often never left her side unless to do chores around the house. Today, Miriam only managed a few morsels of eggs before she gave up – sick from her medication and her injuries. Miserably, she leaned her head against his shoulder and listened to his soft, deep voice fall around her like a children's lullaby.

Following their meal, John examined her injuries. Miriam took a deep breath to steel herself as he did. He started with her cheek as he massaged ointment into her scar. The bruising around her eye had mostly gone. Then John took her broken hand which was still stiff and sore. However, she had much more mobility than before. To distract herself from his examination, Miriam would marvel at the way he studied her and administered his treatment. He was an absolutely assured doctor.

Every time, she would earnestly say, "You must go back, John."

"We've discussed this," John replied in a matter-of-fact manner, "not until you can move around by yourself."

To prove his point, John took her hands and they tried to get her out of bed. She could barely move without being winded from the pain. She breathed and wheezed heavily, trying not to scream out loud. He laid her back down on the bed.

In between breaths, Miriam groaned. "It's been over a month; your patients need you."

"You need me."

"Well, quite frankly, I have grown rather tired of your face."

"Oh, you liar!" he exclaimed, and the pair laughed loudly together. It was the first joke Miriam had made since the attack. She sounded so much like herself that John nearly cried again. He beamed and celebrated each one of her giggles, even as they subsided.

For it was a fleeting moment. All of the laughter would go when John removed Miriam's nightgown. He had to, of course, to inspect her broken and bruised ribs amongst other injuries across her body. But the thought of being naked in the bright daylight bristled in her. She winced as he touched and massaged her. He muttered curiously, "There appears to be little bruising and swelling. I am concerned that you are still in a considerable amount of pain.

Miriam shook her head dismissively. "I am positive it will heal soon."

Though he eyed her curiously, John nodded before taking the laudanum from her bedside drawer. He poured her a spoonful to take to help ease the agony. As she swallowed the tincture, he said cautiously, "May I bathe you?"

She took a sharp intake of breath. "Yes, John, you may."

He brought round a basin of warm water and a cloth. This was a part of their routine that they both hated. Neither would talk about why, nor would they admit to themselves the reason for such anguish. Instead, they tried to meet the task with aplomb. As John gradually glided a warm, wet cloth over her chest and arms, he would talk to her about the new book he was reading, or he'd divulge an interesting surgical fact that she may not know. Every time she would watch his mouth and face, and cling onto his words, so she didn't have to think about how his hands were gliding down her nude body. When John reached her privates, Miriam grabbed hold of his arm tightly and listened intently as he spoke about stuff and nonsense.

Afterwards, he got a fresh towel to clean up her tears.

He dressed her in a new white nightie but then handed her another brown paper package. Inside was a deep purple dressing gown. It was lavish and made of silk. She glided her fingers over the soft material in awe whilst expressing her gratitude once more. As he helped her put it on, she smiled, stretching out her arms as though she had grown new skin.

There was a hesitant moment before John said, in barely a whisper, "How do you feel about visitors today?"

Miriam's smile dropped suddenly causing John's cheeks to burn. Immediately he wished he hadn't said anything. Since her return from the hospital, Miriam hadn't had many visitors. Certainly not many that she could remember, having been heavily sedated or lost in her own agony for the first few weeks of recovery. In spite of her many well-wishers, only a handful were allowed to see her this way and even then, they had overwhelmed her completely. However, as she mused on the prospect, she turned to John, "Who?"

"I have Adelaide and Michael waiting in the wings," John replied in a rhythm that he had been rehearsing all day, "and your father has expressed interest in seeing you."

Miriam scrunched up her nose at the last sentence. "Perhaps another day for father?"

"Indeed." There was a pause. "Adelaide and Michael?"

Taking a deep inhalation, Miriam wavered over the question. John's heart was unexpectedly racing in his throat. He was excited in many ways about seeing their dear friends; joyfully so because it had been a long time since they all had spent time together; happily so because he found great comfort in seeing familiar friendly faces; terribly so because John needed a break from tending to Miriam and she needed a break from his attentiveness. Above all these things, John knew that Adelaide would bring nothing less than her warmth. Miriam still looked unsure at the prospect, but when she caught her husband's eyes, she softened into a gentle smile. "That would be nice, John."

Instead of him visiting, Sir Fredric had sent a large bouquet of flowers for Miriam - brightly coloured gerbera daisies - and a bottle of port for John. His note was just one word, though it conveyed his meaning exceptionally. It read: Understood.

Adelaide and Michael Jenkins had arrived promptly at 3pm. They lingered with John in the hallway for a long time in silence after exchanging pleasantries, all three of them unsure what to say or do. John hesitantly looked over at Adelaide, who was far more pregnant than he realised. He wondered if the very sight of her would cause Miriam to take a backwards step in her recovery and was on the verge of nearly sending the pair away.

However, Adelaide took a breath to dismiss the turgid atmosphere. "Are these adequate John?"

In her hands, she held a comically large bouquet of roses, requested from John. They matched the present that sat in his jacket pocket. He hoped to present Miriam with both, alongside her two closest friends. Reaching over to take them from Adelaide, John smiled brightly. "Exquisite, Adelaide. She will adore them."

"Well, let us not dither any longer, I wish to see my darling Miriam." Adelaide chucked slightly as she gestured to the stairs before pulling up the side of her skirt. John nodded. Despite carrying the flowers, John extended his arm to her to loop through and then began charily guiding Adelaide up the stairs.

"If you'll permit me, I'd rather stay here," Michael suddenly said in a frightfully childlike whisper. He was practically trembling when he looked up the staircase. All colours had left his face and he gripped onto the rim of his bowler hat to steady himself. Apologetically, he turned to John. "I shall fix us a drink, however."

John looked at his friend bewildered. He was frustrated that Michael would waver with such uncertainty when Miriam needed support. Though his cheeks were reddening, John simply nodded and carried on.

However, when Adelaide and John reached the top of the stairs, she grabbed his arm to stop him. "Do not think less of him,

John. That night haunts him also," Adelaide quickly explained in a hurried whisper, "he wakes from the most awful dreams."

This didn't do much to alleviate John's anger at his friend. For a while, he stewed on what Adelaide had said, thinking of how this household knew nothing but nightmares. How Miriam awoke screaming or crying. How John could not close his eyes without seeing the bloodshed.

Then he remembered how Michael was the first to attend to Miriam. He had seen it too: the gruesome carnage of the attack. It would haunt anyone. Still somewhat enraged, John pursed his lip. "I understand."

"He won't say but I think he feels a tremendous guilt too. Oh!" Adelaide paused, lifting her hands to her lips, unsure on whether she should've said it. John breathed out heavily because his mind too had wondered before to the very notion of Michael's complicity. Michael had, after all, led those two women to Miriam and those two women had led Miriam to the claws of that beast.

"Perhaps, Adelaide, it is best if you were to go in alone." John swallowed, unwilling to let his bad mood temper a possible happy moment for Miriam. He handed the flowers and his own small present over to her, trying his best to muster a smile. "I suspect that Miriam has grown weary of me anyway. Michael and I shall have a drink together."

Without giving Adelaide much room to argue, John was already pacing down the stairs.

Propped up in bed, Miriam waited for Adelaide and Michael to walk through the bedroom door. She patted her hair, which she had attempted to put up in a neat bun, but strands were already falling out. She fiddled with a loose thread of her new dressing gown, scared to pull it in case it unravelled completely within her grasp. She then placed her arms beside her, then she folded them, then she rested her hands on her stomach, then she placed her arms beside her once more.

It was a strange sensation not knowing what to do with your arms but all at once, as the anxiousness rippled through her, they just didn't feel like hers anymore.

Throwing her hands to her face, Miriam tried to stifle a scream, frustrated with herself. But this is more than just nervousness. Miriam didn't know how to exist anymore, uncomfortable with the weight of her bones and the texture of her skin. There was a part of her that wished to see her closest friends. More than anything else, however, Miriam wished to curl up inside the blankets and close her eyes. She would happily will the world away, too monstrous to belong within it anymore

She shuffled uncomfortably in this position. Her backside was already aching, but she had to stay in this stiff, lifeless manner. She feared if she moved, John would realise that her side had all but healed. It was only really sore if there was massive pressure applied. However, if she winced and groaned during John's examinations, then he'd think she was still in agony.

The duplicity didn't help Miriam's feeling of monstrosity. However, it was necessary, she knew that if she wasn't in physical pain anymore, then people would encourage her to get out of bed and try to be human. That she couldn't bear. She was not ready to be herself.

A tear fell down her cheek, and she brushed it away, keen for her friends to not see her upset. She was so pathetically useless. What's more she was bored of being this way. She was tired of being mentally unable to do much but stare and think – exhausted by all those sad morose thoughts that now occupied her mind. She could not eat, sleep, or read books without the memories attacking her very core.

Once she was a brilliant doctor who championed wonderful causes and a dynamic woman made electric love to John when the day was over. Now Miriam couldn't even let her husband bathe her without getting upset. She hated how perilous it felt. Sometimes she would wonder if she would ever let him make love to her again. More often than not, she'd swallow that thought to the deep caverns of her stomach, and let it burn. She could not face it yet.

There were several creaks of the stair floorboards and Miriam took a sharp intake of breath to steel herself. There had been visitors before, but Miriam had been too despondent to really interact with them. Through ebbs of sleep or medication, Miriam pretended not to listen to them speak about her condition as she lay there completely flat.

Her father and her Aunt had been the only people that she tried to stay awake for and it was awful. Though Isobel tried to make conversation, her lips tight and taut, Sir Fredric struggled to look at her, and when he did, his eyes were filled with anguish. The heartbroken wails that sounded out through her home afterwards were still fresh in her mind. She couldn't be sure he wouldn't be the same today and didn't want to spoil the nice day that John had planned for her birthday. She hoped her father wouldn't mind, despite having only come to London to visit her.

Miriam could hear heated whispers outside her door. Panicking, she started her routine again. She placed her arms by her side, then on her chest, then on her stomach, and then she folded them. As the door began to open, she took another breath and settled on placing her arms at the side.

Tentatively, Adelaide poked her head into the room carrying a huge bouquet of roses and the little parcel. Nervously but brightly, she said, "Well, hello there."

In a similarly quiet voice, Miriam said, "My little chuckaboo."

As Adelaide saw Miriam lying there, in an elegant purple gown and an uncertain smile upon her face, her heart melted into nothing but care.

She had been in this room only once since Miriam's attack. She doubted that Miriam would even remember, being mostly asleep. It was a few days after Miriam had returned home. Adelaide had to battle Michael and John in order to see her best friend. Both were adamant that seeing Miriam the way she was then would impact Adelaide, causing stress to herself and the baby.

Walking over, Adelaide's eyes darted over Miriam's face, and she tried to focus on how much better it looked now. Still, the image of her friend broken and bruised stalked her mind. John and Michael were right. The aftermath of the attack was a nightmare, indeed. Miriam was unrecognisable for nearly a fortnight as her face was black and blue from the beating.

But what haunted Adelaide most was how Miriam had disappeared from her very being. The loud and loving friend merely moaned and mumbled through Adelaide's first visit. Though Adelaide did not show it in front of her friends, she cried in her husband's arms all the way home - aghast at the entire affair.

Even though Miriam looked more like herself now, she still was different – sitting statue-like in her bed with a forced smile and a distance in her eyes. It was as though something was missing from her very mettle. There were echoes of the event etched on Miriam's face. The scar on her cheek that would never heal, for example, was a permanent reminder. Not that Miriam would ever forget, that was for certain.

Adelaide tried not to stare but she was unsure what to do as she entered. At first she tried to hide her pregnant stomach behind the flowers. She held them stiffly in front of her as she slowly walked around the bed to the brown velvet armchair on Miriam's left.

Miriam furrowed her brow at her friend's caution. "Please Adelaide, I invited you here. You do not have to hide my future godchild from me."

There was a pause. "Do you truly mean it?"

"Whatever makes you comfortable."

Adelaide sighed out of relief before grinning broadly. She placed the roses down next to the daisies on the bedside cabinet and carefully took the seat in the armchair. In her hand, she still clutched John's present, Whilst Miriam had been completely earnest in her permissions, she still stared at Adelaide's protruding belly, full of wondrous, and blossoming life. Miriam was unable to hide the clear longing and sorrow in her eyes. Adelaide sighed again only this time out of pity.

As Miriam began healing and became more cognizant, John, Adelaide, and Michael all decided it was best that the Jenkinses stayed away for fear of upsetting Miriam. Though she understood, Adelaide hated the prospect of leaving Miriam without support. Over the month, she missed her friend and all her silly little ways. On top of this, Adelaide pined for someone to talk to about her condition and other small things that her husband would dismiss as too womanly. For a short while at Easter, Adelaide grew excited about the possibility of sharing this time with her best friend and watching their children grow together. Now that was all gone, and Adelaide grieved for that too.

Perhaps, Adelaide thought to herself, dismissing her own selfishness, *there will be another time.* She blew out all her calamitous thoughts and gripped onto the parcel as her hands were shaking. "How the blazes are you, Miriam?"

"Positively cadaverous." Miriam started to look around the room, realising that there was someone missing from this picture. "Where's John?"

"He and Michael are having a drink downstairs."

"Oh." Miriam's chin quivered and she tried to hold it all back. To no avail. She suddenly started crying profusely. "I fear John has grown weary of me."

As Miriam sobbed, Adelaide blinked somewhat bewildered. Then she erupted into unexpected laughter. When Miriam sniffled and tried to stem the tears, she looked at Adelaide miserably, albeit a bit furiously. Adelaide stopped but with a bright smile said, "Oh I wish not to offend Miriam. It is just that John echoed a similar sentiment only moments ago." Adelaide reached over and grabbed Miriam's good hand, giving it a kindly squeeze. "And if that does not confirm his affections, Miriam, he also charged me with giving you this."

Adelaide handed Miriam yet another brown paper package. Inside was the most extravagant and expensive gift John could give her – a pure silver charm bracelet sitting in a red, velvet jewellery box. Dangling from the precious chain were rubies, all carved to look like roses. Miriam marvelled at the intricacies. Beneath the chain was a small note in John's handwriting. It read:

A sepal, petal, and a thorn
Upon a common summer's morn,
A flash of dew, a bee or two,
A breeze
A caper in the trees, --
And I'm a rose!

The poem by Emily Dickinson was one of Miriam's favourites. It reminded her of John and the budding moment he spilled his devotion for her in the rose garden. She had found the poem one afternoon in December and read it over and over to him. Each time with increasing affection for the words and her husband. John had remembered it all. This gift, Miriam surmised, was a delicate reminder of their ardent love for one another. Miriam gazed upon it with utmost wonder, the tears from before drying stickily upon her cheek.

"You mustn't chastise yourself in such a manner, Miriam," Adelaide whispered, giving her friend's hand a kindly squeeze. "John's love for you endures. It always will."

Holding onto the ornate piece of jewellery, Miriam's heart thudded in her chest. Even as broken and hollowed out as she was, no one truly knew her as well as John did. This gentle, kind, and handsome man was so acutely aware of her current limitations. She knew he was sporadically delivering gifts so as to not overwhelm her and had organised the day the best he could. It was a kindness that, on top of his round-the-clock care, spoke volumes of his character. In this wondrous moment, as she studied the glistening red rose-shaped jewels, Miriam let the memory and the man flood her senses. The way he read books, the way his lips tasted, and the way his eyes lit up when excited: That stirring calm that set off chaos in her. How lucky she was to find someone as compassionate as Doctor John Bennett.

"He is beautiful," Miriam said to herself, forgetting that Adelaide was watching. Her cheeks flushed from saying the sentiment out loud. She turned to her friend and corrected herself, "*It* is beautiful."

"Come, let us put it on you," Adelaide said jovially, taking the bracelet from Miriam's grasp.

But a hesitation gripped hold of Miriam as Adelaide took her wrists. All her happy thoughts of her husband were abruptly invaded by the image of a putrid green necktie worming violently around her hands. She looked darkly on the little cuts that still clung to her skin. Adelaide must've noticed the breaths that had stalled in Miriam's throat and the shaky nature of her being because she gave Miriam's hand another little squeeze. In a kindly manner, she said, "What we shall do, Miriam, is place it upon the wrist as gently as we can, but we shall not clasp it shut until you are ready."

"Very well." Miriam nodded in agreement and Adelaide did exactly that. She slipped the bracelet on as though it were the lightest piece of fabric, a feather of a thing, and she only clasped it shut when Miriam told her to.

Miriam breathed out precariously before admiring the silver piece of jewellery, hoping to replace the thoughts of that dreaded night with shinier and more hopeful ones. After giving Miriam's hand another squeeze, Adelaide whispered in a shaky breath. "One finds nightmares in the tiniest of places."

A sudden realisation hit Miriam. Her face fell into absolute sadness and grief. "Oh Adelaide."

"Fear not, Miriam, it was a long time ago."

"When?"

Adelaide huffed as though the subject was nothing of note. As if the weight of it didn't still impact her. As though she didn't think about it most days. She waved her hand as if to dismiss the event and yet tears filled her eyes as they always did when the memory took root. "Oh, I was fourteen or so. One of Daddy's gambling acquaintances. Found his way to my bedroom whilst intoxicated. "

"My darling girl," Miriam said in a gentle whisper. She was swallowing her own sadness as she hated that such an agony had befallen her beautiful and brilliant friend. Especially when she was so young.

Adelaide leaned back in the armchair and chuckled to herself, causing a few unexpected tears of her own to roll down her cheek. "The next time it transpired, he found himself on the rather sharp end of a cheese knife which I had squirrelled away."

"Does Michael know?"

Adelaide nodded.

"What did he say?"

"Not much. Which is a triumphant achievement for my husband, as well you know." Adelaide smiled tenderly. "He took me in his arms, held me tightly, and told me that I was safe now. That was all I needed."

"Michael is a good man," Miriam said agreeably, causing Adelaide to grin broadly. It was the first time, out loud, that Miriam had ever complimented Michael.

Miriam didn't really notice the weight of what she had said. Instead, she let her mind drift. She wondered on her own husband and how his arms had become her shelter. She pondered on the manner in which he bathed and dressed her without judgement. She thought on how safe she was around him, even if her thoughts were dark and dangerous. Perhaps that was why Miriam stayed in this state – to never leave the sanctuary of John's arms.

For a short while, Adelaide watched Miriam in this deep thought, and knew she had to say the niggling notion that had been sitting on her mind for a month. Sighing, she rubbed her hand over her stomach with an unease. "Michael is sorry, Miriam."

Miriam cocked her head, confused at such an admission. Then she pieced it all together. With the echoes of the night rippling upon her, Miriam shook her head vigorously – both to dismiss the notion and the images that screeched through her mind. "Oh, you mustn't fret. I do not see Michael as culpable. There are no recriminations there."

"Truly?"

"Unequivocally." Miriam did not say this to be kind. She had thought about this very notion quite a bit. However, the conclusion was always the same. There was only one responsible for all this torment – Harry Wright. Though other people were involved, and even held her down against her will, it was all entirely his awful orchestration.

There he was again, lingering in her head. Miriam stared out from across the bed as though he was standing at the end of it, grinning repulsively with his yellow teeth. Memories of his violent smell began to linger around her. She wished for her own sharp knife to violently end this nightmare. In an instant, Miriam was keen for a distraction. She very quickly said, "Let us not dwell on such matters anymore. Come, Adelaide, you must tell me everything."

As Adelaide spoke fast, mimicking her loquacious husband, Miriam smiled the best she could. She leaned her head back against her pillow and simply watched her beautiful friend speak about everything and nothing at all.

An unexpected, contented calm washed over her, and Miriam was lulled into sleep – thinking, for once, only of all the love she had in her life.

Sitting by the unlit fireplace, the two men tried to enjoy a drink together. However, it was not the quiet in which John was hoping for. Whilst still clutching his bowler hat in one hand, an untouched glass of whisky in the other, Michael spoke fast. John only listened to ebbs. "Peters had a patient punch... A new X-Ray machine… Caught a nurse stealing medicine… Beat Crystal Palace by 100 runs to…"

"Do they speak of us?" John said unexpectedly when Michael had stopped for a slight breather. John didn't really want an answer, but he hated the idea that Miriam was being poked and prodded by gossip when they weren't at the hospital. "Of her?"

"Only that they miss her terribly." There was a pause. "And you."

John let out a large guffaw before quaffing the entirety of his whisky. Then he poured himself another, letting out an incensed breath. His friend was an appalling liar.

Michael swallowed nothing but air. The long-drawn-out manner in which he stretched out the silence meant that he hesitated over something damning. People with sins to confess usually spoke in long pauses. Except chatty people such as Michael Jenkins who loathed every silence that he found himself in. To make up for the void, and to distract from his gnawing insides, Michael liked to speak about anything and everything.

However, for the first time in his life, he halted over what to say next. Especially as John was clearly brooding on the subject. On his jittery tongue, Michael wanted to say so much. The apologies stuck to the roof of his mouth, causing him to suffocate with their meaning. He was deathly afraid of making a mistake – which was often the cause of all his ridicule. If he said the wrong thing this time, he could damn everyone involved.

At once he wished he wasn't so pitiful but also hoped his wife would return soon to save him. She could explain better to John about how utterly heartbroken Michael was that he played some part in Miriam's undoing. Adelaide knew all the right words to express that Michael was plagued by Miriam's bloody near-lifeless body. Michael's dear wife would help John, and subsequently Miriam, understand everything.

Sipping at the whisky, which Michael had never had a fondness for, especially as it burned his mouth and throat, Michael tutted. He knew he couldn't wait for Adelaide to return. With the warm liquid coursing down his throat, Michael started, "John I…"

"Please Michael," John said calmly but there was a trembling to his tone. "I cannot bear any more platitudes or conversations on the matter. Let us enjoy this nice whisky in peace. For once."

Michael nodded. The manner in which John shut him down burned his throat further. He had never seen John so despondent – so lost in his own terrible musings. This poisonous cloud and embittered fog. Instead of this grieving silence, Michael wanted John to chastise him or yell out his frustrations. Perhaps, he wondered, if he continued prodding, he could get a rise out of John, and it'd be better for everyone. He put his glass down and leaned forward to speak again.

However, there was a creak from the staircase causing the pair to both startle. They rose together and stood awkwardly next to one another as Adelaide crept into view. She stood in the frame of the living room doorway hesitantly.

"She's asleep," Adelaide whispered even though she was far away from Miriam. "I thought it best to let her rest."

"Indeed, she doesn't get much at night. I am sorry." John wasn't entirely sure why he was apologising but he feared, for a moment, that Adelaide would think less of Miriam. He bowed his head in shame. "Alas, I am afraid she isn't the same."

Adelaide walked over to him and kindly touched his cheek, causing a few tears to sprout and glide down his cheek. He squeezed his eyes shut, worried about dissolving into all his emotions right in front of his friends. Adelaide exhaled. "Of course she is, John."

She had meant it as a kindness, but it burned in John. There was no use denying that the voracious and boisterous woman they all knew was now disconsolate. He held his eyes closed for a long time, trying to steady his breathing.

When John opened them, Adelaide gave him a sympathetic look but there was sorrow in her eyes also. Michael hovered unsure in the background, clutching onto his bowler hat to settle his agitated fingers. John smiled feebly at his friends. "Forgive me."

"There is nothing to forgive." Adelaide wrapped her loving arms around him. She squeezed him the best she could. When they broke apart, she said jovially, "We will come back tomorrow, won't we darling?"

"Yes," Michael mumbled. He wasn't entirely certain that John would let him but when John nodded at both of them, Michael grinned with relief. "Yes, of course."

As John said goodbye and closed the door on his friends, he let out the longest and most guttural breath. The day had exhausted him in so many different ways. He was tired of trying to be strong when he was so useless. He was tired of the pitying way in which people looked at him now. He was tired of their sympathies when he was not the one in utmost agony.

Heading upstairs, John tried to sate the rage that bellowed within him, but it was useless. He was undone. What gnawed and gnashed at his insides most was the fact he hadn't protected Miriam from the world and its thorns. They sliced into her brutally; she was left bloody, cold, and alone on the ground. He had failed in his vows. He had failed *her*. He had failed. And John found that was truly unforgivable.

John climbed each step, counting them mindlessly along the way. Each one sounded in his head like a drum. He thought of the number of villains that still roamed this city. He memorised their names over and over again, inking them into his mind. When he had reached the guest room, he grabbed the doorknob with a final resolution. As he unobtrusively opened the door, he knew he had to save Miriam from the world, and he knew exactly how to do it.

Closing the door behind him gently, John leaned his head upon the wood. He dare not take these thoughts to the bed that was not quite his, and the wife that was not quite herself. In a shaky breath, he tried to swallow the pain away.

"John?" Miriam said in a solemn voice. Despite the calming way she had drifted off, her mind was suddenly full of monsters again. She had jolted awake from a terrible nightmare, heavy in their aftermath. Her skin was cold like the cobbled street she had been left upon, and the scents of that night rolled over her. As John turned to her, she expected him to look at her as though she were a pitiful creature of darkness. Like Adelaide, John would never look at her in that way. Instead, as their eyes met, she saw him completely. Handsome and strong. *Her bright saviour.* She yearned for his warmth.

When Miriam lifted her arms up to him, John sighed. He was caught by her tenderness and beauty. He realised that Adelaide was somewhat right. As Miriam lay in bed, through her agony and torment, John could still see her wholly. *His dark goddess.* He trembled before her and found himself nearly on the verge of tears again. He longed for her solace.

It was John who wasn't the same. He crawled into her arms but did not cry. As she tucked his brown locks behind his ear, he let her add some much-needed tranquillity into his furious mind. Instead of crying, he listened to the beating of her heart. She was as fragile and as human as anyone else. He felt as though those rhythms belonged to him.

For the first time since that night, Miriam held John against her. For a while she was afraid that the weight of him would cause unease. Yet as he rested her head carefully against her, so as to not cause too much pain or discomfort, Miriam remembered how at home he was in her arms. Even if she didn't feel very much like herself, this sensation was familiar. She allowed his breath to skim her chest and it bristled throughout her somewhat blissfully. He was strong and powerful unlike anyone else. She felt as though that breath belonged to her.

Her heart panged with all the adoration she had for him. Miriam knew she never had to say it. Yet in this tremendous moment, as wrought and frightened as she was, there was nothing else she could do. In a rough breath, she whispered, "John, I love you."

John let out a soft, grief-stricken sob, he didn't deserve such heavenly praise. Still, he gripped onto her tighter and replied, "I love you too, Miriam. More than anything."

As Miriam and John held onto one another closely, spending the rest of the evening in that embrace, they didn't share all that they were feeling and thinking. Even though their thoughts and aches were exactly the same. That they were monstrous against the light of the other. That there was a darkness stirring and whirring within and all around them. That they were broken beyond belief, and it was hard to piece their shattered existence back together.

Instead of sharing this similar sorrow out loud, Miriam and John clung desperately onto the other, allowing their breaths and rhythms to synchronise perfectly. They were as one entirely. In each other's arms, they could slip into their own timeless place together and know that, in spite of the sadness, their love could conquer.

In the sanctity of their shadows, that small, sweet, shared thought, was all they had.

An hour after Miriam had fallen asleep again, John removed himself from her arms. His mind was too alive and burning with a different type of desire to join her in slumber. In an oddly calm manner, he clamoured out of the bed and made his way to their bedroom up the stairs, at the top of the house. His thoughts were quite practical as he changed out of the cream suit into his blue and white striped pyjamas. He pulled on a new dressing gown that matched Miriam's purple one and went through the day and the presents that were still left unopened. As he buttoned his shirt, he thought on how best to deliver them – especially the books and chocolates.

Unhurriedly, he walked all the way downstairs to the front room and poured himself another drink. From the bookshelf he removed a deep red journal and took it with him, back to the guest room where Miriam was sleeping. The behaviour was clinical. It was almost as though he were prepping for surgery. After all, he found the best practice to combat nerves was to dilute your mind with odd bits and bobs. Often, he found himself slicing into another human whilst thinking about picking up sausages from the market or the scores from recent cricket matches.

Sitting in the armchair by the fireplace, John readied himself for a different type of labour. One that required great skill and expert planning. He placed the glass on the small table in front of him and opened the red journal coolly as the roll call of names rang in the caverns of his soul.

The front page added to the rage that was transforming him bit by bit.

He had only five minutes to celebrate. Five minutes of being a father. The last five minutes of his absolute pure bliss.

In less than five seconds, John tore the page from the binding.

After he screwed up the paper and placed it in his dressing gown pocket, John looked up and took time to watch his wife. He listened to her gentle breathing - that slightest bit of heavenly peace. For a little while, he reminisced on how divine their union was. He thought of their first meeting, their passionate lovemaking, and the rain that fell on their wedding day. How lucky John was to have found Miriam Clayton and been afforded all these blisses. Even now as she lay broken, his heart thundered. His love knew no bounds.

But the power of it had unleashed something pure and otherworldly within him. It roared with an unholy fire – as though Hell had unhinged its jaw and was screaming wildly within him. The flames that had started in The Furnace over a month ago were finally consuming him. The smoke and darkness had created a bloody mission – and John knew that there was work to be done. If they were ever to rest again in this household.

Caught between the memories of their heaven and these moments of their hell, John breathed out assuredly. Turning a new page of the journal, and thus a new chapter in their story, John Bennett started to write his dark thoughts. He put to page his new resolution. He scribed the acts he was destined to commit.

As he finished the first entry, John stared at the dark and damning declaration. With his heart racing, he flicked his eyes to the clock on the mantelpiece and memorised the time. It seemed silly, childish even, but he knew he'd never forget that time as long as he lived.

For at thirteen minutes to midnight, on the 13[th of] May 1896, Doctor John Bennett had begun a diary… a diary of murders.

ACKNOWLEDGEMENTS:

Thank you to everyone for your undying support through the release of Diary of Murders and this short story collection.

From family and friends to brand new author connections and amazing readers that I have made along the way, you've helped bring my biggest dream to life. I am forever grateful to have the network that I have in my life.

Most importantly, thank you to everyone who has read Diary of Murders, and subsequently Several Glorious Months.

Thank you for loving Miriam & John as much as I do – I hope this book brought you closer to them.

I'll see you in the sequel!

Doctor Miriam Bennett will return
in Secrets Unbound – Diary of Murders Book 2

Printed in Great Britain
by Amazon

52888462R10162